TOGETHER

Book Five

THE NEW LIFE SERIES

By

Louise Bouck

Permissions

Volume one
Book Five in "The New Life Series."

This book is a work of fiction. Any resemblance to actual events or persons living or dead is entirely coincidental.

ISBN 13 978-1-943984-14-5 EBook
ISBN 978-1-943984-04-6 Paperback
Published in the United States
Hisgivenstories LIB Publications

DEDICATION

This New Life Series is dedicated to Jesus and my family, those that have gone before me, those who are with me and those to come, and all my brothers and sisters in Christ.

†

ACKNOWLEDGEMENTS

Thank you to all the people who have encouraged me and kept me in their daily prayers, some since the very beginning of this series. A special thank you goes to Mary Koestner for her prayer support. She continues to refresh my spirit. To my husband, Dale Bouck, my first editor, thank you hugs. He somehow managed to keep my computer running in spite of the monsoons. Thank you for not complaining when meals were late and simple. Thank you for not expecting a house that looks like the page of a magazine. Well maybe the "before" page. Thank you to my other family members and friends that suffered through reading rough drafts. A big thank you hug goes to RJ who was the first to want to read the story of Ben Slater in "More Than Survival" and to Brenda Dick who read "The Story of Sarah" to RJ when he was ill. She continues to cheer me on. Thank you to Donna Shaw, who enthusiastically helped me to keep Sarah's feet on the right path. She revives my focus with positive efforts.

Most recently, I have been inspired by the remarks of Weston Burge after his reading of the manuscript for an Epilogue that I am preparing.

Thank you to all those who gave me technical help. A special Thanks to Ray Shaw for his time and patient repetition until I got it... Without his technical help, this series of stories would still be files in my computer and, what would any of us do without the public libraries and the wonderful people that work there?

CHARACTER LIST

Benjamin Slater, Young man that survived an Indian raid
Sarah, Ben's sister raised as Brave Sparrow
Mary Parker, Pioneer woman with two sons
Joshua Parker, Mary Parker's oldest son
Adam Parker, Mary Parker's Younger son
Eli Slater, son of Mary and Ben Slater
Beth, Elizabeth Ann Wilson, wife of Jedidiah Jones
Jedidiah Jones, close friend, like a brother to Ben
Jonathon, (Johnny) first born of Beth and Jed
Lily, daughter of Beth and Jed
Sam and Helen, run the trading post in Silverville
Henry and Abe, sons of Sam and Helen
Tom and Gentle Fawn, Tom owns the saw mill
Stormy and Anne, twins of Tom and Gentle Fawn
David Sharpe, Sharp Knife of the Winahatah
Zack, Rachel, and Margaret, family rescued from the raft
Rose, the teacher
Mathew Morgan, blacksmith
Liz, wife of Mathew Morgan
Rev. James Brown and Melanie
William and Violet Brown, their children
Calvin, Minnie and Melanie Briggs, settlers
Nicholas and Norah Russell, helpful settlers
Sweet Grass, young healer trained by Sarah
Night Hawk and Spotted Fawn of the People
Singing Wind, the one who made and played the flutes,
Gray Cloud, herd watcher and flute player,
Father Bob and Father Peter O'Riley, Missionaries

TABLE OF CONTENTS

4 ACKNOWLEDGEMENTS
5 CHARACTER LIST
6 TABLE OF CONTENTS
7 INTRODUCTION
9 PROLOGUE
11 CHAPTER 1 HER REAL FAMILY
26 CHAPTER 2 EXCELLENCE IN EVERYTHING
37 CHAPTER 3 WILD RIDE
52 CHAPTER 4 ZACK AND WILD HORSES
67 CHAPTER 5 THE LAKE CABIN
77 CHAPTER 6 BRAVE SPARROW OFFERS FRIENDSHIP
92 CHAPTER 7 CONSEQUENCES
104 CHAPTER 8 ON THEIR OWN LAND
113 CHAPTER 9 I AM DAVID SHARPE
123 CHAPTER 10 A MAN TO HELP
139 CHAPTER 11 AN INSPIRED VISIT
154 CHAPTER 12 HEADING HOME
164 CHAPTER 13 THE AMAZING STORY
176 CHAPTER 14 YOUR GUESTS HAVE ARRIVED
193 CHAPTER 15 GENUINE BLESSINGS
209 CHAPTER 16 A SERIOUS INTERRUPTION
225 CHAPTER 17 THE STRENGTH TO CARRY ON
237 CHAPTER 18 CAN WE DO IT?
250 CHAPTER 19 GOING HOME
266 CHAPTER 20 AT THE CAMP OF THE PEOPLE
284 AN INVITATION
285 ABOUT THE AUTHOR
286 TITLES IN THE NEW LIFE SERIES

INTRODUCTION

This is book five in "The New Life Series." The Christian fiction in this series is written to offer the reader a wholesome entertainment, starting back in a simpler but not easier time. Their example of spiritual strength and "never quit" attitude is refreshing and inspiring. The adventurers follow the trail to a new land and challenges they never imagined.

In book one "More Than Survival", follow Benjamin Slater as he copes with the wild isolation of the new frontier and the lessons of self-preservation. He experiences the pain of loss and joys of accomplishment. He travels "Life's Many Journeys," in book two and learns to appreciate "The Land's Heritage," in book three.

In Book four, you will find out "The Story of Sarah"

As you read the books, Ben develops into a man of physical and spiritual strength. His problem solving mind is challenged many times.

When Sarah, his sister returns to him, they are finally "Together," in book five. You will find out how her life affected the Indians that took her and how they became "The Blue Stone People," a chosen nation in book six.

A change of scene takes you to the camp of the Sentu and three survivors enter the story, in book seven "Teewahpanyee the Boy, Two Feathers the Man," Willow and Water Bug bring new strength and young blood to an old people. With Willow at his side in book eight he becomes leader of "The People of The Lion". They are chosen by the Lion of Judah to be rescuers, and are rewarded in book nine, by being allowed to discover "The Lion's Den."

In book ten, the land that Ben Slater's father chose has miraculously remained with the family as time has gone by and generations were born. In a day beyond today, the series skips to the final times after the rapture. A new heroine stands up bravely to the soldiers of the anti-Christ. She finds Ben's Bible, Mary Slater's journals and the gift of faith. Emily spreads the Good Word and struggles to survive the time of tribulation as she finally realizes that this is "Just the Beginning" for those who believe.

PROLOGUE

Joshua Parker had watched from the top of the bluff. The rider was coming at a comfortable pace, leading a packhorse. The white horse she rode and the streaming blond hair soon brought recognition. Joshua yelled with excitement causing others to scramble to the top to see.

"Sarah! Sarah! Sarah is coming!"

It was Sarah! They hurried down to stand at the river's edge at the crossing. Each one anticipated this day with joy for many reasons. Ben's sister was lost to his family for a very long time. Now she was coming back. They could only hope that this time it would be to stay.

After the Indians raided the Slater's covered wagon and killed their parents, Benjamin had been left for dead. Alone and wounded, he managed to survive.

His sister Sarah had been taken to the village of the Winahatah. Dark Wolf, son of Chief Rising Eagle, had given her to his wife. She had been raised, not as a slave, but as his daughter.

Jedadiah Jones came along in a canoe just in time to help Ben after a cougar had seriously injured him. Jed became a big brother, and stayed with Ben.

Ben and Jed had taken a journey, walking, to visit the growing settlement down river. Stump, their dog, discovered a very frail, ill woman in the forest when they stopped to camp. With care and prayer they nursed her back to health.

Elizabeth Anne Wilson had been on the same wagon train as Ben. She had barely survived the winter. She and Jed soon fell in love and they were married.

A year later, they had a son that they named Johnny. He was tiny and premature, but thrived under the loving care of his family.

Sarah had discovered her brother, Benjamin Slater, was still alive when she had left the Indian camp trying to warn the white men of the increased danger to the wagon trains as the hostilities grew, the number of Indian villages involved in attacking the wagon trains had also increased. Their resolve to protect their hunting grounds strengthened.

When Sarah, called "Brave Sparrow", by the Indians, realized that she could not stop the wagon trains, she had returned to the Winahatah, to warn them that the wagon trains would be more heavily guarded, and that soldiers were near to guard them.

She took back with her a plan to bring peace and prosperity to the people that had killed her parents. Her heart was torn and loyalties divided.

Mary Parker and Adam had escaped the Indian village with Sarah's help. Growling Bear had taken Mary during a raid on her homestead. Her young son, Joshua had managed to cross the river, avoiding capture. He sought help from Ben and Jed. A new army post had provided soldiers to ride with Ben to find Mary. She and the boys had safely spent the winter in Ben's cabin and in the spring Mary and Ben were married.

As time passed the "Slater and Jones" ranch grew and the family bond was strong with God's blessing.

Now, Dark Wolf and Moonflower his wife, had to let Sarah go, but they longed for her return one-day. They had grown to love her.

CHAPTER ONE
HER REAL FAMILY

Sarah hugged the little rag doll that her mother had made for her. Ben had kept it all the long years, hoping that one day he would find her and be able to give it back to her.

Now here she was, standing beside him, a grown woman, with the doll in her arms! Her eyes filled with tears as she looked at her brother Ben, so much had happened to both of them.

She wanted to try to learn the story of his life and to share some of hers.

"Where do we start, to fill in the missing years? Is it even possible?" He asked.

"I doubt it Ben, but I want to try," answered Sarah.

Ben wrapped an arm around her and the other around Mary, his wife, as they all headed up the path around the small lake, to Jed and Beth's house. It stood looking lovely and cared for in the late afternoon sunshine.

As their family grew, they had added rooms on both ends. The size of the house was quite impressive, but not intended to be. It was a matter of practical space for their family.

The flowers in the beds beneath the front windows were in full bloom. Curtains moved, behind open windows and an old dog moved away from the mat by the front door when he saw them coming.

"What is that marvelous aroma?" asked Sarah.

"That is my wife's wonderful chili!" answered Jed. "If she didn't make it for us once a week we would all feel neglected."

"It smells delicious," said Sarah.

As they settled around the table and Sarah looked from one smiling face to another, she felt sad for all that she had missed in their lives. I am nearly as old as these women she thought, but I haven't a husband or child. Perhaps here, I will find someone that I know God has sent just for me.

"Jonathon was a baby when you were here before Sarah and Mary's Adam was small, too. They have grown."

"Yes, they are big boys! Beth you must have had your girl, the year after I was here. She is lovely." Beth and Jed beamed with pleasure at the compliment.

"This is Lily," said Beth, stroking the child's head of soft, shiny, dark curls. Her dark brown eyes sparkled with the look of both intelligence and mischief. Like her mother, Lily was small boned and would always seem delicate but that exterior hid a strong will and Tom-boy attitude.

Sitting on the floor with a pile of blocks was a small version of Ben. It was easy to see that this was his son. Joshua bent down and stacked the blocks for him saying,

"This is Eli. He is my baby brother."

"What a nice family. I hope that I will have a child and a home of my own someday, but until then I know that I will enjoy spending time with yours. They are precious," she said.

They sat around the table kidding Beth about the fire in the chili, and enjoying the fellowship of being together at last without asking the many questions that entered the minds of everyone at the table. No one mentioned the cabin they had worked so hard on, either; they were saving that as a surprise.

After the kitchen was cleaned and things were back in order, they all went outside to sit on the grass. Sarah's eyes searched the corral but couldn't see a white horse there. She was afraid to ask about Moon Boy and Dart Away. Ben saw the sad look that entered her eyes.

"Sarah, Jed and I have something to show you in the barn if you are not too tired," said Ben, taking her hand to help her get up off the grass but not letting go after she was standing. He treasured being able to be near her and knowing that she was here, well and safe at last.

She followed half-heartedly thinking of the many times she petted Dart Away, her father's horse, and had taken him little treats when he was with the herd of the Indians.

Beautiful, white, Moon Boy was so spirited. He must have gotten away from them, she thought as she crossed the yard. She had brought him with her as she rode Pretty Mother. He was young and although she wanted him near her, because she knew Ben would give him attention and train him gently, she had left him here, as a sign of her promise to return.

Jed opened the door to the big barn wider and the smell of fresh hay and horses swept over her. There in the largest stall was Blaze, with a new foal that looked just like Dart Away!

We call him Dash Away. He was born just two days ago. He is pretty special. We have another well-bred mare that we bought from the Army that should have her foal any day now. She is back here." Sarah had a grin from ear to ear as she followed him to another stall near the back, where an open shutter allowed fresh air and sunlight into the area.

"This is Star," Jed said with a grand wave of his hand.

"Jed, she is beautiful. Her black coat is so shiny and her face is so pretty, with the white star on her forehead."

"Yes, Dart Away thinks she is gorgeous."

"Dart Away? Oh I was afraid to ask! Where is he? Oh, Please let me see him."

"Right this way," said Jed. Both men were enjoying her excitement.

Jed opened a side door and stepped out. Dart Away stood in the middle of a large green field.

"He is king of his domain," said Ben. She clacked her tongue, but he was too far away to hear her. Jed made a shrill whistle and Dart Away lifted his head and walked slowly toward them. Sarah clacked her tongue when he came near and he walked directly to her. She hugged and scratched and discovered that tears were escaping down her cheeks.

"I have missed you, my friend. I have often thought of you and Moon Boy."

She turned her face to Ben, hopefully. When he said nothing, she asked.

"Where is Moon Boy? Is he here?"

"He is more beautiful than ever," said Ben. "We can all take a ride over to see him and some others in the morning if you like," he said.

"Where is he?" she asked.

"We keep him and a few others separated from Dart Away," said Jed. The answer satisfied her for now. We keep a couple field companions in here with him for company but not Moon Boy.

Jed pointed out the small herd of mares and foals in the field next to Dart Away's. "We have three yet to deliver," he said and then he showed her their growing herd of milk cows. "We have 15 cows now, and several will be having calves in the next few weeks." Over here is a small barn we built for Beth and Mary to experiment making different kinds of cheese. We take some of it and butter and eggs to Silverville. We dug a cold cellar near the river and packed it with blocks of ice and that keeps things fresh. The soldiers come with a wagon and pick up milk, butter, cheese, and eggs, too."

"Someday we hope to have a herd of horses big enough to sell mounts to the Army," said Jed.

"We have been selectively breeding the mares for the smooth gate and endurance that soldiers need. My, Big Boy is the father for several of those in the field over there. I'll ride him in the morning," said Ben. Sarah smiled and said she remembered that big horse.

"Well, he is dominant. He thinks he owns all the mares."

"I can't wait to see all the new foals," said Sarah. Ben laughed at her enthusiasm.

"We will all be up at night when they start arriving. I'm sure."

"Sometime, I will tell you about my first foal, Ginger. That was sure a day to remember," said Ben.

"I remember Ginger. She is so sweet. You told me about rescuing her from the mud bog. That was dangerous. I hope you are more careful now that you are older."

"Sarah you must be very tired," said Ben. "We will walk you to the house and then I will take Mary and the boys home," he said.

"Beth has made up the same room for you that you used last time," said Jed. "Josh put your bundles in there after we ate."

"That does sound like a good idea," said Sarah. "We can talk more tomorrow."

When the trio stepped back into the house they found the cozy glow of lanterns and the smell of mint in the air. Beth had prepared some chamomile and mint tea for them all to sip before heading to bed. This had been an exciting day and she thought it might help them all to relax. Johnny and Lily had been put to bed and they were sleeping. Joshua was already at the hut after climbing the bluff to check the lookout and making sure that they had an all clear. Eli was asleep curled up with the old dog, on the bearskin in front of the fire.

As Ben carried Eli down the path, Mary walked behind with Adam, carrying the lantern and rifle. Ben couldn't help but say what he was feeling.

"Mary, I can't believe it! She is here. She really came back and this time I think she intends to stay! I have to admit that I wasn't sure that we would ever see her again. It is good that we kept thanking God for her return as we built the house. God has blessed us and honored our prayers."

"She looks well, but old for her years," said Mary. "I wonder if she will ever tell us all, that she has gone through. I doubt it."

"Mary I think the best thing is just to love her and be kind and if she wants to talk, then we will listen," said Ben.

Joshua had added wood to the fire and told them that he had checked the lookout. "Mom I checked the chickens, too. They are fine."

"You are such a responsible young man. Thanks Josh," she said.

"I'm going out to the barn to check the horses and then we should all turn in," said Ben.

"Dad, what do I call Sarah? Is she just Sarah or should I say Aunt Sarah?"

"Josh, if you are comfortable with it, I think she would like to hear you say, Aunt Sarah."

"Then, that's what I'll call her." Joshua hugged them both and went to bed. Eli and Adam were tucked into bed together. Eli curled around Adam the way he had around the dog on the floor and they were asleep before Ben returned from the barn.

The next day everyone was greeted by a glorious, golden morning. The men prepared the wagon for the short trip to see Moon Boy. The wagon was packed with soft hay and two big picnic baskets were added. Joshua put a soft bridle on Little Mouse and jumped on her back without blanket or saddle. Adam rode the same way on Dixie, his father's horse. Jed stepped up onto the wheel of the wagon and helped the ladies to all climb in and handed the little ones over the side into the hay. Lily wrapped her arms around her Uncle Ben's neck and didn't want to let go.

When they arrived at a fence and gate Ben stopped the procession long enough to tell Sarah that here against the bluff, Mary and He would be building their new house someday. Mary chuckled and decided that it was a good time to share the news that she thought that another child was on the way.

"Ben, you may need to start that house soon. I think we will have another child before spring." A big grin spread across his face as he hugged her. He was proud of the family God had given him.

"That's great Mary," he said swinging up and hugging her and then handed Lily to Beth. "Do you think it would help if we all think girl? It would be nice for you, to have a girl." Everyone congratulated them and Sarah watched as Beth placed her hand on Mary's tummy and prayed out loud.

"Father God, You are a big God, filling our lives with good things. You give us blessings before we ask for them. Thank you for this baby that is on the way. Bless Mary and the baby and make them strong and healthy."

"Amen," They all said. Sarah beamed with joy to hear her family pray together. Everyone started talking at once, filled with excitement over the announcement and the coming events of the day.

Once they were all through the heavy, very tall gate, Ben made sure that it was secured before riding on ahead to open yet another gate. This unusually tall gate was at the end of a long narrow trail they had just traveled. It was fenced high on both sides and merged into the strong branches of ancient trees with underbrush. All these fences and gates puzzled Sarah but she didn't comment. I guess I have lots to learn about the way things are done here, she thought.

In the field to her right, Sarah could see four white horses grazing in the shade of pine trees. It was too far to tell but she was sure that one of them was Moon Boy.

"Ben is that Moon Boy over there?" Sarah asked.

"Yes. He is with my Buddy and two young fillies that we bought from the army. Moon Boy is the whitest one and the biggest too. We could put Pretty Mother in there with them if you want."

"They are beautiful together," she said. "Have you had the time to ride him?"

"Yes, I have been working with him when time allows," said Ben. "He is spirited and takes a firm hand, but he is a good strong mount and usually willing to do what I want. Boy, can he jump! He and Buddy both like to jump the fences once in a while. That's why we have the double fences here and they are in a section against the bluff, with higher fencing there too. We use box fence for all our horses. We don't want them running into barbed wire and getting cut.

"It looks like you have all worked very hard," said Sarah, just as the trail they were following turned around a grove of trees to reveal a small cabin tucked up against a stand of huge pine trees. Wild lupines were in bloom and wild grape vines trailed over a dead stump to the right of the house. A stack of neatly cut wood was nestled near the wall and a braided, colorful, round mat lay in front of the door. Four posts held a roof over the porch and a large willow bench was set invitingly in the morning sun beneath a window displaying flowered curtains inside.

"What a beautiful little house," exclaimed Sarah. "Who lives here?"

"No one yet," said Ben. "We built it for you. We all worked on it together. The women have worked hard on the inside. They made all the bedding and put the finishing touches on everything. Jed and Josh and I have been working on it every spare minute we had, all the time you have been gone."

"Oh this is too much to believe!" she said, as she jumped from the wagon before it was totally stopped. "Ben this is wonderful! Thank you, Thank you everyone!"

"Well don't just stand there. Let's go inside," said Jed. He was anxious to see her reaction to the bed and chest that he had helped to decorate with carvings of beautiful scenes. On the front of the big door they had carved "Home Sweet Home."

She ran her hand over the smooth wood and deep letters and turned to Ben,

"What does it say?" she asked. It was then that they realized that she couldn't read.

"It says, Home Sweet Home," Ben answered.

"Gosh, Aunt Sarah, I think you will have to start learning your letters the way I did," said Joshua. "Mom keeps getting me harder books to read and bigger numbers to work."

"I know that I can learn, Joshua, if you will help me. I would like that," Sarah said with a smile.

"Sure Aunt Sarah, we can work together."

When they opened the door and stepped into the cool room, Sarah was amazed at what she saw. The floors were wood planked, and sanded to a soft patina. The stone fireplace mantel held a tintype of their grandparents, young and handsome as she remembered them. A pair of willow chairs stood near the window and a small table and benches waited to have a meal served, on a blue and white, checkered tablecloth. A large wooden bowl set in the middle of the table, held an arrangement of dried wild flowers.

She was puzzled as she passed the table to a small counter. A sink was in it and a pump just to the right of the sink. She looked to Ben for an explanation.

"It's a pump to bring the water right to your kitchen. You have the first well in the family Sarah!" He levered the handle up and down several times before a small stream of water started to pour into the sink. She couldn't believe her eyes. She couldn't remember having ever seen anything like it.

"This is all so unbelievable. You are all so very wonderful and kind." She began to sob. She couldn't force herself to be strong and in control any longer. Somehow now she knew that she could completely let go of Brave Sparrow, the persona that had always been strong and the best possible at everything.

Now she could be Sarah Slater. She had a family and she was accepted and loved, just the way she was. All the tension flowed with the tears until there were no more tears to cry.

Beth had held her against her shoulder, with arms wrapped around her.

"There you are Sarah. You are home. You can cry, laugh or yell if you want to." She wiped her face with a cool wet cloth.

"There now, no more tears. The "S & J" is a happy place!"

"S & J," asked Sarah?

"Yes, that's what we call this ranch, for Slater and Jones. We put it in the ear of every horse and cow," explained Beth, "to mark them as ours."

"Oh Sarah, I did put that in Moon Boy's ear, too, in case we lost him. I hope you don't mind," said Ben.

"I can see that you all take good care of everything and everybody. I feel so blessed to be here in this family. Thank you again for this house and taking care of Moon Boy, and Dart Away," said Sarah.

"We are all very glad that you are finally here Sarah," said Mary.

Jed knelt and quickly started a small fire in the new fireplace by using the firebox that he had stealthily brought. Beth pulled the crisp white curtains back and opened the little kitchen window.

"You haven't even seen your bedroom yet," said Mary. She led the way, pushing the drape in the doorway to the side to reveal the beautiful hand carved bed.

"Oh, how lovely everything is." Sarah gently ran her hand over the carving. "The people would say that the person that did this has great medicine." Jed and Ben were both wearing big grins.

"I am learning to carve, too," said Joshua. "I made the cross on the wall for you." Sarah touched the small rose in the center of the wooden cross and smiled. "I copied the rose from the rifle," he said.

"Josh, it is perfect. I will cherish it always." She hugged him so tightly that he could not breathe.

Jed pointed out a door in the floor. "You have storage down there and a door that allows you to slip out to the bluff. The cache is empty though. We didn't want to fill it until you came so that everything would be fresh." He lifted the door and revealed a ladder that led to a small room with an even deeper cache in the floor. The walls were lined with shelves waiting to be filled with whatever she wanted to put there. "The end shelves swing into the room so that you can slip out and then pull it back shut."

"But who would I need to hide from?" Then at that instant she realized that they feared the Indians just as the people feared the white men.

Ben changed the subject.

"Let's go outside and visit Moon Boy." A clack of her tongue brought him to the fence, and Beth slipped her a couple crackers from the picnic basket to use as a treat.

"You have grown into a handsome man, my Moon Boy. Do you remember me, and all the scratches? I have brought your mother with me. She will be proud of you when she sees how handsome you are. Maybe tomorrow we will go for a long ride on the prairie." She gave him a final pat and walked back toward the beautiful log cabin. "This is all so wonderful that I can't take it all in yet. You have accomplished so much, and worked so hard."

Ben looked at Mary to signal that it was time for her final surprise. Mary pulled a piece of paper from her pocket handing it to Ben. Ben grinned broadly as he held it out to Sarah.

"Sarah this paper says that this house and the land around it belong to you. No one can take it from you. It is yours to keep forever." Sarah's hand shook as she took the paper and starred at it blankly.

"I can't read it now, but when I learn, I will read every word," she said.

"Mom, can we eat now? I'm starving!" Josh said it with a grin.

"Yes I think that is a good idea." They all filed back into the little cabin carrying the picnic baskets. They settled at the table or on the braided grass rug on the floor. Beth and Mary had packed far more food than could be eaten by a small army. The leftover food was wrapped and placed in the empty cupboards. Sarah discovered that she had a set of six blue china plates and six carved bowls. On a shelf she found two wooden cups. A large kettle sat on the stone of the fireplace hearth. Leaning against the wall next to it was a large wooden spoon.

"I made that spoon," Aunt Sarah, announced Josh proudly.

"That will be useful to stir the soup that I will make for you in that big kettle, Josh. Thank You," said Sarah.

"The next time we go to the trading post, we will get you a coffee pot, lantern and any other supplies that you will need before winter," said Jed.

"I have never been to a trading post. What is it like?" she asked. "We take things there in the wagon, vegetables, baskets, bowls, anything extra that we have and exchange them for supplies that we need,' said Beth.

"You can go with us when we go. Silverville is getting to be a good sized settlement, with a school and church and blacksmith shop," answered Ben.

"Do they have cloth to make a dress there?" Sarah asked. "Yes, lots of it in many colors," said Mary enthusiastically.

"I would like to make a dress like yours and Beth's."

Sarah was excited when Beth announced that tomorrow was Sunday. "I think we should read the Bible here at Sarah's new house and ask God's blessing on it before we help her move her bundles here and start to fill the cache." Everyone agreed.

The next morning when Ben placed the bible on his lap, Sarah reached over and tenderly touched the cover of the book.

"You have Father's book with God's words in it! It isn't lost!"

"What do you mean Sarah? It wasn't lost," said Ben.

"When Growling Bear and a scouting party came looking for the wagon and this book, they couldn't find it. They said that the wagon had disappeared."

"Well in a way it had. I took the wagon apart," said Ben, "board by board I brought everything across the river along with the few things they left behind when they took you."

Jed immediately got concerned.

"Do you mean they were here at the river looking for the wagon?"

"Yes," said Sarah, "but they couldn't find it or any sign of it. They were looking mostly for the book, because I told them about it. I guess they thought they would have God's power if they found it. I'm glad they didn't find you Ben. I didn't have any idea that you were right here all that time!"

"We have much to thank God for, today and every day," he said.

As Ben read Psalms of praise, she closed her eyes and drank the words into her thirsty spirit.

"Lord I have longed to hear your word for so long," she prayed silently. She thanked God for her family and the beautiful little house they had built for her.

As the words drifted to her, she pictured her father reading to the family. "Ben, your voice sounds a lot like Father's did," she said. "I remember our Bible time each evening on the trail."

CHAPTER TWO
EXCELLENCE IN EVERYTHING

It didn't take long for Sarah to fit into the routine of the ranch. The very next day they stocked the little cabin and Sarah was able to move in. The idea that everyone helps and everyone shares was not new, since it had been the way of the people. Beth and Mary soon discovered that there were many things that they could learn from Sarah.

She wandered the woods nearby, collecting supplies for a new pharmacy. Soon chokecherries were waiting in baskets to make a mauve colored dye. Grass near the lake was turned into an olive colored concoction that colored anything it touched. She helped with the garden and with the making of soap. Bee's wax was used to make candles.

The forms for brick making had been retrieved from Mary's land and had been stacked in Ben's barn. Mary hauled them out and took them to Sarah's, along with a few new ones that she had coaxed Ben to make. There, beside the cabin they made bricks and after a string of very hot days, the bricks were tapped out of the molds and a new batch of clay filled the forms. When they had enough bricks, they built a large oven. Sarah had deliberately shaped the opening a little larger than Mary thought wise.

"Won't you lose heat out such a large opening?"

"I want to bake more than bread in there," Sarah said laughing, but she didn't explain. The men provided her with a piece of slate to close it, which she promptly chipped into a large disk that was easier to move by rolling.

Late-summer as they readied the wagon with produce, to take to the settlement, a tall stack of the most beautiful baskets was included. Patterns and pictures woven in colors decorated each one. Watertight baskets with secure lids, sealed with wax, held many colors of dye for trade. Small baskets with lids, held various kinds of dried medicinal teas with a description of its uses written by Mary on small pieces of birch bark, fastened with cords made of strong grass. Each one was a treasure.

Sarah had bundled and dried plants for poultices and worked many skins to a lush softness. Only time seemed to limit the things that Sarah could do.

Mary had lengthened one of her own dresses with a white ruffle and added a white bow on the back of the skirt to match and gave it to Sarah to wear, the night before they left for the settlement. Sarah was grateful and felt warmed by Mary's thoughtfulness.

Mary and Sarah rode the wagon, while Ben led the way on Sundown. Josh followed along on Little Mouse. Adam had decided to stay and play with Jonathan. Beth insisted that Mary leave Eli, too.

"He will have fun playing here and you can use the break, Mary," she said. Ben had promised them all a stick of mint candy when he returned.

Sarah's stomach hurt from nerves as they neared the crossing of the Silver. The bridge was strong and had been widened but Ben got off Sundown and led him and then Ginger pulling the small wagon across on foot. Tom bellowed a greeting before they got all the way across. Gentle Fawn came out wrapping Mary in an embrace.

As soon as Sam and Helen saw Sarah they quickly ushered them all into the house at the back of the store. Everyone was talking at once.

When Ben proudly introduced Sarah, the room grew quiet. Finally, Helen said that she was glad that Sarah had been found and rescued from the savages!

"It is good that you live out far enough that Sarah won't have to interact with the people of the Settlement, Ben. You know how people are." Sarah gasped at the words. She could physically feel the wall that had been put up by Helen's words. It sounded as if they thought that she had a disease that they would catch. She rushed outside fearing that she would lose the small breakfast she had managed to eat. She leaned against the wall of the store taking deep breaths, squeezing her eyes shut tight, trying to close out the stinging words and white man's world.

Mary's eyes bore a hole into Helen's.

"How could you? She was raised as the daughter of a Chief! She was treated well, with respect. They treated her better than you just did!" She ran out after Sarah, not knowing where she had gone. When she found her, Mary folded Sarah into her arms.

"Don't cry Sarah. They don't understand," said Mary, trying to console her.

"She looked at me like I am a filthy thing! Why?" Sarah sobbed. Mary didn't answer. She shook her head, knowing full well why. She thought that most of the white people in the settlement would not accept Sarah for the precious, person she was.

Helen busied herself with her children in the back, too upset to show her face as the men went outside. Sam wanted to carry the contents of the wagon into the store, but Ben was so angry that he nearly left without trading.

Sam couldn't believe his eyes at the quality and variety of goods they had brought.

"These baskets are fantastic! I have never seen anything like them. They will bring a good sum."

"Sarah made them all," was Ben's reply.

"What do you have in these?"

"Be careful with those," said Ben. "Each one holds a different color dye the color of the lid. These are dried teas." The wagon was emptied of all the garden produce, carved bowls and small carved animals and big stirring spoons that Josh had made.

Ben quickly handed Sam the list of supplies they needed.

As soon as he had them in the wagon, he told Sam that when he figured out the credit for his trade goods, that he should hold it. Ben would put it toward windows and lumber for his house. He would come for it when he could, perhaps he could get it soon. Josh chose a new pocketknife for carving. At the last minute Ben remembered the candy for the children.

Ben tenderly gathered the ladies into the wagon and they were back across the bridge before nightfall. His jaw was set and he was angry through and through. How could people that he thought were his friends treat Sarah so badly? He glanced at her and saw that she held her chin high. Mary's overly pink complexion showed that she too, was very upset. Ben knew that the tight jaw and unnatural color of Sam's face meant that Helen would soon hear from him.

He slowed the wagon to a crawl as soon as they were out of sight of the settlement. He knew that Ginger and all their horses were tired. He found a clearing just off the trail and pulled the wagon into it.

"Well I hope you all feel like camping out tonight," he said cheerfully as he cleared debris from a circle of stones to make a safe place for a fire. This spot had been used many times.

Sarah hadn't said a word since they had left the front of the store. She turned to Ben.

"Ben, I am sorry that you were embarrassed in front of your friends. I had no idea that they would feel that way about me. I would not have come here, had I known."

"Sarah they will change their minds when they get to know you. They really aren't bad people. I'm the one that is sorry for subjecting you to that."

She took her blanket from the wagon and spread it in the grass near the trees and lay down closing her eyes. Once again the pain of the remark overwhelmed her emotions. She was fighting back tears. Ben and Mary sat on the grass quietly, beside the small fire for a long time.

Mary went to her.

"Sarah, please eat a piece of jerky and have some water." Sarah sat up and decided that she had to stop feeling sorry for herself. If they act like that because they don't understand then I must help them understand, she thought. Father how can I do that, she wondered? You will show me the way. Immediately her mood brightened. Sarah had learned well, how to cope. She could do it again. The others could feel her change even though they didn't know what had brought it about. They were glad for it.

Sarah was amazed when all the supplies were delivered to her house. Not only did she have a kitchen with all the basics of flour, sugar, salt, baking powder, coffee and a coffee pot, Ben had thought to buy a bolt of white cotton and thread and a pack of sewing needles and a pair of scissors. It was enough to make lots of things. She could color it any color she chose from the many dyes she had made. He had spools of ribbon and lace, and many balls of white wool and knitting needles, too. He had a lantern for her and oil enough to last all winter and beyond. The many new pans were truly amazing to all the women. Loaf pans, pie and cake pans were in the bundles, a set for each kitchen. Fresh tins of ground black pepper, hot red pepper, cinnamon, ginger and cloves were included.

Sarah had gathered bundles of weaving supplies and neatly stored them in her little room beneath the floor. Some of the shelves there already held new baskets with lids, filled with dried vegetables from the garden. She had hunted the edges of the river diligently for just the right large stone to use as a base and found another one that was long and smooth for her hand to rub back and forth to grind corn. Jed had brought her a huge bag of dried corn and carried it down the ladder for her. He had thoughtfully carved a scoop and tucked it into the top.

"This corn is from last fall. The new crop won't be so rock-hard."

"I am sure it will be fine. I am so impressed with all the bounty here at the ranch.

After a visit from Ben she found that she had a new wood box near her fireplace, and a set of two wooden mixing bowls. She had woven a large net and hung it above the kitchen counter, between two beams, to hold some of her larger utensils. Another beam held bundles of herbs and dried medicines hanging in a neat row. Wild onions and garlic, hung in strings on the wall against the logs, along with bright red peppers. On the top of her cupboard, ears of popcorn lay in a basket covered by a grass mat, and two bags of hickory nuts still in their leathery casings rested in the corner of her kitchen area.

Apples were in one of the caches, along with space for squash and pumpkins. Wild cherries had been dried and grapes would be gathered and dried, all adding to the wonderful aroma of her home.

She had dug a second cache for meat in the floor of her storage room and discovered that the hardest part of it was taking the loose dirt out of the room.

When she hit a vein of yellow clay, at first she was annoyed by the difficulty it offered in digging, until she realized that this was the same clay that she had seen used to make wonderful pots, at the summer council. She had traded several baskets for one and given it to Moonflower. She wadded the sticky clay into neat balls and placed them on a mat in the corner. I will have fun experimenting with that later on, she thought.

Once the cache was lined with grass mats and a strong lid in place, Sarah decided that she would go hunting and see if she could fill the cache herself. It had been a while since she had used a rifle and wondered if she would be able to shoot accurately.

She knew the best horse to use would be the brown hunting pony she had pulled from the herd and used as a packhorse when she left the camp of the people. She had never shot a gun near Pretty Mother and didn't know how she would react. I will use a small saddle so that I can tie a rope to it and lead Pretty Mother. It will be good exercise for her, she thought, and I want her near me when I fire my rifle. She needs to get used to it. Sarah tied an old hide in a roll on Pretty Mother's back, to use if she got lucky enough to have meat to bring back. With a few pieces of roast and a water bag, she headed up river walking the horses slowly along the trees that framed the river.

She saw the buck just as he spotted her. He turned, made one big leap and then collapsed. She couldn't believe her eyes. I didn't shoot! I don't understand this, she thought as she slid from her horse and tied the reins to a bush.

Upon examination she saw that the deer had been wounded with an arrow and had been bleeding for a long time. He was just too weak to run. She mercifully ended his suffering. She cleaned him on the spot and used the old hide across Pretty Mother's back. A rope thrown over a branch, helped to leverage the deer up on Pretty Mother's back and tie it on.

She headed up the path to the spot in front of Beth's house where it had become customary for the women to dry their meat. The young buck was large and fat, but the three women made quick work of slicing the meat and putting the fat in a kettle to melt down. Joshua was given the job of watching the meat on the drying racks, while the women went inside for a well-earned cup of tea. Eli and Lily were put down for a nap and all was quiet.

"That was quite a beautiful deer, Sarah. He had a big rack of antlers. How did you ever learn to hunt like that?"

"The people feel that it is important for women to be able to hunt. If the men go to war and are killed, babies still need to be fed. Many women are good providers, sometimes better than their men. Women gather too and grow the corn. I haven't hunted for a while. I was just lucky," Sarah said.

She didn't tell them that the deer had been shot with an arrow. She had put the arrow in her bundle to look at later, wondering which tribe was hunting so near. She was not ready to share her concern yet.

"Now that the meat is sliced, I think I will take the hide back and start processing it," She said, but when she got away from the fire, she suggested to Joshua that he check the lookout. I will tend the meat for you until you get back down. She felt uneasy. Joshua hurried away to the path they used to climb up on the bluff. Although seeming to be glad to be temporarily free of his duty, he returned promptly and said that it was all clear.

Ben and Jed returned from the woods with Angel pulling the wagon filled with logs for the porch of the new house for Ben. They took it to the location and unloaded it. When they returned they were surprised to see the racks filled with drying meat.

"Who shot the deer?" asked Ben as he looked at the nice set of antlers.

"Aunt Sarah did," answered Josh.

"I didn't hear a shot," said Jed. "We were probably making too much noise." Ben picked up the antlers. "I am going to fasten these onto a board for her wall. This is the first thing she has hunted since she was here. I didn't realize that she could."

"You know Ben that the property really isn't hers until she turns twenty one. When is her birthday?" asked Jed. "It was about a week before mine and we usually celebrated together."

"How old will she be this fall?"

"Let me see," said Ben. "I'm going to be twenty six so that makes her nineteen."

"We better explain it to her, just in case something happens. The people in town saw you sign that paper for the land, but now that they saw her, they might figure out how young she is. Well I wouldn't put it past some of them to try to take it from her."

"They wouldn't do that. Would they?" Ben said. He couldn't believe that the people he knew would do such a thing.

"They could and they might if they knew what a nice place it is. We couldn't do a thing to stop them," said Jed.

"What should we do?" asked Ben.

"Nothing, the less said about her and her place for the next two years the better!" said Jed.

"Jed I am worried. I never knew she had to be twenty one. They didn't ask me her age."

Ben and Jed walked over to the shade where Sarah sat on the grass resting.

"You look warm and tired, what have you been doing, Sarah?" Ben asked.

"I was scraping the deer hide in the sun but decided to take a break and move it over here into the shade. It is really warm today. What have you two been doing?"

"We brought a load of wood for the house porch and decided to say hello and see what you were doing or if you needed anything."

"That's nice. Are you hungry? Would you like a drink of water?"

"No thanks, we're going back now for lunch with Mary. I'm sure she has it ready. That's a good sized buck you got."

"Yes," she agreed with a smile, "and he is young enough to be good meat."

They noticed that she had a fire started outside and the big kettle hung over it.

"What are you cooking?" "Oh, that is dye that I am heating. I want to color some of the cloth you brought for me."

"I think we better just tell you the real reason we are here. Sarah, that paper I gave you, it does say that the land is yours, but what we didn't tell you is that legally it can't be until you turn twenty-one years old. That won't be for two years yet."

"Ben, do not look so worried. We are here, the house is here, God is here and what a paper says or doesn't say, can't make any difference. He is in control. Let's pray about it and put it in His hands."

Ben looked from Sarah to Jed and reached for their hands to form a circle. He prayed.

"Father, we thank you for all that you have given us. You are our provider. We thank you again for bringing Sarah home to us. We thank you for helping us build this house for her. We ask you now to help us trust you. We ask that you protect Sarah and this place and keep them safe and secure. We ask that you hide her youth from anyone that might want to take this place from her. We pray in the holy name of Jesus. Amen"

"Amen" they said together.

CHAPTER THREE
WILD RIDE

That night, Sarah sat on the edge of her beautiful bed. The room was filled by the warm glow of a small grease candle. She looked out the open window, into the field to see her horses and realized that she could see a herd of wild horses milling around near the fence on the far side. I need to tell Ben right away. No maybe I should try to scare them off. They may steal Moon Boy, and Pretty Mother. They could empty the field if they knock down the fence.

She hurried out the door and jumped on the brown pony she kept near the cabin for easy transportation. She rode hard to the hut, yelling. "Ben Hurry! There are horses near the field with Moon Boy!"

Ben threw open the front door of the hut, pulling on his shirt.

"What's the matter?"

"Horses, lots of them, and I think they are trying to take our white ones. They are right by the far fence!"

"This is what we have been waiting for! I am heading over there, go tell Jed and then come back. We may need your help."

"She was puzzled and excited as she raced the horse down the trail to Jed's house yelling. Her voice carried into the open windows.

"Jed, get up! Horses, lots of horses are here. Jed, hurry, Ben needs you!" He was up and out the door in a flash. He ran all the way to Ben's corral and jumped on Dixie's back taking time to only add a bridle. Ben had taken Big Boy. All the horses were showing excitement.

With a little luck and good timing they thought they could catch the entire small wild herd. Ben and Jed had created a section in the far fence that would drop down to form an opening to the trail that surrounded the small field where Pretty Mother and the other white horses were kept.

The stallion stomped his feet and called to the horses in the enclosed field. He watched Pretty Mother as she circled the fence that held her. Suddenly the section of fence in front of him dropped to the ground, as Jed and Ben released the clasps that held it in place by jerking at the same time on separate ropes. He raced inside, with his herd behind him. He soon realized that Pretty Mother was held by yet another tall fence. He turned to retreat to find that the section he had entered was no longer down.

As soon as the last horse in the wild herd had crossed the down fence, Jed and Ben had replaced the fence and fastened it securely. He was trapped, in a long narrow channel of fencing, high above his head. He raced along the length of it building speed. Hoping to clear the end, only to find that it meshed into tree branches and brush with no space to get near it. He turned into the face of his following herd, pushing through them, dashing back the way he had come. There was no escape! He was frantic! In his prime, and he had never been stopped from going where he wanted. Over and over they ran the length and back until they were all exhausted.

Sarah sat on the brown, watching the horses dash past.

"Ben, you are a genius! By making the fence high and the area between narrow they can't jump over."

Jed and Ben were already busy reinforcing the section they had dropped.

"The stallion saw this down and will think that it is weaker here. We will leave them in there only a few days until they get used to the fence, and then, one by one, we can start bringing the more docile ones out and deciding where we want them."

Sarah was amazed at how quickly they had caught the entire small herd.

"What are you going to do with so many?"

"Some we will keep as breeding stock. Others we will train and sell to the army."

"I don't think you will ever ride on the back of that stallion, Ben," said Sarah.

"Well he won't be easy!" replied her brother.

"You are right about that." Jed laughed. "I can't wait to see him try!" Then they all laughed. They worked nearly until morning, getting hay hauled and tossed In to the wild herd and a large wooden tub filled to the top with fresh water.

"At least now we can let them relax and calm down," said Jed, as they all headed back; to let the waiting women know what they had accomplished. Mary had a meal ready of wild oats with honey and crushed nuts, coffee and eggs.

As Ben entered the hut he kissed Mary on the cheek and asked how she was feeling. "I'm fine but all of you must be exhausted, you were up all night."

"Wait until you see the horses we have caught in the long pen. It worked better than we could have hoped," said Ben. Adam and Eli came out and both got up into Ben's lap.

"Adam, if you get any bigger I am going to have to sit on your lap instead," Ben kidded the boy. Adam laughed and jumped down.

"Dad I heard what you said. How many horses did you catch?" asked Joshua as he came out rubbing his eyes.

"We thought we would leave the job of counting them for you this morning. You can go over with Adam after breakfast, but stay back from the fence. I don't want either of you getting kicked. They are pretty angry right now."

"I was worried about all of you last night. I spent my time here in prayer for the safety of all of you and the horses, too. I thank God that you managed to catch them without any injuries," said Mary.

"I'll be careful and I'll be sure that Adam keeps back. Hurry up Adam, get your shirt on so we can go see how many they caught." Both boys bolted out the front door and ran to the corral to get their horses without a thought of eating.

Joshua stuck his head back in the door and asked if someone had used Dixie last night.

"Yes, son, Jed did. We were in a hurry and I think Jed didn't want to take Angel near the wild herd."

"I thought he looked a little tired. We can both ride on Little Mouse, if you think it's alright. That way I will know for sure Adam is back from the fence."

"That's fine. Adam do you want to ride with Josh on Little Mouse, or would you like to ride on Missy?"

Adam's face lit up with a big grin.

"I have never ridden on Missy. That would be fun!"

"I'll help you get her ready," said Ben.

"Don't get near the fence with the wild horses," he reminded the boys as they headed down the trail.

Beth rode slowly, walking Princess with Johnny and Lily in front of her.

"Mary, do you and Eli want to ride over to see the horses?" asked Beth.

"Yes, just give me a minute and I'll be ready," said Mary.

"Sarah, do you want to ride back with us?" asked Beth.

"Yes, I will. I have a hide to work and snares to check. I think I will boil some of the softer apples and make jelly today."

"Sarah, where do you get your energy? You were up all night."

"I'm not very tired. I will sleep well tonight." Mary and Beth glanced at each other wondering why Sarah felt it necessary to continue to work so hard.

Joshua tried to count the horses but they continually moved, so he couldn't be sure that he had an accurate count.

"I think we have thirty one, but I'm not sure," he said to Beth, as she rode up beside him.

"Aren't they beautiful?" she said. Mary sat quietly for a moment and then agreed with Joshua.

"I think you are right. I counted thirty-one. They are good horses. Most of them look young enough to train for riding." Just then Mary noticed the palomino.

"Look at that one Beth. It is almost golden, and the white mane and tail are beautiful. I wonder if Ben or Jed noticed her." Sarah had stopped to appreciate the beauty of the horses and then slowly rode on toward her cabin and the chores she had decided to do. In her mind she was thinking about the herd of the people and wondering how many of the wild herds of the prairie were being captured. Soon we will not see the horses running free, she thought. Sarah felt sad.

Joshua told his mom that he was going to check the lookout. Adam turned Missy, intending to follow him.

"Adam you stay here. Please ride back with me," she said. "I don't want you climbing up there until you are bigger," said Mary. Adam pouted all the way back to the hut. "We have a big job to do today. While Dad gets a little sleep, you and I are going down to the woods with Eli and gather some more nuts. Maybe we can find a honey tree." She said with a smile. She knew that Adam loved honey. His face brightened.

Joshua treasured his times alone on the top of the bluff. It was his time to do what he wanted. Usually that was carving, but today he felt restless. He was about to climb down, when he noticed movement on the river. It was hard to see what it was at first. He thought maybe a tree had fallen in the water. Then he realized that it was a big raft. It was moving along swiftly and tipping dangerously. No one was steering it. A woman and child clung to each other in the middle of it as it spun and bobbed along banging boulders dangerously.

"Dad, Dad, hurry," Joshua called as he opened the gate to the corral pulling out Big Boy and Dixie. He tied their bridals to the corral fence and hurried in the hut. Ben was standing near the fire pulling on his clothes as fast as he could.

"What is the matter Josh?"

"Dad there is a raft heading down river with people on it. No one is controlling it. I saw a woman and a little child on it. They looked like they were in big trouble Dad!"

"They are son. We have to help them before they reach the falls." Ben buckled on Big Boy's saddle in record time and galloped down the path at the edge of the river. He couldn't see the raft until he had rounded the bend. Big Boy seemed to sense that this was no ordinary trip for exercise and he stretched out into a distance-eating stride that surprised Ben. They had to get ahead of the raft in order to stop it. Ben decided that the only chance he had was to take Big Boy into the water. He would need his powerful muscles to stop the raft and pull it to safety. The woman screamed as the raft slammed into a rock and banged past it, dumping a crate that bobbed along beside it.

As Ben got closer he could see that someone else was on the raft lying under a blanket. Still he raced on until finally he had gained enough distance to plunge in. Big Boy pulled against the current and neared the middle of the river as the raft came near. Ben readied his rope and threw it, catching on a post that at one time had held a tiller. He wrapped the rope on the saddle horn and hoped that Big Boy's strength would be enough to anchor the raft without it swinging so wide that it would spill its precious cargo, but just then, the raft did swing wide and tilted dangerously against the current. The water washed over the raft in response to the restraint. Big Boy instinctively backed up, avoiding being slammed by the rafts corner as it spun out of control. Knowing what to do, he headed for the bank pulling with all his might against the current, with the raft in tow.

The big horse's sides heaved as he stood on the bank and Ben tied the raft securely to one of the trees.

Big Boy had used all the strength that he could give and it had been just enough. He was spent. He had worked with Ben the night before spending nervous energy as he saw the frantic horses trapped by the fence. Now he had been asked to stop a heavy raft that was rushing down the center of the river. He had succeeded. Ben hugged Big Boy for just an instant.

"Well done my big friend. Well done."

The woman and child were crying. The man beneath the wet blanket seemed unaware of his surroundings. Joshua had not immediately followed Ben, but had hurried to get Jed. Their horses came, pounding up a moment later. Jed gently helped the woman to shore and then lifted the child into a blanket that Joshua had ready.

Ben saw the arrow sticking out of the man's chest before the woman said that they had been attacked the night before.

"We were with another family. We were traveling the river together. The others were lost, but our raft was carried away from the fight quickly by the current when my husband fell from the arrow. We had a pole that I used for a while but I dropped it and couldn't get it back. I was so scared, that we would tip and fall off. We have lost most of our things, but that doesn't matter. I am afraid for my husband. He has been still like that since this morning," she said between sobs. "Thank you, Thank you for helping us."

"It's alright now Ma'am. We are glad that we were here to help," said Ben.

"We need to get him back to the hut as fast as we can," said Jed. Ben was already cutting poles for a travois. They tied the wet blanket between the poles and stretched it tight. After hugging Big Boy and telling him how wonderful he was Ben led Big Boy as he pulled the travois slowly down the trail. The woman rode with Jed. Joshua held the little girl in front of him. She seemed to have made a remarkable recovery from her frightful journey down river and was riding quietly with Joshua.

As they neared the hut, Sarah was there.

"Keep going, take him to my house," she said as she rode out swiftly ahead of them.

When they arrived, the front door stood open. She had cleared the benches away from the table and the curtains were all pulled open. The fire was going brightly and a pan of water heated a poultice. A second pan held a concoction that smelled terrible and probably tasted even worse.

"Put him here on the table," she directed. "Jed, please cut his shirt off. Ben, get more water into that pan. Joshua, ride back to the house and see if your mother or Beth have soft hides or cloth for bandages." Sarah took charge as she was used to doing when someone was injured. The chest was bathed in the concoction and the arrow pulled free. The man moaned but didn't wake. She handed the arrow to Jed. "I have another just like it over there on top of the cupboard. It was in the deer that I hunted. I think we have people near here that we do not know."

Mary had gone down to the river and waded in pulling a few pieces of floating clothing to the bank. She watched as a barrel sped by out of reach. She felt bad for the woman.

"Please God spare her husband. Heal him and watch over the little family and watch over us, too. That was an arrow I saw in the man's chest, Lord. That means that Indians are near. Please don't let them come here to harm my family. Thank you Father, for loving us and hearing my prayer, Amen"

As Mary prayed on the riverbank, Ben, Jed and Sarah were also joining in prayer in the cabin for help with the man's injury. Sarah raised her hands as she had done before, many times in the community tent of the people.

"God once again I ask your help, to guide my hands as I work to help this man. Be with me Lord Jesus. Touch him; heal him, as I know that you can. Thank you, Jesus. Amen." Ben, Jed and the man's wife said "Amen."

Joshua returned with the leather bandages and strips of white cloth that Sarah had requested. He put them next to the man on the table and took the little girl by the hand out to the porch. He lifted her onto the bench and gave her a piece of meat and some water in a cup. She swung her feet and was content to nibble and smile at Joshua. It was then that he realized that he had seen her cry, but she had not spoken a word. "What is your name? Mine is Josh." She didn't answer. She slid off the bench going back inside and stood leaning against her mother.

Ben looked at Joshua and realized that once again Joshua had acted very responsibly. He thought back to the time when Joshua had stayed with Beth and Johnny, after the Indian raid while he had ridden to the Parker homestead to bury Slim Parker, Mary's husband and Josh and Adam's father. He breathed another prayer of thanks, that they had found Mary and Adam after they had escaped from the Indians that had captured them. Joshua had cared for Johnny like a grown up when Beth had gotten very ill.

"Dad, is something wrong?" Joshua asked. "You were staring at me."

"No Josh, I was just thinking. It might be a good idea if you made sure that we have an all clear. Maybe you should take a water bag and jerky and stay at the lookout for a while, if you don't mind."

"Sure Dad, I'll go right away."

After the man was made comfortable on a pallet near the wall, Sarah cleared the table and scrubbed it. Ben put the benches back in place. Jed had helped with the lifting of the man and supported his weight while Sarah had applied the poultice and wrapped the wound. They had gotten very little of the concoction in him but set the cup and spoon nearby where they could try easily whenever he stirred.

Beth came slowly up with the wagon pulling it into the shade of the trees and motioned to be quiet. Lily and Johnny were both asleep on the hay in the wagon. She lifted down a pot of stew and Ben took it inside and set it near the fire. She brought in a loaf of bread she had baked the night before. The aroma of the food filled the little cabin and lightened the mood.

"Hello, I'm Beth," she said to the woman now sitting in the chair near the window. "Rachel," said the woman softly as she continued to rock her little girl. The child's eyes drifted shut and she slept. Sarah motioned for Rachel to carry the girl in the bedroom where she was placed on Sarah's bed and gently covered.

After you have something to eat you should rest, too. I will care for your husband as well as I can. He is in God's hands now. There isn't much more I can do for him.

Mary stepped in the open door quietly. She had noticed the children sleeping in the wagon.

"I stopped down just to leave this food," she said as she placed the food near the fire. She had brought cooked greens and vegetables, boiled, new potatoes and a roasted rabbit.

"Thank you Mary," said Sarah. "You work too hard. We will be fine here. We are just waiting and praying."

"If you need anything at all let me know," said Mary. "I am going back to the hut now. Joshua is with the boys and he is waiting to go up to the lookout." Mary left as quietly as she came.

Joshua was eager to go. He had seen the arrow Sarah removed, and had heard her say that the deer had been shot with the same type arrow. He hurried to the top of the bluff where he scanned the prairie and the trees along the river as far as he could see. Nothing was moving. No animals were in sight either. It was a shame to take the horses off the prairie, he thought. He liked watching them out there, but he felt more would come.

He got out his new jackknife and began to work on his latest carving of a deer, but put it back down. He selected a new chunk of wood and began again. He wanted to make a doll's head. He would ask his mother to make the rest of it out of cloth. He had seen Sarah's. It can't be that hard to do. He thought. I think that little girl would like a doll. It was late in the day when he came in the hut with a smile on his face.

"Hello Son. You have been up on the bluff a long time." His mother hugged him and said, "It helps me to feel safe when I know that I have a responsible son as a sentry. I made cookies. Would you like some?" she asked. He picked up a handful and took a big bite of one before he said,

"Thanks, Mom. I was getting hungry up there. It is boring without the herd of horses on the prairie. I didn't see any big animals at all today."

"Joshua, there are lots of wild horses. More will wander this way. I'm sure of it."

"Mother, would you do me a favor?" he asked.

"What son?"

"Well it's not really for me. I made this doll head and I was thinking that if you would make a cloth body for it, then the little girl from the raft would have something to play with."

"Josh it was thoughtful of you to think of making her a doll. Let me see what you have made." She looked at the carved face and hair. It was pleasant to look at and smooth on the surface. He had done a good job. "This is very nice. I'll see what I can do this evening after we eat. You can give it to her tomorrow."

"Do you think we could brush the hair part with brown dye?"

"Yes, I think that would work and we can rub a little of the pink I made from the beet peelings into her cheeks and lips," said Mary with a smile.

He went out the door smiling, with Adam by his side. They began the evening chores of caring for the animals. Adam brought in the eggs and reported that the chickens were fed and watered and that they had put some new hay in some of the nest boxes.

The boys knew that the barn was empty of horses. Only a couple yearlings were in the corral. Joshua tossed in a bundle of hay for them and opened the channel so that the little pond would fill. He smiled, thinking of how Rusty would like to be in there to stomp in the water as it filled. Now Rusty and Missy were grown and out in the fields with the rest of the horses. Dad will be back from Aunt Sarah's with Big Boy. I guess I better throw another bundle in there. He shut off the channel with the slate and rock and heard Ben coming on the trail.

"Dad, I am glad you are back. How is the man?"

"He is still not awake," said Ben. "His wife says his name is Zack. Her name is Rachel and the little girl's name is Margaret. She is a sweet little thing isn't she?"

"She doesn't talk though," said Josh. "Mom and I are making her a doll. Supper is almost ready. Mom is boiling potatoes and making fried rabbit." "That sounds really good. I am hungry."

Joshua knew that anytime his mom cooked rabbit, it was his job to check the snares and reset the ones that needed it. She had already pegged the two skins in the grass ready to process. He and Adam went together to check the snares.

"Maybe we should put out more snares. Then we would catch more rabbits and have some extra skins to trade when we go to the trading post this fall," said Adam. "I am going to ask Dad at supper, if he will let me go this time."

After they sat down at the table, Ben led a prayer for Zack and his family. He thanked God for allowing him to save them from the river, and for bringing them into their lives. He asked that God help them to be a blessing to the small family and that Zack would be made well quickly. He thanked God again for the herd of wild horses and asked for wisdom in their care and kind training. He thanked God for the bounty of food that He always provided. And they all said, "Amen."

Silently he added that he hoped that God would grant his wish for Mary to have a baby girl.

After they had eaten, Mary got out her sewing basket and bits of cloth and they fashioned a body for the doll. When it was nearly finished and they were adding tiny roses of color to the face, Joshua took the doll and dunked both its feet into the brown dye. There he said. She has shoes on. They laughed at his cleverness and set the doll on the clothes tree to dry. "She is pretty Mom, Thanks a lot. I think Margaret will like her."

"I'm sure she will," said Ben, "You both did a great job! I'm going down and check the water on all the horses at Sarah's and make sure she has everything she needs. I won't be long," said Ben. He swung back up onto Big Boy who had munched through nearly the entire bundle of hay that Joshua had put in the corral for him. He turned around before leaving and asked Josh to make one last trip to the top of the bluff to check before dark.

"All clear," Josh announced as he came in. It is cold up there. The wind is strong," he said as he rubbed his arms and sat down by the fire.

"Tomorrow we should work in the garden and bring in anything that is ready to be dried. We won't need to get the rest of the potatoes and squash, or pumpkins but we should put a layer of grass over the green tomatoes," said Mary. "I hope we don't have an early fall. We have so much to do before winter."

"Mother, after we get everything out of the garden will we get to have popcorn?" asked Adam. "How can you remember that? Yes we will have some popcorn like we did last year and maybe we can take some down to Margaret," said Mary.

CHAPTER FOUR
ZACK AND WILD HORSES

Finally Rachel slept. She was exhausted after her ordeal on the raft. Sarah had made a batch of chamomile tea and added a few crushed wild cherries and honey for a sweet flavor.

Zack mumbled during the night but never came fully awake. Sarah spoon-fed the concoction into him each time he stirred. He had a fever that was climbing. The arrow had started an infection in his chest. Sarah changed the poultice and each time her concern deepened.

When Ben stopped by in the morning to check on Zack, Sarah stepped outside to talk.

"Zack needs more help than I can give him. He needs a doctor that can remove the infection and give him strong medicine. Is there a doctor at the settlement?"

"I don't think so. I have never seen one there."

Jed rode up and joined the conversation. They explained what they had been discussing.

"I think we need to open up the wound and make it drain. Then we can put on a poultice like I used on your shoulder Ben. His wound is sealed over and the plants can't draw out the infection."

"Let's do it right away, said Sarah. "Let's do it now before his wife wakes up. She doesn't need to watch that." Sarah heated a knife at the edge of the fire while Jed pounded more fresh plants and willow bark. Those were put on to boil in a little water. They removed the poultice and Jed made one quick slash into the spot that the arrow had entered.

Zack cried out, even in his unconscious state. Rachel jerked up awake.

"What has happened," she shouted racing to his side? They explained and showed her that infection and blood now flowed out of his chest. They covered it with hot wet compresses to keep it open and flowing and when it finally seemed clean, they covered it with the disinfectant solution from the pan and applied more of the poultice. They spooned medicine into his mouth, time and again. Rachel and Sarah's vigil continued. During the night he improved and his fever broke. By morning he slept peacefully.

Sarah was so glad to see the improvement that she met Jed and Ben at the door with tears glistening in her eyes.

"He is much better. He is going to live."

Jed hugged her and said, "We make quite a team, the three of us."

"Three?" questioned Ben. "I didn't help."

"No, I was thinking, God, Sarah, and I."

"Yes, Big Brother well said." And with that Ben went out to move the white horses from the double fenced field so that he could use it to transfer some of the wild herd.

It wasn't difficult to put a rope on Buddy, Moon Boy or Pretty Mother so he took them first. He put them into the field where Dart Away had been. Dart Away was now in a stall in the barn, for the time being. The two white fillies gave him a challenge but eventually he was able to rope them and lead them to the new field, too. He hoped that all the activity with so many horses around would keep Buddy and Moon Boy entertained so they wouldn't jump over the fence and need to be caught and brought back.

Jed and Joshua were on horseback and ready to help any way they could. Ben couldn't see any other way to start, other than going in the long pen with the herd. He had selected several that he thought were good candidates to start with. He eased through the side gate. It was only big enough for one horse with a rider.

Getting the younger horses to bunch together where he wanted them was nearly impossible. They gave up on driving them into the field. Instead one by one they roped them and took them to the field between Ginger and Angel. It worked perfectly until the stallion decided that he would not stand for these humans taking members of his herd away and he charged at them with hooves flying. Ben rode out of the gate and it was closed just in time. They waited for him to calm down.

Jed could tell by the look on Ben's face that he was in his problem-solving mode again.

"What we need is several long poles that we can slide across, dividing him from the rest, while we move them. We will need some kind of a rack on both sides to support the poles. The fence isn't enough." "Let's let him think he has won while we go cut some poles. We can be thinking about the racks while we are working," said Ben.

"Ben is foolish going into a narrow pen like that with that wild stallion. Doesn't he know how vicious they can be?" said Rachel. She stood on the front porch of Sarah's cabin watching the men work with the horses. "He knows," said Sarah, "but he has to get them out of that narrow pen and into a field where they can graze and they can begin to gentle some of them."

"That Stallion will never be gentled," said Rachel. "One like that almost killed my Zack."

"What happened?" Sarah asked. "He was working on a ranch and they got in some new horses. The owner offered one hundred dollars to the man that could ride a big gray stallion in the bunch. That beast threw Zack clear over the fence. He landed hard. He broke an arm and his leg and didn't wake up that time for nearly a week. Even after that, he still loves horses and training them." Sarah was amazed that Zack would want to work with wild horses after an ordeal like that.

Joshua rode up on Little Mouse, and jumped off with a flourish. He walked over to Margaret and pulled the doll out of his shirt.

"This baby keeps crying. Do you think you can do something for her?" He said, as he handed it to Margaret. She tucked the doll into her arms and rocked it gently. Her smile was the sweetest thank you anyone could ever ask for.

Joshua winked and smiled at her as he rode away on Little Mouse. He hurried to the trees along the back edge of the lake where he could see Ben and Jed working. They had laced two logs together and Sundown was ready to pull them up near the pen. They were tall straight saplings, perfect for the job. Josh volunteered to lead Sundown while they cut two more.

"Stay back from the fence Josh," said Ben. "That stallion is all fired up."

"I will," answered Josh.

Mary was glad to see the men and her oldest son coming with happy voices. It must have gone well she thought. She was surprised to see them leading old Dart Away. Ben put him in his corral and tossed in some hay and filled the pond.

"He has never been in there. I hope he likes it here near the hut. It has lots of shade and he can go in the barn anytime he wants. Later I'm hoping that we can introduce him to some more of our ladies. It can't hurt," said Ben with a grin.

"Dad and I got the wild herd moved. Uncle Jed helped, of course," said Josh.

"How did it go?" asked Mary. Ben wrinkled his forehead before answering.

"Not bad."

"What is bothering you then, Ben, you look a little concerned."

"I am. I can't figure out what to do with the stallion. There can be no doubt that he is the strongest horse in the herd and has certainly proven his worth in the beautiful young ones he has sired, but he is dangerous. I will have to pray about him."

"Jed you are quiet. What do you think we should do with him?" Mary asked.

"Well we sure can't let him go. He would return here to try to get his herd back."

"Mary have you seen Beth today?" asked Jed.

"Yes," answered Mary. "She helped me in the garden for a little while but then she went back to the house. She is making a batch of apple jelly I think."

"That sounds good. Guess I'll go up and see what she is fixing for lunch and tell her about moving the herd."

*****

Zack's strength started to return and after a few days, there was no keeping him down. He wandered around Sarah's fields and even ventured down as far as Ben and Mary's looking at everything, and always asking questions.

One afternoon while Rachel and Sarah were sewing, he wandered down to Jed's barn. Finding Joshua there alone, cleaning stalls, he asked him questions about everybody.

"Your Mom's older than your Dad. Ben's your second Dad isn't he?"

Yes, my dad was killed by Indians. They took my mom and Adam, too. Ben helped the soldiers to get them back."

"How old is Ben?" Without a thought Josh answered.

"Dad is twenty six. He was just fifteen when the Indians attacked and killed his folks and took Sarah. We only got her back early this spring. I was six years old when the Indians came and killed my first Dad.

"How old is Sarah?"

"I'm not sure, but she was about nine when they took her."

"Is Sarah married?"

"No but she is sure pretty. Mom says any man would be lucky to marry her."

"Well, I've got Rachel so I don't think I will even consider that." They both laughed. "Whose place is that?"

"It's hers. Uncle Jed and Dad built it for her before she came back."

"I see." Then Zack changed the subject. "I saw you climbing up on the bluff yesterday. What were you doing up there?" "That's our lookout post. We make sure that there aren't any Indians around. We can see forever up there. It is a good place to spot game, too."

"When I feel strong enough I'll come up there and have a look with you, if that's alright."

"Sure anybody can go up there."

Zack headed back to Sarah's and lay down on his pallet closing his eyes. He wasn't tired. He just wanted to think and not be disturbed. He had to keep calm and not let on. He was planning. He got back up and went out to the porch where the women were sewing.

"Sarah when I get stronger, I'll be glad to break some of those horses for you. I have to do something to earn my keep," offered Zack.

"Well I appreciate you wanted to do that for us, but at the "S & J" we believe in gentling a horse, not breaking it. Ben starts them out with a small weight strapped on their backs and lots of love. He has never used a whip or spurs on any of the horses," she said.

"That can't be true. I saw spur scars on that big beast that Ben rides."

"That's Big Boy. He had those scars when Ben got him. He had been badly mistreated by his first owner. Ben treats him kindly and that horse would do anything for Ben now."

"That's hard to believe young lady, hard to believe."

Suddenly Sarah felt a strong dislike for Zack. She wished that they would move on. She no longer liked having them there, and she certainly didn't want to continue living with them all winter in her small cabin.

Sarah needed to be alone to think. She told Rachel that she needed to do something but thought it would be nice if Rachel continued sewing and finished putting the buttons on Margaret's dress. Rachel had a bad feeling. She could tell that something was bothering Sarah. She had been vague about what she had to do. She watched her as she walked to the fence and slipped the soft bridle on Pretty Mother. Sarah rode away toward Ben's but then entered the trees along the river and disappeared from sight.

She crossed the river and rode out onto the prairie toward the tall grass. For a while her thoughts were jumbled as Pretty Mother plodded on. Sarah had not realized how much she enjoyed the solitude of her little cabin until circumstances had abruptly changed it. She slid off the horse and walked along leading her.

She knew that she had to deal with the feeling that her sanctuary had been invaded. She had passed judgment on Zack and she had found him lacking. What is the matter with me? I shouldn't feel this way. He hasn't done anything wrong. What did he do anyway? He just disagreed with me. That's all. Rachel is nice and hard working. Margaret is sweet. I wish I could figure out why she doesn't talk though. They have been through a terrible time, and they lost everything they had on the river. I am ashamed. I need to be patient and kind. God always has a plan. She knelt there in the grass of the prairie. At first she was quiet and listened to the wind moving the tall grass around her. She also listened to the voice inside her heart.

"You are a healer. Sometimes it is necessary to treat more than a person's body."

"God forgive me for not wanting to share my cabin. Forgive me for judging Zack so harshly. He was offering to help us in the only way that he knows. It is our job to teach him a better way. I know that now. Give me wisdom and strength so that I can be your hands to help this little family."

It's funny, she thought, as she rode back toward the river. I never feel threatened by predators in the tall grass. I just feel closer to the Lord.

As she crossed the river she decided to visit Mary before going back to her cabin. She stopped at the hut and just as she suspected, Mary was not inside. The path to the lake was empty, but when she rounded the trees she could see Beth, Mary and the children all outside at the house. They were all gathered around a sweet treat that Ben had brought from the woods. He had discovered another bee tree. This time he had paid a painful price for the honey. He had several welts from bee stings on his face, neck and arms.

Sarah immediately made a paste of mud mixed with baking soda and applied it to the stings.

"Look at all the honey. We are going to have good treats this winter," said Johnny. Ben had asked that the honey be divided between the three houses. The women were trying to do just that between pauses to remove sticky little fingers.

"Sarah was there something that you needed?" asked Ben.

"No I just stopped down to visit."

"I am glad that you are here, because we wanted to talk to you, where Zack and Rachel can't hear us. We are thinking about building a cabin near the backside of the lake and let them use it this winter. We can use the help with all the horses and they need the time to try to get back some of what they lost. Since you are part of the "S & J" now, we want to know what you think."

"Well, Zack did say to me this morning that as soon as he is strong enough, he wants to help with the horses to repay us for helping his family," said Sarah. She didn't mention how upset she had been at Zack. This may be God's answer to my prayer. He didn't waste any time, she thought.

After her time alone with the Lord, and now finding out that they were planning a cabin for the little family, she returned with a much lighter heart.

Joshua had watched Sarah ride out onto the prairie alone and had felt relieved when she had returned. He scrambled down the bluff in time to join in the fun of tasting the honey.

"Where's Uncle Jed?" Josh asked. "He is missing out on the treat."

"He was here. He has gone to the woods, to cut trees for a new cabin we are going to build down by the lake," said Beth.

"Now that I have delivered the honey, I need to go help. Do you want to help, Josh?"

"Sure," said the boy with enthusiasm, "I'll bring Sundown. He is good at pulling logs."

The cozy cabin was built in record time. Experience made the job a lot easier, and after a couple weeks, Zack was able to help with some of the lighter chores, making more time for work on the cabin.

Ben, Jed, Joshua and Zack went hunting several times in the next few weeks. Joshua divided his time between the lookout and the cabin site.

Whenever he spotted game, the men would ride out and they usually returned with meat to be dried and shared for winter. They knew they had plenty of garden produce and the woods would give her bounty of wild apples, cherries and nuts, but they had a new cache in the lake cabin to fill with meat.

The women sliced and dried meat and kept fires burning. They gathered food from the prairie together. They took baskets into the woods returning tired and happy, with baskets filled with God's bounty of wild onions, coltsfoot and mushrooms. The garden was tended and the last few potatoes and seeds harvested.

Rachel had set traps under the willows near the lake and had a growing stack of small furs for hats and mittens.

The women sewed coats for the little family from their many big game hides. Beth knitted a sweater for Margaret and a shawl for Rachel for Christmas; being careful to work on them only when she was sure she would not be discovered. Mary had taught Sarah how to knit and she was working on a dark green sweater for Zack. Mary had showed Sarah the one she had finished for Ben. She had kept it hidden from him only with a great deal of difficulty. Jed had cut slices of bone for the buttons and drilled holes in them. After they were sanded they could be waxed and left cream color, or soaked in the dye to match the yarn. Beth had one almost finished for Jed. She had dyed the yarn and buttons a rich dark brown with nut casing dye. She was sure she had made it big enough, but when she took it out and tried it on, she wasn't so sure. The sleeves were not as long as his shirt sleeves. She sat by the window picking the shoulder seams out and unraveling the yarn, when she saw the men approaching the house. Quickly she stuffed the unfinished sweater back in its hiding place.

They did their best to provide the necessities for the new cabin. By pooling their resources they found they had pans and dishes enough to share.

Sarah pointed out the brown Indian hunting pony and told Rachel that she was welcome to use her anytime she wanted. Zack had begun to work with several of the wild mares. He was learning that any force or rough treatment was met with fierce disapproval from everyone. Ben explained what he had done first with Ginger and then others and that it was the way that he wanted all the animals treated. Zack was learning.

The problem of what to do with the stallion solved itself. One morning when Ben went to check on him and give him water, he was gone. He had kicked the fence down in one section and sailed over another. Ben had to admit to himself that he was almost glad. It is a shame to fence in a wild spirit like that horse, he thought.

When the first dusting of snow covered the ground, the wagon was taken to the trading post and along with the usual things, they returned with two windows and supplies to make the new cabin comfortable. Ben had asked Jed and Beth to go. He didn't want to see anyone in the settlement. He was still hurt and angry about the way Helen had treated Sarah. Rachel stayed at their house with Margaret and cared for Lily and Johnny.

Zack had become a real asset. Ben was beginning to see progress with many of the horses. Zack seemed tireless when it came to patiently working with them.

Rachel helped Mary daily with some of her work, as she prepared to have the baby. It was expected soon. Mary's walk seemed more like a waddle as she and Rachel made their way slowly past the empty garden, leading Eli and followed by Margaret.

"It almost seems like we were meant to be here. I love all of you and I like where they have put the cabin for us. It is far enough from the lake to be safe if we get a lot of rain, but not too far from you or Beth or Sarah. I think Sarah will be glad when we get moved. Her place is small and I get the feeling that sometimes it is trying on her to have us there this long." Mary looked at Rachel realizing that she was probably right.

"Well it won't be long now. They have most of the work done on the cabin.

"The trading post had all the supplies on the list. The windows they brought were a couple that Ben had ordered for our new house," said Mary. "Jed ordered more, when he picked those up. We will be building against the bluff where the trees are near the gate to Sarah's surround. I like it just fine in the hut, but he seemed to think that we should build a house like Jed's. It does seem a little small in the hut sometimes, and now the new baby is almost here I guess we will need a little more room," said Mary.

"Mary, you are so practical. Don't you know how much money this place will be making in a few years when they start moving the cattle and selling saddle ready horses?" said Rachel.

"I guess I never really thought about it. I'm just grateful that the boys and I found a man like Ben to love us and take care of us. When the Indians killed Slim I thought my life was over!"

"Zack and I are going to have a place like this," said Rachel. "He says he has a plan that will get us off to a fast start. He won't tell me what it is. It is kind of exciting to think about though."

"I can tell you this Rachel. There is nothing quick about building a ranch like this," said Mary. "Ben was only fifteen when he started and Jed joined him here later that year. They have worked hard every day since."

"Maybe you should go back to the hut and rest for a while," suggested Rachel. "I'll take Eli with me." Margaret skipped happily along carrying her doll.

Rachel looked down at her daughter and couldn't help wondering why she wouldn't or couldn't speak.

A few days later, Beth sat on her porch with Rachel having a cup of tea and watching Margaret pet a baby rabbit that Johnny had brought home. Eli grabbed a handful of its fur and Margaret gently disengaged his hand without hurting the rabbit.

"How long do you think it will be before the men let us move into the cabin," asked Rachel?

"I think any day now," said Beth. "They made two beds yesterday, and Jed said that they had the wood for a table and benches all cut. They just need to put them together."

"Zack said that it is a good cabin and will be warm and comfortable this winter. Did you know that Ben gave him a horse yesterday, one to keep I mean, not just to ride? He says that before long it will be gentle enough for anyone to ride. It is brown with white legs. He calls it Socks," said Rachel.

"That's good." Beth said, "He should be rewarded. He has been working really hard and is doing a good job with the horses. Jed said that he can't imagine what they would have done if he hadn't come along."

Beth glanced in the direction of the little cabin by the lake, and saw that Jed and Ben were done for the day and heading toward her on Ginger and Surprise.

"Surprise looks like he wants a good run," said Beth. "Look how he is prancing."

"Yes he is full of energy. You have so many beautiful horses. It will be hard to sell them to the army or anyone else. Won't it?"

"Yes, I don't like the thought of parting with any of them. I love all of them," said Beth. "I know that Ben and Jed feel the same way. God has been so good to us. When I think of the winter I spent alone in a cave with so little to eat and only one thin blanket to wrap around me, I am amazed at what we have now."

In the hut, Mary sat down heavily in one of the willow chairs by the fireplace and looked around knowing that she was not in a hurry to have anything change. She was happy in the hut. It felt warm and safe.

Rachel followed the fence back, and saw that Sarah had nearly finished a waterproof basket and lid. She had been preparing items that would be needed by Rachel and her family in the lake cabin. Several large grass mats were stacked in the storage room along with extra carrying baskets. Sarah had made several long ropes of different strengths from different materials. One small basket sat on a shelf loosely covered by a rabbit's fur. It held bars of strong soap for laundry and a milder version for skin and dishes.

Sarah had made several clay pots in the oven but each time they proved to be fragile and crumbled at the slightest bump, until the last one. It was ugly, and black, but strong. She filled it full of water and sat it on the grass beside the oven to see how it would hold up. If it stays strong, clay pots will be useful in all the houses. I will make lids and anything can be stored in them.

CHAPTER FIVE
THE LAKE CABIN

Sarah kept busy as the days passed. She rode Moon Boy and he responded as if he knew what she was thinking. She always took her rifle with her, but it still troubled Ben when he would see her ride off alone.

One afternoon Joshua hurried down the path of the bluff just as she arrived at the hut on Moon Boy.

"What's the hurry Josh?"

"I want to tell Dad that there is a mountain lion on the other side of the river."

"Well get your gun and Dixie and lets go see if we can find him."

"You mean it?"

"Yes I do, but bring Dixie not Little Mouse. He is used to people firing from his back. He won't spook and leave you lying in the grass."

"Good idea Aunt Sarah." Joshua was so excited. She had included him as if he were grown. He took a deep breath, and tried not to show how excited he was as he put a saddle and bridle on Dixie. He added a water bag and a coil of rope and slid the rifle he had been allowed to use for practicing, into the sleeve as he had seen Ben and Jed do many times. They rode side by side as they crossed the river and headed in the direction that Joshua indicated.

"I think it was just up ahead that I saw it. It wasn't too much farther." Sarah put her finger to her lips and slowed Moon Boy to a walk and finally stopped all together. They studied the grass of the prairie, trying to spot any movement that was caused by anything other than the gentle breeze.

"There," she said softly, as she pointed to a sway in the grain heads. The big cat parted the stems as it moved through.

"How can we shoot it if we can't even see it?" He asked in a whisper.

"She is hunting. Just wait and watch. Suddenly a flurry of action and sound betrayed that the cat had taken its prey.

Now we know right where she is. We go slowly and quietly. She is well entertained. As they crept up on the scene, suddenly Sarah realized that she had made a serious mistake. If the cat sensed their presence she would attack instantly to guard her prey. Sarah had placed Joshua in grave danger.

"Stay a few paces behind me," she whispered. Joshua had not heard her. In his excitement he had circled to her right and was nearly on top of the cat before he could see it in the chest high grass.

The warning roar told Sarah what was happening before she heard the rifle. She ran to the sound and saw Joshua standing there as white as a ghost. The cat lay at his feet. It is not dead yet Joshua you must shoot again. He put the gun near the head and pulled the trigger with his eyes closed. Sinking to the ground on his knees he was instantly sick.

"She has killed a wild pig," said Sarah. "We will skin it too and you can take the tusks. The meat will feed other animals. You must skin the cat yourself. It is your first big kill. Today you are a man, a hunter." Joshua's hand shook as he made the incision. She worked on the boar, keeping busy so that he would not feel embarrassed by his lack of skill at removing the skin of the mountain lion. Finally as he pulled the skin free from beneath the cat a wide smile spread across his face. He pried the long tusks from the boar and a pair of teeth from the cat from top and bottom and planned to start a necklace like Jed and Ben's.

"Thank you, Aunt Sarah, for trusting me. I was foolish for rushing ahead of you, but I promise I will do better next time."

"I know you will." And then right there on the spot she knelt and thanked God out loud for protecting him. When she had finished he was still grinning.

"You know, I think next time I would like to hunt a deer," he said. They laughed together as they rolled the skins and tied them both behind the saddle on Dixie. She pranced nervously, not wanting the smell of the lion on her back.

When they crossed the river and rode up to the hut, they caused quite a stir.

"What have you two been up to?" Mary asked. Ben knew with one glance.

"What happened? Did she jump you?" he asked. "Are you hurt?"

"No Dad. I spotted the cat from the bluff and Aunt Sarah and I went after it. It downed a bore and then I shot it."

"Are you crazy, Sarah? You don't go into the tall grass looking for a cat even if you are an experienced hunter. You certainly don't take a boy that has never hunted!" His face was red and he was shouting.

"I deserve every bit of your rage. Forgive me. I did a stupid, dangerous thing. I thank God neither of us was hurt, but Joshua has had his first successful hunt. Let's all celebrate with him tonight. He has a story to tell. We can have a big fire and sit on blankets and maybe Mary will make us some popcorn."

Mary was very upset. She knew that her son could have been killed. She sat down in her rocker and tried to tell herself that it was alright now. That he was safe and here with her. She laid her hand on her stomach and felt the hard surface as the contraction came on. Instantly Sarah sprang into her role as healer. She started water in a small pan adding this and that from the dried bundles hanging nearby. As soon as the tea turned dark, she poured Mary a cup and added hot water to the rest and served it to everyone.

"I am so sorry. I caused all this concern. I will never do such a dangerous thing again, I promise," said Sarah.

"Nonsense," said Mary. "This young man has done well and I don't see any reason to wait until tonight to celebrate! Ben, would you ride down and tell Beth and Jed. Adam, go get Rachel and Zack. We are going to have a party. Tell the children that we are going to have sweet tea and popcorn!" Mary was beaming. The medicinal tea had done the trick. She was feeling fine now, and the news of her son's accomplishment was making her giddy.

Beth arrived bringing in two loaves of bread she had baked that morning. Jed carefully carried a big pot of her spicy chili.

"It can't be a party without Beth's chili," he declared, as he set the pan near the fire. Rachel and Zack arrived, bringing dried apple cakes, still warm from the oven.

"This is a feast fit for a king!" said Josh, as he sniffed the cakes. Margaret sat as close to him as she could. The doll sat on her lap and was fed pretend bites of everything that Margaret ate.

Adam looked at his big brother with admiration.

"Josh now that you have the lion skin for a new coat, do you think I can have your old one? The sleeves on mine are close to my elbows."

"Sure, Adam, and you should give your coat to Johnny. He is getting bigger every day," said Joshua.

"Good idea," said Beth, "and Eli could wear Johnny's."

"See how God provides for us Joshua. You brought one skin home and four people will have coats that fit, for winter because of it," said Mary.

"What will you do with the pig's hide?" asked Jed. "Gosh I don't know. What do people do with them?" Sarah answered his question.

"We can make you a new pair of boots. The hide of a boar is very thick."

"Great! That's a good idea, but how can you get the smell out? It sure stinks!" They all laughed.

"Rachel, the cakes are delicious," said Ben. "You are a good cook."

"I used to cook for all the men on the ranch where Zack got hurt," said Rachel.

"They said they would keep me even if I couldn't ever ride again just to have her cooking!" said Zack with a hearty laugh.

Mary and Ben had a warm feeling in their hearts as they prayed together that night. They thanked God for watching over them and protecting Josh on his first hunt. Then Mary thanked God for their growing family. When she said it she was referring to the baby coming soon, but Ben thought that she meant Rachel, Zack and Margaret. He silently asked God to help him dispel the uneasy feeling he had when he was around Zack. Something isn't quite right Lord, but I don't know what it is, he thought.

All the women spent the next day making trips to the new cabin by the lake. The wagon was called into service, transporting bedding and supplies. A second cache had been lined and was ready for a share from the bounty of the fall harvest. Baskets hung from beams filled with dried fruits, vegetables and nuts. The dirt floor was nearly all covered with tightly woven mats that the women had made sitting together while their hands kept busy. The young apple trees, planted by the ladies of the settlement now stood tall on the lawn in front of Jed's house. They too, had provided a small harvest. It would be just enough to make wonderful pies for Thanksgiving for everyone. The last two apple trees, Ben had planted on the far side of his barn, near the bluff. He looked at the spot where he had buried Bold One and without any trouble he had planted the trees so that they were on the left and right of her grave. They would get plenty of sun and runoff from the bluff. The grave of the baby that Beth had lost was there too. It would rest in the shade of the trees.

The fireplace was ready for a tiny fire. Ben lit a twig from the lantern and placed it in the bundle of kindling. As the fire crackled everyone cheered. Rachel walked around the kitchen area looking at the supplies in a neat row on a wide shelf. She put a handful of ground coffee into the new pot and poured it full of water from the barrel and placed it near the small fire.

"I feel like I am a little girl playing house," she declared. "Everything is new and fresh."

"We have a few surprises for you yet," said Jed. He pulled a bolt of fabric into view. A hide rolled over it before it was tied on his horse's back, had covered it.

"You can use this for curtains and dye some of it for a dress for you and Margaret. You can do whatever you want with it." Tears slid down her cheeks as she said thank you. All of you have been so good to us."

Small pieces of wood were added, maintaining the very small fire throughout the day to dry the river rocks and mortar. Rachel had made her little family a pot of stew for their first meal in the new cabin. That night as they went to bed in the new beds she sighed contently.

"Zack this is the best we have had it for a long time. I like it here. Everyone has been so nice to us."

"Honey, it's going to get a whole lot better," he said, as he turned to the wall and quickly fell asleep. She wondered what he meant. I know he is planning something. His comment triggered a feeling of excitement. She was eager for the day when they could have a place of their own.

As weeks sped by, all the storage areas of the houses were bulging with the fine harvest. Baskets hung on beams, full of good things to see them through the cold winter.

"Zack has done a good job with the horses. We have at least a dozen right now that are ready to offer to the army," said Ben.

"Do you plan on just taking them without going to the post and talking to them to see if they want any?" asked Mary. "What if they don't need any horses?"

"Mary, the army always needs good horses. But I do plan on going into Silverville first to see what they are willing to pay and when I should take them. Zack says he will go with me. He sold horses for the ranch where he worked before. He has an idea what they are worth."

"When do you think you will be going?" she asked. "Well tomorrow is Sunday, I think we should go Monday morning just to inquire. Are you going to be ok with me gone?"

"Yes of course, I won't be alone."

"Dad let's go hunting and see if we can get a deer," said Josh. "If we are lucky and the weather holds, we can all get together and roast it at Uncle Jed's for dinner and Sunday Bible reading on the grass by the new cabin."

"Sure Josh that would be fun. Do you want to go up on the bluff and take a quick check or just take our chances?" "I think it is a better hunt when we don't know where they are to start with but I'll make sure we have an all clear before we go," said Josh. "While you do that, I'll go over and tell Jed we are leaving. He is over by his barn working with a couple of the yearlings."

As Ben and Josh road up river and into the trees, Zack watched them go. Resentment burned in his eyes. I feel like I have been here a thousand years. I am just barn help, he thought. Just because they have land they have homesteaded doesn't make them better than us. Things will be different soon enough.

Zack had hunted with them many times, but he felt left out, because they had not asked him to go along on this particular hunt.

Rachel was baking bread in Sarah's oven. She had rabbits ready to fry and a pan of vegetables placed to the side of the fire. Coffee was made and the meal would soon be ready.

When Zack returned to the little cabin he noticed Rachel had filled the forms for making the adobe bricks and they were set in a neat row in full sun in front of the porch. She works too hard and all for someone else's place. He swung up on Socks and walked her to the field where he turned her loose for the night. She is a good animal, he thought as he patted her flank and closed the gate.

"See you at first light, girl." He spoke to her softly. It was for her ears only.

He heard the shots. They came from up river where Ben and Josh had gone. He was thinking that they would have fresh deer meat when he heard three more shots. That had to be trouble. He ran back to the gate and called Socks. She came to him and he slipped the bridle on and swung up quickly as another shot rang out. Rachel ran to him holding up his rifle. He grabbed it by the barrel and hurried away, hoping that he wasn't too late. As he reached the bend in the river he saw four Indians ride out of the trees into the tall prairie grass. He continued on slowly looking for any sign that would help him find Ben and Josh. The area was silent. The birds had flown away. Then he heard a horse coming through the trees. He ducked behind a clump of pine as Josh rode by on Little Mouse.

"Josh, stop. What happened?" Zack shouted.

"We ran into Indians!" Josh yelled back, as he turned Little Mouse around.

"Where's Ben? Is he hurt?"

"He is back there with the deer. He told me to go warn the women and to help put out the fires."

"Josh, how many Indians did you see?"

"Four, I think. They were hunting and after the same deer we were. Dad shot the deer and then they shot at us. No one was hurt, but we better be ready in case they come back." Joshua headed back toward the houses sounding the alarm at each and then he hurried up to the lookout where he stayed until dark.

When Zack and Ben returned with the deer and hung it in a tree for the night, everyone had gathered at the hut to talk.

CHAPTER SIX
BRAVE SPARROW OFFERS FRIENDSHIP

"It was a hunting party, not a war party," said Ben. "Everyone should calm down."

"The problem is, now they know we are here. They may come back hunting for us!" said Jed. Mary and Beth and Rachel were glad that they had tucked the smaller children into bed. They didn't need to hear discussions like this. It would frighten them. The women were already frightened.

"What should we do Ben?" asked Zack.

"I guess we should keep the place quiet, keep the fires very small and work without any loud noises. Let's put our best horses inside, as many as we can, so there is less activity around. Zack I want to ride up river tomorrow morning. Will you go with me? I want Jed to stay here with the families in case there is trouble."

"Sure Ben, but why go up river? Shouldn't we go to the fort and tell them we have Indians in the area?"

"No, first, I would rather check and see if they are still around and if so, how many," Zack frowned knowing that Ben was right, but he didn't really want to go looking for Indians. He rubbed his chest, remembering the pain from the arrow.

He admitted to himself silently that he was afraid, for himself and his family but his real reason for asking Ben to go to the fort was because he wanted to go to the settlement to the land office. He wondered if he could get Ben to let him go to Silverville alone. It might be worth thinking about.

"Zack will you meet me here in the morning at first light?" asked Ben. Zack nodded, but he wasn't happy about it.

Before dawn, Ben and Zack rode out quietly keeping to the trees along the river. After they cleared the first big bend in the river they both began to relax, thinking they weren't going to find anything of concern. It was then that they could smell a faint trace of smoke in the air. Ben silently slid off Sundown and motioned to Zack to dismount.

They tied the horses securely to a tree and crept closer to the small-banked fire on the other side of the river. In the dim light they could just make out the outline of five tents nestled among the trees. Ben put his finger to his lips warning Zack not to speak. They crouched in the bushes watching as the camp began to come awake.

Each tent held at least one man, plus women and children. Ben studied them for a moment longer before he recognized them as the same band he had seen so long ago in Mary's woods, camped in the clearing, when he and his dog Stump had discovered the spring.

The men were perhaps no more than Mary or Rachel's height but much stronger looking, with wide shoulders and stocky builds. Everyone that he could see had coal black hair. He watched their behavior as they moved about camp. There was an air of affection and gentleness. He found it hard to believe that these were the same men that had ridden in and shot at him and Joshua the day before, until he recognized the brown and white paint as one of their horses. The blue and white striped blanket was hooked near it on a tree branch. It was then that he remembered finding a piece of the same colored blue yarn hooked on the barbed wire of his downed cattle fence on Mary's land. So you were there too, thought Ben, as he and Zack backed away from the scene and quietly returned to their horses.

"Well now that we know that there aren't that many, what do you want to do?" asked Zack.

"First I'm going to take that deer back to them. They look cold and hungry. I can't imagine what it was like living through last winter in those tents in the open. They would have been much more comfortable in the clearing in the woods by the spring. The trees would have offered them protection. Here the wind came across the prairie and there was nothing to stop it."

Zack was totally puzzled. "Why not just hide in the trees again and shoot them as they come out of their tents?"

"I don't want to kill them, Zack. I just don't want them to kill us!" Ben hurried Sundown into a fast gallop and entered the hut without looking back at Zack. He wondered how he could get Zack to understand.

Ben directed Joshua to saddle Dixie and use him to tell Jed and Beth that they were going to have a meeting as soon as they could all get together. "Then go tell Sarah and Rachel, too," he said.

Zack shuffled his feet uncomfortably. Mary encouraged him to sit down at the table to have some coffee and fresh bread with Jam, while they waited. She poured a cup for Ben and tea for herself.

She watched Zack spread a thick layer of butter, followed by mountains of crab apple jelly. She cut wedges of cheese and cold roast, adding them to the food on the table. "You must both be very hungry, getting up so early." Mary scrambled a pan of eggs and fried up some sliced potatoes. Josh stuck his head in the door long enough to ask if he should put Dixie back in the barn. Ben said no, just put him in the corral. We will need him. Both boys slid up on the benches and were ready to receive a scoop of eggs and a piece of bread with butter and new jam. Josh downed his first glass of milk and asked for a second, saying that Uncle Jed would be a few more minutes because he was just finishing the milking.

"Aunt Sarah said she was on the way in a couple minutes. Rachel has dough rising for bread and said she would only be able to stay a little while or it would ruin. She said she would be here right away, too."

"Good job Josh, you are always dependable. Your job today is to take warm clothes and a lunch and stay at the lookout all day. It is very important that you be extra alert."

"I'll go up right after breakfast."

"Adam I want you to help your mom with Eli. It is crucial that he is quiet."

"Sure Dad," Adam said.

"I will take good care of Eli and play with him."

"Good boy," said Ben, as he affectionately hugged both the boys.

After everyone had arrived, Ben got right to the subject at hand. Sarah listened to Ben's suggestion that they make friends of the Indians in the little camp. She could hardly believe her own ears. He was laying out a plan that followed the story of Jacob's reconciliation to Esau in Genesis Chapter 32.

"First I want to send a horse across the river, right into their camp, with the deer I shot. Next we will send one with a bag of grain. Then last I will walk and lead Ginger with the wagon and take them dried meat and dried vegetables and some blankets, too. I want them to know that I am sorry that my fences stopped them from camping where they used to by the spring."

Sarah do you think you can understand their language. I don't know Ben, but I am so glad that you are willing to make this effort instead of driving them away."

"That's ridiculous! They are Indians! They will kill us all once they know we are here!" shouted Zack. "You can't tell me that you plan on supporting all those Indians from now on! They won't thank you. They will kill you in your bed!" Zack slammed the door as he left.

"I'm so sorry," said Rachel, "but you can't blame him. After all he was almost killed by them."

"You don't know that Rachel. All the Indians in the world aren't responsible for one arrow," said Sarah.

"Ben, I think it is a good plan," said Mary. "I think so too. What can I do to help?" said Jed. "Help me get the deer on Ginger's back."

"No Ben! Don't use Ginger. What if they want to keep her? We all know how much she means to you," said Beth, with a look of concern.

"If we could talk to them, it would make it a lot easier," said Mary. "Before you do anything, let me go near their camp and see if I can understand their language. I don't think they will know that you are offering help. I think they will fear it is a trick of some sort," said Sarah.

Sarah was concerned for Ben's safety, but she didn't want to say so.

"Let me go with you. Or better yet, let me go instead of you. If I can explain to them about their old camp and the fences then maybe they won't resist the help."

"Why should they trust you?" asked Mary.

"I think they will trust Brave Sparrow, of the Blue Stone People. They are known now, as peaceful people."

"It could work," said Jed. "It won't work if I can't talk to them," replied Sarah.

"Let's pray and ask God's help," said Ben. As they held hands and bowed their heads, Ben prayed.

"We praise you, Lord. We praise you, as the Father of all life. We praise you, as the provider of all we have. We praise you, Father of wisdom and we praise you, Father of peace. Father, we ask that you help us to share with the Indian camp. Give us wisdom as we plan to help them and make peace with them. Father we are your children and so are they. Help us Lord Jesus, to help them and help Zack to understand."

"Amen," everyone said.

Sarah went out the door and hopped up on Dixie. She had ridden Pretty Mother down to the hut, but now she wanted to use a horse that would blend into the trees. Pretty Mother's white coat was just too easy to spot.

"I'll ride there with you," said Ben. Sarah was surprised to see the big smile on Ben's face considering all that was going on. Well why not, she asked herself. We put it in God's hands. He knows that it will all work out for the best.

"This sure is a beautiful day," he said as they headed for the trees along the river.

"I wonder what is taking them so long," said Mary. "It seems like they have been gone for hours."

"Have patience Mary," said Rachel. "It really hasn't been long at all."

"I can't help it. If she can't understand them, how will we get them to understand that we just want to help them?"

"Don't worry. It will all work out," said Rachel. "Here Mary, have some tea and rest now. You got up early."

"You don't need to fuss over me, I'm just worried over Ben and Sarah," said Mary, as she sat down heavily.

"Ben is a smart man. He will take care of it," said Rachel, as she poured the cup of tea.

They felt relieved when they heard the horses return. Sarah hurried in the door with a big smile saying she understood nearly every word.

"Rachel, I need to go back to my cabin and change and get ready. Will you come with me?"

"Yes, I'll bake that bread and you can give that to them too. I will come over as soon as I put the bread in the oven."

Jed said he was wondering where Zack was and went to look for him. He finally spotted him up on the bluff with Josh, looking in the direction of the Indian camp.

Sarah had suggested that Ben use the brown hunting pony. He decided she was right and Jed helped him load the deer onto an old hide and tie it securely. A gentle brown mare was chosen from the ones that Zack had worked with. This one carried the grain. Ginger was harnessed to the wagon, carrying the much-needed supplies. They all waited for Sarah to return.

When she did, they were all in awe of the vision before them. She was dressed completely in white. With chalk dust on Pretty Mother's coat, she was like nothing they had ever seen before. She hoped it would have the same effect on the people camped by the river. A necklace of large blue stones testified to her status with the Blue Stone People.

"I am ready," she said.

The hunting pony was often used to carry game. She carried the deer to the edge of the river, across from the Indian's camp, where she stood hesitantly waiting. No one was leading her. Ben nudged her flank and gave her a light slap before ducking quickly into the bushes.

The Indians couldn't believe their good fortune, when the horse crossed the river and walked into their camp with an unusually large deer on its back, it stopped by the first tent and just stood there. The men held their weapons at the ready. The women and children hid in their tents.

Finally one of the men pulled out a knife and cut the deer free, pulling it to the ground. Still the men looked around expecting an attack.

The second horse came a few minutes later, bringing grain and fresh baked loaves of bread. Still they suspected a trick, but the smell of the fresh bread was more than they could stand to ignore. The basket was lifted down and pieces were handed into each of the tents. The men held their guns with one hand and ate bread with the other.

After sending the horse with the grain and bread, Ben and Sarah backtracked and crossed the river farther downstream. The wagon had to be rafted. When they were dry and ready, Brave Sparrow came into view, approaching the camp from down river. It was as if she had materialized from the prairie.

"In the name of the Great Spirit, I greet you." The woman in sacred white clothes, with white hair and white horse struck fear in the hearts of the small Indian camp.

"I am Brave Sparrow of the Blue Stone People. I have come to tell you that you are welcome here. The meat, grain and bread are gifts from your brother. He sent the food. He wishes you to know that he is aware now that his fence has stopped you from camping in the clearing by the spring. He is sorry for the discomfort that this has caused you this past winter and he will change the fence so that you can camp there again. He understands now why you broke his fence. He is not angry. He asks that you forgive him. They nodded agreement. He comes.

At her signal Ben pulled forward with the wagon very slowly. Not knowing what to expect. Sarah wasn't sure what they would do. They had not lowered their rifles.

"Put your weapons down. This man comes as a friend." Only then did they lower the guns and bows. The women peeked out of the tents with gasps when they saw Sarah all in sacred white.

Ben stepped from the wagon and reached inside it starting to unload the many bundles of produce and blankets. He smiled at the men and held out pieces of jerky. Finally one stepped forward and took a piece, then another. The women and children came out of the tents to stand around him giggling and touching the blankets. Wisely Ben picked up the brightest blanket and gently wrapped it around the shoulders of the oldest woman. She nodded her head and smiled a toothless grin and hurried away. He handed warm furs or blankets to each of the women.

Brave Sparrow reached into her pocket and took out several small pieces of the blue stone. She placed one in the palm of each man.

"When you look at these stones you will be reminded that today this man has made it known that he and his family and camp are under the protection of the Great Spirit. He brought an offering of friendship. I tell you that he is brother with the Son of God, the Great Spirit." Murmurs filled the camp.

"Ben, I think now would be a good time to leave, just as slowly as you came," said Sarah quietly. He turned the wagon around, and from the corner of his eye he saw Sarah take the reins of the two horses and hand them to the man she perceived to be Chief of the small migratory band.

"Be well and live long, my Chief," she said as she rode away as swiftly as she could, disappearing into the tall grass.

For a long moment the people stood looking at the waving grass, marking the path she had taken. When they could not see her or any sign of movement in the grass, they began to open the bundles. The squash and pumpkins rolled onto the ground. The sack of corn was carefully taken into the Chief's tent. The dried fruit was nibbled and smiles spread across the children's faces as they were each given a small ration. The men examined the horses, patting and touching their coats.

Sarah waited all day, to move slowly under the cover of darkness, to return to her house. She rubbed pretty mother down with a piece of wet hide after brushing her to remove the chalk and make her shine again. She changed into her tan leather pants and top and rode to the hut. Everyone was ready to celebrate. Beth and Rachel had made a rich stew and baked more bread. They hugged and laughed and thanked God for His Son and the power in His name. They praised Him for the bounty they were able to share with the Indians.

Zack came in looking cross and sat beside Rachel and Margaret without saying a word.

"Zack, I just want you to know that we understand how you feel. You had every right to speak your opinion, after all this affects you and your family, too." Ben had said the words that Zack needed to hear. He relaxed.

Jed looked across the table at Ben and could see that he was in his problem-solving mode.

"Ben you have that look on your face again. What are you planning?"

"Well, I couldn't understand what was said down there, but I did notice that they had some nice horses and maybe they would like to help us with some of the mustangs. Jed didn't know If that was such a good idea.

"Once you get those guys here and comfortable, how will you get them to leave?"

"If they are as good as I think they will be; we may not want them to leave." Let's give it some time and pray about it," said Ben.

He looked over at Mary, rocking by the fire, noting the smile on her beautiful face and very round tummy. Eli was in his favorite place on the floor, curled up on the big bear fur with Rascal beside him. Adam and Josh were still at the table. Ben felt his heart would split wide open with joy and love. He looked at all the people gathered there and felt that he was the most blessed man on earth.

*****

"Zack," Rachel said, "isn't it wonderful how everything turned out?" Rachel couldn't see the look on his face in the dark as she got into bed beside him.

"Yah, I think it's just great," he mumbled.

When Rachel got up the next morning and looked out the window, she knew something was different. Zack usually went out to the barn before it was light out. She looked at the field near the barn, but couldn't see the mares and foals. He always let them out first. She wondered why he hadn't. She went to the other window and looked at the bigger field. Socks, his horse was gone. That's odd. He didn't say anything different was going on this morning. Maybe he and Ben left together for the settlement to talk to Major Bennet about buying the horses, and if that is it, I can expect Jed here soon. She put on a pot of coffee. Why would Zack head out without telling me? She wondered.

She hummed as she brushed Margaret's hair and tidied the bedroom. Suddenly she thought about the fact that it was Monday and they were so busy with the Indian camp yesterday that no one thought about getting together to read the Lord's word. I suppose that it was the Lord's work that was done and we sure did do a lot of praying, but I think it would be nice if we got together today and spent a special time with the Lord.

Joshua had brought a different horse for Rachel to use. It was standing near the gate. He is a thoughtful boy. He knew that I would need a horse to ride since they gave the other one I was using to the Indians. She lifted Margaret up, and slid on behind her. Missy was a gentle horse. She plodded along the path around the lake and it wasn't until she was near Jed's house that she noticed Jed and Ben standing near the porch talking.

If Ben is here then where is my Zack? She wondered. A bolt of fear entered her heart and jolted her stomach at the same time. She rode up beside them.

"Have either of you seen Zack this morning? He didn't put the mares and foals out and Socks is not in the field." A note of alarm could be heard in her voice.

"Jed, you don't think he went back there to bother the Indian camp do you? He wasn't in favor of us making friends with them," said Rachel.

"I don't think so. Maybe he has gone to the fort to tell Major Bennet. That was what he wanted us to do," said Ben.

"Jed, I have an uneasy feeling about this," said Ben. "I think I am going to get ready and ride to the fort myself right away. Do you mind taking care of things here while I am gone? I was going to go to the fort anyway, to talk about the sale of the horses."

"No, that's fine. I'll go over and check on the foals and their mothers' right after I tell Beth what's going on."

When Ben and Rachel arrived at the hut, Josh came scurrying down from the look out.

"Dad, why did Zack leave for town alone? I thought you were going with him."

"I was, son. I'm not sure why he preferred to head out. I will be leaving soon. I'll need you to be very vigilant while I'm gone. Did you take care of all your chores?"

"Yes I'm done, but Adam is slow this morning. He is still in the chicken pen gathering the eggs."

Ben stepped in the hut and found Mary had already prepared his pack to take. His water bag was filled, too.

"That was nice of you to get things ready for me."

"I did it first thing this morning," she replied. He hugged her and tickled Eli, getting a big giggle. Eli stretched his arms up wanting to be picked up. Ben picked him up and swung him around in his usual playful way.

"Daddy is leaving right now to go to Silverville. You have to stay here with Mommy and be a good boy."

"Candy," said Eli. "Yes I'll bring some, if you will be a very good boy for your mommy." Eli smiled his broadest and nodded his head up and down. Mary hugged Ben again, handing him his packed food, as he walked out the door. Adam came running, and nearly spilled his basket of eggs.

"I had to hurry," he apologized.

"I am done. I just wanted to be in time to say Bye to you, Dad." Ben laughed and hugged him tightly.

"You give your mom extra help while I'm gone."

"I will Dad.

Sundown easily slipped into a distance eating pace. He was a wonderful strong horse. Ben favored him because he was a beautiful blend of Ginger's sweet gentle nature and Big Boy's strength and endurance. Even with those qualities, Ben knew it was best to take a break halfway. He didn't expect to see Zack until he reached the settlement.

When he arrived and crossed the bridge over the Silver, he glanced down the growing row of buildings. Socks stood in front of the registrar's office. She was lathered and had been ridden hard. Ben was very irritated that Zack had used Socks that way needlessly.

Ben was puzzled but thought that perhaps Zack was looking for a way to get a nice piece of land. Maybe he wanted to surprise us, thought Ben.

He was trying to take Sarah's land!

"I tell you she is not twenty one years old. That paper with her name on it isn't any good!"

"Here's Ben. He signed it. Just ask him about this." The clerk's face was red and it was apparent that he was upset. Zack on the other hand, was cool as a cucumber.

"What's going on?" asked Ben. "It's nothing the truth can't take care of. This man is trying to sign for Sarah's land. He says she isn't of age. Is that true Ben? I'm sorry Ben, but I have to ask you, now that he has raised the question." The clerk didn't like asking. He considered himself Ben's friend.

"What?" Ben turned toward Zack and stepped very close.

"You are a miserable, ungrateful, son, of an evil spirit! What devil's work are you doing here, Zack?" Ben didn't answer the clerk. He rushed out the door and jumped on Sundown. His first impulse was to race to the fort to blow off steam, but he remembered another time when he had not used good judgment. He had ridden hard until Big Boy was exhausted. He headed Sundown in the direction of the fort at a normal pace.

It was the best thing he could have done. Without proof, there was nothing that Zack could do to get that piece of land. He did sign for another piece on the Silver. It was the first piece available anywhere near the fort.

CHAPTER SEVEN
CONSEQUENCES

Zack wondered what he should do now that he was found out. I guess I better head over to the fort and see if I can apologize to Ben.

When he got to the fort, he found Ben sitting on the ground with his back against the fort wall. Sundown stood beside him munching grass.

"How come you are out here?" asked Zack. Ben didn't answer, but when he raised his face, Zack could see the tears and rage on Ben's face. "Hey I didn't take her place. I signed for one down halfway to the wagon trail on this side. I'm sorry Ben. I'm really sorry. I guess I was jealous. It seems like everybody has a nice place but us." Zack forced a little smile as Ben rose from the grass. Ben's fists curled automatically. The next thing Zack knew, Ben had hit him on the chin so hard that Zack was lying on the ground looking up.

"Now I feel better!" said Ben. "Don't you get up," he warned, "or I'll put you down again because I have something to say to you and you just lay there and listen and I mean really listen! Don't you ever mess with my family or our ranch again or I'll give you a lot worse! Next time you won't just be sitting on the ground, you will be under it with a pile of rocks on top! Do you understand me, Zack? I mean what I'm saying! You were going to take Sarah's place and add more pain to all that she has been through. God is the only one that knows all she had to endure to survive in that Indian village. I told Sarah that she would always have that place! That it was hers." He was so angry that his face was purple as he shouted at Zack between clenched teeth. Both Ben's hands were still made into tight fists. "Zack, I will try hard to forgive you. I know just how much you and your little family have been through but that's no excuse for you to be deceitful. Now, you get up."

Zack rubbed his bruised chin and got up nodding and backing up, watching to be sure that Ben wasn't going to hit him again.

"Let's go talk to the Major about those horses that we trained."

Later, they rode out together. Ben was pleased with the interest that Major Bennet had shown in buying Ben's horses. Zack became more and more excited about his land as they headed out to see it. We can camp and then take the wagon trail across the Silver and go home that way, said Ben.

He hadn't stopped at the trading post. He had forgotten, but he really didn't want to go there. He was still feeling angry inside and hurt by the way they had treated Sarah. He knew that he needed to forgive them, too, but he was finding it difficult. He wouldn't stand for anyone to ever inflict any more pain on Sarah. He stopped Sundown and asked Zack to go back and buy candy sticks for all the children.

He slid down onto the grass after handing Zack enough money to pay for it.

"If you don't mind I want to wait right here." Although Zack was eager to see his land, he also wanted to please Ben and be helpful in some small way and so he did the errand willingly.

He was back in less than an hour to find Ben sound asleep. Socks began to eat the grass beside the river as soon as Zack stopped. He realized that the horses had to have time to eat and rest. He tied Socks to a bush where she could reach both grass and the water and gave her a rub down with dry grass that had grown against the trees and then he sat down and rested until Ben woke up.

Zack had, without knowing it, picked a very good piece of land. It was bordered on the front by the Silver River. The back left side had a small hill backed by pine trees. The entire center was rolling prairie dotted with ancient trees. The right side included part of a dense virgin wood of oak, maple and pines. The ground looked fertile enough to grow anything he would want. As they strolled through the grass, leading their horses, Zack was already picking a place for his cabin.

"Ben, I think it is back and high enough there that it will never flood from the river," said Zack enthusiastically.

"I think you are right," said Ben, "but did you know that farther down on the other side of the river, it turns into a mud bog? That's where I found Ginger. She was just a small foal and stuck halfway up her sides. She was my first horse."

"No wonder everyone thinks she is so special."

"I am glad that you didn't choose land on the other side of the river. It would have been worthless."

"Yes, it was just good luck that I didn't pick that side. I just wanted to be on the same side as the fort and Silverville."

"Zack, I think it would be best if we never mention to anyone back at the ranch, what happened at the registrar's office. Let's just try to forget it."

"I certainly do appreciate that, Ben. I had an evil intention, but look at the good piece of land I have now!" Ben watched, as Zack cleared a spot and made a small fire.

"Zack, God had a good piece of land ready for you. It is beautiful here. He loves you Zack. He loves all of us. We are his children. It will be hard work for you and Rachel, but if you trust Him, it will all work out."

They ate the food that Mary had packed and sat drinking coffee, as it grew dark. Zack handed Ben half of a candy stick.

"There was enough money left to get us one to share," he said, with a little chuckle.

"Peppermint is my favorite," said Ben, as he held the candy in his mouth and unrolled his bedroll. Zack stood up, broke his half into three small pieces and gave Socks and Sundown each a little piece. He stepped back to Socks.

"I am sorry for running you so hard earlier." He took the small piece from his mouth and gave it to her, too, while scratching her ears. She blew a soft response and laid her head over his shoulder.

"She sure is special. I couldn't have a better horse than Socks. Thanks Ben. I guess I owe you for a lot of things. I promise I'll treat her better from now on."

He banked the little fire and then crawled under a blanket he had hastily grabbed before leaving the ranch. They both were asleep when the moon peeked over the trees and reflected in the river. It was a scene that Zack would appreciate many times in the years ahead.

While Ben was gone, Mary had her fourth baby. Sarah had rejoiced at the blessing of the easy birth. Beth, Sarah and Mary all praised God for the ruddy faced, noisy, red haired, little fellow. Mary gave him the name Nathaniel after her Grandfather.

"He and my father both had red hair, too," she explained. I wonder how it is that I have four boys and only this one has red hair."

They were all eager for Ben to return. Josh had kept watch and met the returning men at the river yelling.

"I have a new baby brother. I have a new baby brother."

Ben knelt beside Mary and gently kissed her. He picked up his new son and marveled at the tufts of red hair. "

"Mary, I am sorry that I was gone when your time came. You must have had a rough time of it. He is a beautiful big boy."

"Oh Ben, don't worry about it. Having babies is women's work. Sarah was here and this was the easiest birth of the four."

"Four! I have four sons! Can you believe it? Look at his red hair. Who had red hair?"

"My father had red-brown hair, but my grandfather's was carrot red. Ben, his name was Nathaniel. I want to give our baby his name."

"That is a good name. I like it. All right Nattie, you and your mommy need to rest."

"See what you did? You gave him a nickname already. Nattie, I love it. It seems just right for him."

"Rest now Mary. We will all go over to Jed's so that it is quiet here."

After the excitement over the new baby, Zack told Rachel and Margaret his wonderful news.

"Honey, I have something for you." He handed her the piece of paper that said the land was theirs. Her hands began to shake as she read it.

"I'm going to help Ben move the horses to the fort and then we will be going to our own land, woman."

"Where is it? What does it look like?" she asked.

"It's the most beautiful piece of land in the world." He put his arm around her and held Margaret's hand. As the little family left the hut, Zack was still talking about their new land.

Sarah waited until the room grew quiet and then said she had some news, too.

"I rode down to check on the Indian camp, but it was gone. They have packed up and left. All that's there is a ring of stones and ashes where the fire was. I wonder where they have gone," she said.

"With winter coming they probably headed south to follow the buffalo. I will move that fence so that if they return and want to camp in the woods near the spring during winter, they can," said Ben. He had given his word and would keep it.

He rode to the settlement and asked for help from some of the men who originally helped to string the fence on Mary's land. Together they created a small channel that ran water from the Hickory River into a low spot. They hauled load after load of river gravel into it, until it was able to take the tread of the heavy cattle without turning into a muddy mess. They moved the end of the fence and left easy access to the woods, spring and the little clearing.

"We will have to come down here regularly to maintain it but I should check on the cattle more than I have been anyway," said Ben.

"These guys are hardy. They look like they are doing well without anyone babying them," said one of the men with a chuckle. Just keep water in there that they can get at and they will be fine. This piece has good soil. It seems to be keeping up with all those mouths chomping the grass. I think it would grow most any crop you would pick. If you do decide to feed these guys to the soldiers anytime soon, let me know. I would like to buy one from you." The men left, happy with their pay and glad they could help Ben.

*****

"You and Rachel are welcome to use the wagon for your belongings when the time comes, but we would be happy to have you stay the winter in the cabin. You can build your cabin in the spring and work on the other things you will need then."

"Ben you know we don't have much. You have given us most of what we have."

"Zack you can have two of the trained horses to sell as your wages and Rachel can take Missy. She will need a gentle one. She has worked hard every day and deserves a reward. That way we will see Missy when we come to your place to visit.

The next few days, the women spent stitching hides into a tent that was big enough to offer protection from rain or cold nights for the little family until the really cold weather hit.

Ben and Jed strung the horses together so they would be easy to move and none would be lost.

On the chosen morning they piled the wagon full of blankets, baskets of dried foods, clothing and the forms for bricks.

"You will need those forms so you can make an oven, said Sarah. The one you made for the cabin by the lake is a good one. We can get the forms back when you no longer need them. When you sell the horses, you will have money to buy things like a big kettle, some lamps and tools for building your cabin."

Rachel hugged Sarah.

"You have all been so kind to us, but Sarah you have been more than kind. There are no words to thank you for all you have done. I hope that you will come our way and visit us. I have grown to love you and everyone. I will miss you."

"I will come soon, Rachel, and I will miss you, too," said Sarah. Suddenly she realized just how much she really would miss the little family.

After a short rest on the side of the trail, they rolled past the settlement. Beth turned her face toward the Silver River that ran beside them. No one suggested going to visit. The loaded wagon was stopped beside the gate to the fort and the string of horses was taken inside for the Major's inspection. Zack was pleased with the money he received for the two horses that were his wages.

Since they had stopped to rest along the way, the day was spent and it was growing dark by the time the men had finished their business. They camped beside the river eating food that Beth had prepared before they left. They enjoyed their small campfire. The children were bedded down beneath the wagon and the adults rested nearby.

The entire trip to the fort had seemed like a celebration, but now Ben was concerned about the ranch left attended only by Sarah. He knew she was capable of taking care of the necessary work of the animals. He just didn't like leaving her to do the work alone, but she had insisted. Mary was there with Nattie, but not yet able to do much other than care for her new baby.

In the morning they moved out at a quicker pace, eager to arrive at Zack and Rachel's land. As they turned off the trail by the river, into the undisturbed grass and wild flowers, Rachel slid off missy and turned to Zack.

"Oh Zack, You were right. This is a beautiful piece of land."

"Soon, it will be even better."

"Rachel, I am sorry, honey, I wish I could have built us a cabin before the winter sets in."

She didn't want to think of the hardships. It was their land and they would build that cabin and put in a garden as soon as the spring came.

"I want to help build a cabin and then dig a well. I know we can do it all."

"Zack we have water from the river and once the ground is worked up, Margaret and I can plant the seeds and tend the garden this spring. Jed said he would come and work up the ground for it and help you get started. It is going to be a wonderful place." Zack looked out at Margaret playing tag with Johnny.

Eli and Lily played in the grass.

"We will make her a room all her own. I'll make a big fireplace in the end of the main room to cook on and for heat. Maybe someday we can get a pump inside like Sarah has."

"Where do you think we should build?" Rachel asked Zack.

"Let's back it up to the big pines near the top of that hill," he answered without hesitation. In his mind he had also planned where the barn and corral would be and where the garden should be planted.

"I like that. The trees will break the wind," she said. "We will be snug and comfortable."

Ben and Jed carried the tent under the trees and began to cut limbs large enough to support it. As they trimmed off small branches they made a pile to use for drying racks. The rest went into a second pile for firewood.

Before the day was out they had a good camp set up. Rachel and Zack had gone back to the trading post to purchase what they immediately needed while the rest of them worked at various jobs. Beth sat weaving some mats for around the fire, while watching the children. The girls had grown fond of each other. They chased butterflies and collected a bouquet of the wild flowers. Eli tried to follow Johnny and Adam. They were collecting bugs. Joshua stood beside Ben with his hands on his hips watching him stake out the size and shape of the garden.

They camped on Zack's land that night, but headed out very early the next day, eager to return to the "S and J."

When they pulled the wagon up next to the barn, it seemed good to them all to be home. It was so quiet that Ben felt a twinge of concern until he saw Sarah coming out of Jed's barn.

Sarah waved and jumped on Pretty Mother hurrying to hear about the time they had been gone.

"Are they all settled? I hope they are going to be comfortable."

"They are fine and the tent you girls made is really great. They will be cozy in it."

"Thanks Ben. I want you to know that the milking is all done and I think the cows like a woman's touch. They produced more than ever!" Jed smiled and hugged her and asked if she had cans ready to go to the icehouse.

"Yes I have plenty but they are fine for now. The stack of ice you put on the north side of the barn is doing the job nicely." Jed said that he would be going right back with the plow in the morning, and he could take all the milk he could fit in with the plow to the fort for the soldiers.

"Sarah, do you want to leave Ben the job of milking for the next few days? You can come with me if you like and see their place."

"That's a good idea. I want to check her area to see what herbs grow there so she can start collecting them. You never know when you might need them. I have some extra ones that I will take with me. Is there anything else you can think of that they might need us to take?" "No, I don't think so. Rachel doesn't seem bothered by the idea that she will have to camp until the house is built. Besides she knows how to do lots of the things already that Beth had to teach Mary."

Jed chuckled at Sarah when she rode up the next morning on Moon Boy. "You look like an Indian!"

"I couldn't decide what to wear so I went for comfort. You don't mind do you?"

"No, I think you look cute. The beadwork on that shirt is beautiful. Did you do it?"

"Yes, I did lots of it in the winter months. There wasn't much else to do."

Everyone yelled "Goodbye" one more time as they pulled out. Big Boy had been hitched to the wagon. The load was heavy and would have been taxing for a lesser horse. The rest of the journey was much easier, after the soldiers relieved them of several full cans of fresh milk. They took a break to rest the horses and Sarah surprised him with cinnamon apple cake. She had baked while they had left her alone. She had pieces of roast and green, crisp, shoots to munch.

"Sarah, you are amazing! Thanks. That was a great lunch. Let's take a short nap and then the horses should be ready to move on," he said with a yawn.

Sarah was glad when Jed headed down the trail beside the Silver River, and left the settlement behind. Jed wondered if Sarah's clothes had been chosen as a reminder to the little town, for the way she had been rejected, but he didn't ask.

CHAPTER EIGHT
ON THEIR OWN LAND

Zack and Rachel were excited to see Jed and Sarah arrive with the plow. Margaret smiled and gave Sarah a hug. After the greetings, they walked to the back of the hill to see the exact spot that Rachel and Zack had picked for the cabin. Jed set to work hitching Big Boy to the plow. He thought it was almost too late in the year to plow but he did it anyway. It would make it easier in the spring to have the sod broken now. He knew he would come back with the plow then and help Zack get it seed ready.

Sarah noticed that there were some small patches of snow on the north side of the dense trees.

Mary had slipped a piece of sugar candy in Sarah's hand as they left.

"This is for Big Boy after he is done working," she said. Sarah thought the trip, pulling the wagon had been a chore in itself and decided to reward him. She broke the candy in half and gave him a chunk and a good scratch.

Rachel had chosen a spot for the garden not far from the trail along the river. She wanted to be sure that she could carry water to it if the rain didn't come. Sarah saw the modest plot and told Jed to make it a bit longer and a lot wider.

"Why do women always do that? It doesn't seem to matter if it is a garden or a cabin, they say, make it bigger." He chuckled as he said it.

"We will have seeds and a sack of seed potatoes for them," she explained with a grin, appreciating that his comment was meant as humor.

Zack had chopped down two trees in the area of the cabin. He will need a lot more she thought.

They all pitched in to the hard work of removing the thick chunks of sod to prepare the soil for a spring garden. Jed reminded Zack that he would need some kind of fence to keep animals out.

"One rabbit and one morning when you are both busy and you can lose an entire garden!"

"That's a dreadful thought," said Rachel. "After all this work, I would prefer to be the one to eat the carrots myself," she laughed."

Rachel had found several animal trails in the woods and said she had also spotted a maple and planned on a tap right away. Sarah smiled, thinking that Jed was right. She is more comfortable with all this than I thought she would be.

That afternoon Sarah and Rachel took a walk with Margaret, each of them carrying a collecting basket. They walked deep into the property and cut through the woods slowly examining the bushes and trees, and then along the river's edge back to camp. All three baskets were full. They had found nut trees that had dumped their abundance the fall before and the squirrels had collected only a small percentage. The trees were loaded for a new harvest when the wind brought them down. Cattails grew in a backwash in the woods, and a fallen tree marked the spot to look for fennel ferns and mushrooms in warmer weather.

Sarah had found what she was looking for. Her basket held clover, and two of the infection fighting plants. They were brown and bare but their roots would soon send up new plants in the spring. She made a point of where they grew so that Rachel would be able to get more if she needed them. Sarah rinsed the plants and scrubbed the plant roots. She hung them on the branches of a small bush near the tent.

The clover, she spread on a hide to dry. As they gathered them she had explained again to Rachel how to prepare and use them. She had gathered leaves from the tips of the raspberry bushes and fresh tips from the pines. When she returned to camp she had put on a pan of water and added a small amount of each along with lemon grass and mint.

It was nearly dark when they sat down near the campfire to eat and enjoy the unique tea.

Zack said that he was going down to the lumber camp the next day to see if he could get work. He hoped to earn enough to buy the cut logs and windows he would need.

"That's a good idea Zack."

"I don't like leaving Rachel here alone but I guess she can find lots to do."

"Zack it isn't safe here for her and Margaret without a gun. That should be the first thing you buy."

"You are right. I do need to have a rifle on the place. I was planning on that. I had a couple of good guns on that raft but they were lost, too."

The sky was overcast as Jed and Sarah headed for home traveling toward the wagon trail. The empty wagon bounced along with little effort on Big Boy's part.

After crossing the Silver River, they decided to follow the edge of the mud flat back to the Parker place. Just as they turned right, Jed got the idea to take back some of the beautiful carving wood that Ben had collected, and later sacrificed to make a fire for Beth when they were bringing her to the hut for the first time. He chopped down one small tree and by cutting and cording the thick part of the branches on top of the tree trunk they were able to fit all of the usable pieces in the wagon. Jed was excited about his surprise for Ben.

Sarah glanced up and saw that the sky was darker and threatened to dump rain at any minute.

"Let's make a bit of cover here in the trees and wait until the rain has passed," she said.

"That sounds like a good idea."

They quickly dragged branches into a clump of brush and covered it with the only hides they had. Sarah tied it down while Jed dragged their bundles and bedrolls under the temporary shelter to keep them dry. The thunder rumbled and the wind picked up. They had tied Big Boy with Moon Boy close by. He stomped nervously. Sarah wrapped her arms around the big horse and talked quietly to him. It was then that she remembered the other half of the candy. She broke it into several small pieces and as she comforted him with scratches and tiny nibbles of candy the lightning hit a tree close by. He reared and screamed in fear. She jumped on his back as he came down. Lying across his neck, she talked into his ear.

"Jed hand me something to cover his head or we are going to lose him. He handed her his shirt and a cord to fasten it on. Moon Boy acted as if he didn't notice the storm at all. He munched the grass and looked over at Sarah with complete trust as she tried to calm Big Boy. "Jed that loud sound was too much for him. He is still agitated," she said.

"Covering his eyes was a good idea. He can't run away if he can't see where he is going," said Jed. Sarah felt sorry for the big frightened horse. She just thought it would be easier for him if he couldn't see the lightning flashes. The rain started to come down with an unbelievable force.

"I'm sure glad that we are already across the river. When this lets up the river is going to be a lot higher," said Jed.

They sat huddled under the shelter watching the rain pour down. Neither of them spoke for a long time, until Jed finally got the courage to ask the question that had often come into his mind.

"Sarah," he said hesitantly, "was it terribly hard for you?"

"When they took me?" He nodded. "Yes, I guess it was, until I made up my mind that I would be like them. Then I became invisible. I dyed my hair and deliberately got my skin burned, over and over so it would turn darker. It never did match theirs, but they got to the point where my being white wasn't an issue anymore."

"But why did they take you?" he asked.

"The village lost many people when they got the white men's sickness. The only grandchild of Chief Rising Eagle was one of the ones that died. Dark Wolf the Chief's son took me to replace the child they lost. They never intended to harm me. He gave me to his wife Moonflower as if I was a precious treasure.

At first I thought my family would come for me but later on I figured out they had been killed."

"Sarah, you are a precious treasure. You are a beautiful woman and so clever and knowledgeable."

"Thanks. That was a nice thing for you to say, but all the women of the Winahatah, learn to do many things. They work very hard. What about you Jed? How did you become Ben's big brother?" she asked. "Well that's a long story, but a short version is that I came down the river in my canoe when Ben really needed help. His dog had tangled with a bear and he didn't know how to treat the wounds. We got along so well that when I left I told him I would stop back in the fall. All summer I worked in the settlement and then in the fall I headed back up the Hickory. That time it was Ben that needed my nursing skills. Winter came and I ended up staying with him."

"In the spring, we went for a journey with Stump and Ginger and found Beth. She was the only other survivor of the wagon train that you and Ben had been on. She spent that winter alone in a cave. She nearly died. I fell in love with her and we were married. We were staying with Ben in the hut until I could build my own place, when we spotted a war party heading down the Hickory. We were afraid for the people of the settlement, so I took my canoe down river and warned them."

"They all came that next spring and brought the lumber and built my house and put in a huge garden and fixed the hut where a huge boulder had left a hole in the back. That was their way of saying thank you for the warning. They really are good people Sarah, I don't understand why Helen and Sam acted the way they did to you."

She didn't acknowledge his reference to the incident at the Trading Post.

"What about your own family, how could you just stay with Ben?"

"I am like you Sarah. I lost my family."

"Hey look, the rain is stopping," he said.

"Jed, look at the river! You were right. It is frightening. I wouldn't try to cross that now. Let's gather up our stuff and get going." They munched on jerky as the horses trudged through the mud and cold wet grass. They were glad when the fence on the back edge of Mary's land came into view.

"It looks like the cattle went under the trees during that storm. Many of them are still in that area," said Jed.

They checked for any weakened fence as they rode along, stopping now and again to reinforce a post by piling additional rocks against it. The Hickory was higher, but not as angry looking as the Silver had been. They continued on along the edge of the trees.

Josh saw them coming a long way off. He shouted the news to the family and ran smiling to the crossing point at the big oak tree.

Mary and Beth had missed Sarah.

"It doesn't feel right here with you gone," said Mary. "Now with Rachel gone too, it felt really strange. We need to find a new little family to live in the cabin by the lake," offered Ben as he greeted Jed with a quick hug. All the little ones gathered around waiting. They were thinking that someone returning meant candy.

"Sorry to disappoint you, but we didn't go to the settlement, no candy this time," said Jed. "Maybe we can get someone to make popcorn this evening. Would that be a good treat?"

"Yes! I like popcorn." said Adam grinning.

"I like it, too" Said Jed.

Later as Jed and Beth sat at their table with just Lily and Johnny, Jed told Beth about the stop because of the rain, and the conversation he had with Sarah.

"It is good that she was willing to share that with you. It means that she is comfortable with you. She is pretty special isn't she?" said Beth.

"She sure is," said Jed. "You should have seen how good she was with Big Boy when the lightning struck a tree near us. He was about to bolt. She got on his back and talked to him and then asked for my shirt. She covered his eyes with it and talked to him and he settled right down."

"Zack says he is going to try to get a job at the lumber camp so he can get cut logs for the cabin. If he does he will be able to earn money for windows and a rifle or two. I don't like the thought of them being out there with no protection."

"Jed they have protection. Don't under estimate the power of a praying woman. Rachel has that family in God's protection. They will be fine. I just know it."

"Even so I think I am going to check with Ben. If he agrees, I'll take them one of ours until they can buy one of their own."

"Well it would help to have a gun so he can hunt for meat."

"I should have thought of that and left him mine when I was there. I wish I had."

Beth took care of the children while Mary, Sarah and Joshua worked in the garden.

"I hate these weeds, said Josh. "I wish they would just come out and not break off all the time." Sarah moved over beside him and handed him a digging stick she had been using.

"Put the stick into the ground and push it down under the roots and then just pull and lift with the stick at the same time."

"Hey it really works! That is a neat trick Aunt Sarah."

"The women of the People use a stick like that when they gather wild foods for their families.

Sometimes the ground is very hard and a tool is needed to get the plant up."

Mary looked over at her son and smiled.

"Josh if you would like to, you can go to the lookout now. Take a branch with you and while you are up there you can make your own digging stick."

"Thanks Mom and I will make you one, too." He quickly disappeared around the clump of pine trees.

"I think making the digging stick is more appealing to him than using it," said Sarah and both women laughed.

Sarah heard Jed yell as he was dumped over the head of one of the mustangs they were trying to train.

"I hope he's not injured," said Sarah. Just then they heard Ben laughing. They could see Jed tying a big bundle on the back of the horse that had bucked him off. The women continued working the soil in the garden. They couldn't hear Jed say that he would really like to start working more with the palomino that Mary liked so much.

"She is young and spirited, but I think she will make a good horse for Mary once she calms down and decides we can be friends. Zack said he had worked with her and given her scratches, but she backs away when he tries to put even the smallest bundle on her back. She hasn't developed trust yet."

CHAPTER NINE
I AM DAVID SHARPE

Sharp Knife had cautiously entered the settlement that morning. He had ridden in slowly and gone to the blacksmith shop. He had always kept shoes on the lean, long legged son of Dart Away. No one had told him that Dart Away had sired the foal. They didn't need to. He had asked the Chief for the foal as soon as it had been born. He knew with one look that this was going to be one of the fastest horses in the herd when it was grown. He had named him Thunder.

Mathew Morgan, the blacksmith, was surprised to see an Indian ride up in front of his shop, but since there was only one, he wasn't concerned.

"Good morning," said Sharp Knife. "I need some shoes on Thunder. Can you put on a set while I go over to the Trading Post?"

"Sure," said Matt. "I'll do it as soon as I finish the preacher's buggy horse."

"Thanks, I will be back in a little while."

"This fellow looks like he is more thoroughbred than mustang. Where did you get him?"

"Well I didn't steal him if that's what you are implying!" said Sharp Knife instantly defensive and getting his temper a little riled.

"No, I just meant that he looks like a really fine horse. That's all."

"Thanks, I'll be back." Sharp Knife walked across the street and over to the store still feeling irritated by the remark. If I weren't an Indian, he wouldn't dare make a remark like that!

That's when it hit him. He really wasn't an Indian. His mother, Fire Grass, was Spanish. After they had been taken from their home, they had lived with first one tribe and then traded to another. She had been extremely brave and remained strong. Finally his mother had been allowed to marry and she had moved to the Omati village. He had been accepted by Chief Rising Eagle and at thirteen; he had moved to live with the Winahatah. He tried harder than most to be a Winahatah. He had moved in with Night Hawk and his wife Spotted Fawn. They liked the boy right away. The people had treated him like one of their own. His mind had nearly swallowed his memory of his mother's background. He pictured her long, black, wavy hair and black snapping eyes. Maria was her name then, until she became Fire Grass. I remember now. My dad left us when I was small. She took me to live with her brother. We lived with Aunt Nan, Uncle Joe and my cousin. His memory was racing. He hadn't thought of these things for many years. He still saw his mother most years at the summer meetings, but last year he had not gone. He had stayed behind to water the corn.

They took us from the side of a river where we were getting water. They took my cousin, too. I wonder what happened to him.

"Sharp. Sharpe!" I was David Sharpe! I remember now. I remember it all! I wonder how old I was then. I wonder how old I am now. Sharp Knife didn't realize that he had been standing in front of the store for several minutes. He shook his head to clear it and bring his mind back to the present. He acknowledged the chill in the air as he walked into the store.

The bell on the door clanged as he pushed it open and stepped inside. Sam stood behind the counter with his hand out of sight, on his pistol.

"What are you doing here? What do you want?"

"I guess you aren't used to seeing folks dressed like Indians. I hope I haven't upset your wife." Sharp Knife could see Helen peeking with one eye through the center closing of the curtains on the doorway to their private rooms. Helen surprised Sam and herself by stepping out from behind the curtains.

"Don't be silly. White women don't frighten that easily. What did you come here to get?"

"Well Ma'am, I need a pair of pants like your husband's and a shirt, a pair of boots, and a hat." She looked surprised and suspicious. As they found what he needed in the correct sizes, Helen suggested that he would need some socks so that the boots would not chafe his feet and some cotton underwear. They will make your trousers more comfortable."

"That makes sense, Ma'am. I should have two pair of each, one to wash and one to wear. Thank you. Would you know where I could get my haircut?" He admitted to himself that he would hate to lose his long black hair, but he felt that it would be easier to find Sarah, a white woman, if he didn't look so much like an Indian. Finally Sam couldn't keep still any longer.

"Why are you buying all these clothes and trying to look like a white man?" he asked.

"I am a white man. That is, I'm not an Indian. My mother was Spanish and my father had dark eyes and black hair I think but I'm not sure. He left us when I was very little. The Indians took me and my mother when I was a little boy. My mother says that I look a lot like him."

"What is your name?" asked Sam.

"Sharp Knife," he replied and then added that's what the people call me. My mother called me David Sharpe.

"Well Mister Sharpe, you are the second person that has made your way back to civilization in this area. The other was a simple little woman that had been stolen years ago. I can imagine what she went through," said Helen.

"Woman, be still!" said Sam. "Mister Sharpe, you can get a bath and a haircut down the street next to the land registration office."

"That will be two dollars for the clothes and another two for the boots." Sharp Knife placed the coins on the counter and picked up the bundle of clothes he had purchased. Helen had wrapped them neatly in brown paper and tied the bundle with string. He headed for what he felt was a fate worse than death, a city bath and a haircut. He preferred to wash in the river.

The sign on the building had a picture of a man, sitting in a tub, with a cigar in his mouth and a hat on his head. Sharp Knife wondered if that was the way it was always done. He was puzzled.

He found the bath more pleasant than he thought possible. The water was warm instead of cold like the river or lake and he had been given a bar of soap to scrub his hair and body that smelled like a fresh spring meadow. He enjoyed the wonderful soft towel to dry with before putting on his new clothes. He discovered that the pants felt strangely restrictive and the shirt buttons were difficult to push through the little holes. He looked at the boots and decided to pull his soft moccasins back on. He would wait to wear the socks and boots and wrapped them back up in the brown paper from the store, along with his neatly folded leather clothes.

Sharp Knife was ushered into the barber's chair and soon his long beautiful hair lay in piles on the floor. His chin had very little beard. He had been taught to pluck it as soon as the first hair appeared, but the barber shaved his face anyway. The last thing was a splash of sweet smelling after-shave that sent him scrambling from the chair.

"I don't want to smell like that!" said Sharp Knife. The barber laughed and so did Sharp Knife until they could laugh no more.

When Matt Morgan saw him crossing the street toward his blacksmith's shop, he could barely recognize Sharp Knife. The first thing he recognized was the large piece of blue stone resting on his shirt front, held by a tightly braided cord.

"Well it looks like you have made some changes while you were gone!" said Matt.

"Yes, I decided it was time to look civilized." The comment from Helen still rankled in his spirit.

"Your horse is ready and I gave him a good feed. That will be four bits." Sharp Knife glanced at the sign. "That's a fair price, Mister Mathews. I will give you a choice. You can have the four bits or this piece of blue stone for your wife." Sharp Knife pulled a polished piece of turquoise from his pocket the size of a hickory nut and held it out for Matt to see.

"Liz would surely like to have that. I'll take the stone." Matt tucked it into his big pocket and asked, "Where you headed now that you are all dressed up?"

"I'm not sure. I am looking for a woman. Her name is Sarah." "What's her last name?"

"I don't know. I just know Sarah."

"You might try the land office. They might have some information for you. It's right over there." "Thanks for everything. I'll see you again sometime."

"Hey wait. You didn't tell me your name."

"It's Sharpe, David Sharpe."

At the land office two men were seated playing a board game as he entered. Sharp Knife soon learned that it was called checkers. He had played games, too, many times, but the games he liked best were far more physical.

"I don't want to interrupt your game. I will watch and learn how to play, if it is all right." He stood beside them for only a few moves of the buttons before one man stood up.

"That's enough torture for one day. What can I do for you, young man?" asked the clerk as he moved behind the counter.

"What is it that you do here?" asked Sharp Knife.

"We register land for the homesteaders. Do you want to register a piece of land? The clerk asked. The white men have strange ways thought Sharp Knife. All the land belongs to the Great Spirit. It is here for all men to use. How can the white men cut it into pieces? He stood there in thought. "Well, do you want a piece of land or don't you?" He repeated.

"No not just now. I am looking for a woman. Her name is Sarah. Do you know her?"

"Well I don't know if I do or not?" It was then that the clerk noticed the worn moccasins and the new clothes.

"What do you want with her?"

"I am David Sharpe. I am her friend. I would like to know that she is safe and well. She left the people quite a while ago and no one has heard from her."

"We can look in the book and see if her name is here. What is her last name?"

"I do not know her last name, only the name Sarah."

"Well I can't look without a last name." The clerk already knew who Sharp Knife was looking for and where she was, but he wasn't comfortable telling him. What if this man was looking for her to take her back to the Indians? Ben might not be able to defend against a party of raiders looking for his sister. He didn't know what to do.

"I know who you are talking about," volunteered the other man at the checkerboard. "She is Ben Slater's sister. She showed up there a while back."

"Where do I find this Ben Slater?" asked Sharp Knife.

"How do we know that you mean them no harm?" asked the clerk with a frown.

"I will not harm anyone. I am from the Blue Stone People." Sharp Knife thought that was proof of his peaceful intent.

"I thought so, you are an Indian! You are looking to take her back!"

"Yes, that is true. I love her. I would ask her to come back as my wife."

"It looks to me, like she has already chosen. She ran away didn't she?"

"Sarah did not run from me, she took a journey to find her people and learn the white man's ways. I too have taken a journey but now I look for her. I will find her."

"No one here will help you find her. We don't like Indians in this settlement! The best thing you can do for her is to go back where you came from and leave her in peace."

Quickly Sharp Knife decided that he would ask the next person he saw on the street, not for Sarah, but for Ben Slater. He spotted the Barber sitting in a chair in front of his shop.

"Could you direct me to Ben Slater's place? I need to speak with Ben Slater."

"Sure, just cross the bridge and follow the trail up the Hickory. When you get to the biggest oak tree you have ever seen, cross the river and you will be on his land."

"Thank you and thank you for the bath and haircut." The barber watched the beautiful horse with its rider cross the bridge. He sure is a strange one, thought the barber, but I like him.

Matthew Morgan also was watching as Sharp Knife rode out of town. I sure hope that he isn't trouble, he thought, as he plunged the red hot horseshoe into a bucket of water. A cloud of steam filled the air in front of him and when it cleared, he could no longer see Thunder or David Sharpe.

Sharp Knife stopped in the cool shade and could hear the cattle before he saw them. The barbed wire strands held a large herd. They were milling around nervously.

At first he couldn't see the cause of their unrest, but then he spotted the big cat on a branch of tan and gold leaves. It was fixing its attention on a calf. Slowly Sharp Knife pulled his rifle from its sleeve and took aim. He shot just an instant before the cat leapt. It lit on the ground in a heap, just feet from its intended victim. The cattle scattered running mindlessly in fear against the fences and causing further damage to the already unstable posts.

Sharp Knife knew that if he didn't repair it quickly, the herd would soon scatter over the prairie. He tossed the heavy cat over the fence and dragged it down wind of the cattle and then collected many rocks to support the posts and used his own rope to reinforce where the wire had snapped and tangled.

After skinning the cat and rolling the hide he tossed it over the back of his saddle. He glanced at the field as he started away. The cattle were quiet now and the calf and others like it were nursing or standing close to their mothers.

He stopped long enough to let Thunder graze in the grass near the river while he tried to prepare his mind for what he would say when he met Ben Slater. He began to have doubts. What if the man at the land office was right? Maybe she has made her choice. What if she doesn't want me and doesn't want to be my wife? What will I do then? Suddenly he realized that his heart was pounding much faster than normal.

As usual, Josh had been at the lookout. He was a good sentry and had seen the lone rider coming slowly up river just outside the trees. He raced to pass the word. Jed and Ben got their rifles and the women and children were hurried behind closed doors.

Thunder stood beneath the oak tree as Sharp Knife read the names on the tree and felt Sarah's pain as she had learned the meaning of the letters.

After crossing the river, he walked his horse up out of the trees and followed the trail past the hut without even seeing it. He was deep in thought at what it must have been like for her to find her brother and to live here after living so many years with the People.

Just as the house on the hill came into view, Ben stepped out of the trees onto the path near the lake, and Jed blocked the way behind Sharp Knife. Each of them held their rifles ready.

Sharp Knife was caught off guard.

"I am David Sharpe and I am looking for Ben Slater."

"I am Ben Slater. Why are you looking for me?"

CHAPTER TEN
A MAN TO HELP

Although Mary protested, Sarah left her and the children in the hut and crept through the trees near Ben's corral. She felt a flutter in her stomach as she leaned forward through the brown leaves trying to get a better look at the rider. There was something familiar about him and the horse. She could only see the back of his new hat and clothes from the trading post. I wish I could see his face, she thought.

She could not clearly hear what was said, but as she got closer she did hear Ben.

"David, we are glad to have another person to help with the horses. You can use that cabin across the lake. Just follow the path around. It crosses in front of Jed's place first and curves around to the cabin."

Jed extended his hand and introduced himself.

"David, please come meet our family at my house and have a meal with us at sundown."

"You can start in the morning," said Ben. "It will be good to have your help, David." They shook hands and the man rode slowly down the path toward the empty cabin.

Sarah still had a strange feeling inside as she reentered the hut and told Mary that it was safe, and that it had been just one man named David, looking for work and that Ben and Jed told him he could start in the morning.

"They told him he could stay in the cabin by the lake."

"That's good, because this place can sure use another pair of hands."

"Beth wants us all to come to the house tonight for the evening meal," said Mary "I told her that I would bring bread and I'll take over these two cherry pies. Will you be coming?"

"No I have some things I want to do and I will take some bedding over and some kitchen supplies so that our new help is comfortable. I'll make sure he has enough lamp oil and I better check the coffee, too."

"Well if you change your mind just stop at Jed's."

"Thanks, I'll be fine, really."

"Don't you want to meet the new help?"

"I'm sure I will have an opportunity if he stays."

What Sarah really wanted was to figure out why she felt so strange inside, every time she thought about the man. As she loaded her packhorse with bundles for the lake cabin, she had to admit that she was glad that he would not be there when she arrived. Perhaps something would present itself and solve the mystery. She waited until everyone had gone into Jed's house, before she took Pretty Mother and the packhorse slowly down the path that crossed in front of Jed's house.

The little cabin stood quietly with only the slightest glow of a small fire visible through the window. Sarah tied her horses to the railing of the porch and carried in her first load which was bedding. Next were things for the kitchen. She filled the lamp with oil and left a container with more on the floor against the wall. She put the coffee pot full of water on the counter and placed a small tin of coffee next to it. She added a basket with slices of apple cake and covered them with a tightly woven mat.

When she went into the bedroom to make the bed, she noticed a stack of neatly folded clothes and a bedroll lying on the floor near the window. The shirt on top of the stack was tan leather. She recognized the beadwork immediately. She had seen Sharp Knife wear it many times. She gasped and couldn't believe her eyes.

Sarah's face wore a frown as she added wood to the fire and lit the lantern. She checked the storage room. It still held many dried fruits and vegetables in baskets, along with dried meat in the cache. Rachel had been careful to leave some of each. Sarah brought out a jar of wild raspberry jam and placed it on the table and then she remembered that the bread was still tucked in her saddlebag. Sarah's hand shook as she got the bread and put the wrapped loaf on the table beside a plate and knife.

She couldn't help wondering. How did this man, David, get Sharp Knife's clothes? She didn't want to allow herself to think the worse, but on some level she still did. What if this man has killed him? What if Sharp Knife is dead? I'll never get to see him again, she moaned. She began to sob. Her tears filled her eyes as she stepped out on the porch to leave and found herself blundering into the chest of the man. He grabbed her arm to keep her from falling.

"Are you alright? What's the matter?

Sarah jerked away from the man. In the dark all she could tell was that he smelled like the man at the Trading Post. She felt like she was going to be sick. She jumped onto Pretty Mother and grabbed the rope of the packhorse and hurried away, down the path.

He stood there for a long time trying to figure out what had just happened.

"Sarah?" he said softly. If that was Sarah, why did she act like that? He wondered. This may be a lot harder than I thought.

Sarah cried herself to sleep and woke with a terrible headache. She stayed near her little cabin all morning sipping medicinal tea and pressing a cold cloth to her forehead.

Ben came to her door in the afternoon to tell her that he was moving some of the white horses and that he thought she would want to know. He was leaving Moon Boy and Buddy in the front field for her to ride. The mares were going to be put in his corral with a new, large, white stallion, named Cloud. He said that he had traded three saddle ready mustangs to the army to get him. She said she would come later to see him. It was then that he noticed that she didn't look well.

"Sarah you look very tired. You need to rest."

"Really Ben, I am fine, I just have a headache, that's all."

"Well I don't think that rest would hurt you." He turned to leave and then asked if she wanted him to introduce Pretty Mother to Cloud.

"Yes, that would be nice." He took her along with the other white mares on ropes running along behind him. Pretty Mother trotted beside Ben proudly. Ben wanted to create a herd of pure white horses with good lines and durability. He knew the officers of the army would desire them. Sarah spent the evening reading the books that Joshua had loaned her until she knew them by heart.

I want a Bible of my own, she thought. Heavenly Father, Please help me to get a Bible so I can read your Holy Word. I know that Ben said that I can use Father's and I have, but I want one here in my house that I can read each night. She prayed silently as she lay beneath her covers.

Her mind was troubled and she still didn't feel well. She slid out of bed and onto her knees.

"Father, I am ashamed that it took me this long to bring this to you. The man Ben hired, I think he killed Sharp Knife. Please don't let it be so. I give Sharp Knife to you, Father, and I won't worry about it anymore. I know that you have a plan for each of us. You have always taken good care of me and protected me from harm. If this man did kill Sharp Knife, perhaps he is the kind of man that would harm Ben or someone else here. Protect us Father and show us the truth. Amen."

She felt much better the next morning. She decided to take Moon Boy for a run on the prairie. She needed to take a couple days of rest as Ben had suggested. She bathed and pulled on her old tan leather outfit that she had worn when she visited Rachel and Zack. Her hair was pulled back into a long braid and tied with a strip of leather. She put a light saddle on Moon Boy so that she could make use of the saddlebags. With a water bag and supply of dried meat, tucked in beside collection bags and empty pouches, she added a bedroll and small tent. She walked Moon Boy up the path to Mary's to tell her that she was going out for a long ride and that she had a large hide and a blanket as well as a tent and food. "If I am not back right away, don't worry about me," she said.

She rode to the crossing, out under the oak, and turned her horse up river. She wasn't sure where she was going or why but she knew that she had to get out in the open to be alone. She needed time to think and pray. The sky was so bright blue that it was amazing. Winter is coming soon, she thought, but not yet.

Moon Boy stretched out into a full joyous run and as the distance spread before them she could feel the glad spirit in the horse to be allowed to run. Her own body began to relax, too. She felt positively giddy. After his first splash of excited energy wore off, Moon Boy settled into a smooth gate that was comfortable for both of them.

Later as she sat on the grass leaning against the trunk of a tree near the river, she began to think about the Blue Stone People and the family there that she had left behind. I would like Ben and everyone here to meet them and get to know them. It was then that the idea started to form that she would go back to the village in the early spring and invite the Blue Stone People to come visit her family here, when they went to the summer council. She knew that it would take some convincing to get Ben, Mary, Jed and Beth to agree, but the more she thought about it the more she wanted it to happen.

She spent the night there under the trees, not using the tent, just wrapped in a blanket. She needed time to be still and just listen to the voice of God. She was finally asleep as the last stars gave way to the early light of morning. A golden leaf drifted down and landed on her chin.

As she came fully awake she realized immediately what a foolish idea it had been, to want to invite an entire Indian village to come. It is like I told Ben long ago. I still have one foot in each of two worlds and I cannot ever have both, she thought.

"Father, thank you for showing me that before I created a problem," she said. "Thank you for your guidance in my life, and if it is possible, let me see Sharp Knife again, alive. I miss him."

She swung up on Moon Boy and followed along further up river until she discovered an area where the river widened and became shallow and clear. Rocks sparkled in the bottom as if they had captured the sun. She slid off Moon Boy and walked into the water looking at the rocks.

When she picked one up and held it she realized that it looked like it contained the same beautiful yellow metal that had laced some of the blue stones. I think I need to show this to Ben right away. She knew that the white men had always preferred to trade for the stones that had the most yellow metal. She wasn't sure why other than that they were beautiful.

Sarah turned Moon Boy back down river and retraced their route. She knew she could easily find the spot with the shining rocks, anyone could see them that looked. That was what worried her and that caused her to hurry. By the time she reached the crossing, Ben and Jed were waiting for her on the other side. Josh had told them Sarah was coming and she was riding faster than a comfortable pace.

"What's wrong? What happened?" Ben questioned her before she had time to slide from Moon Boy.

"Nothing is wrong, but I may have found something that you will think special. Can you come back with me right now?"

"What is it Sarah?" asked Josh, with boyish enthusiasm. "Wait until you see. You can come, too."

"Why are you being mysterious about this," Jed asked?

"You will see. It is a special secret."

"No Sarah, I think I better stay here. David is working by my barn with some new mustangs and I don't think we should all leave."

"Alright, Ben can tell you when we get back, but I want to change horses. Moon Boy is pretty tired and deserves a good rest and some feed."

"Josh would you go saddle up Little Mouse and saddle Rusty for Sarah? I think I'll use Buddy. He could use the exercise." Moon Boy was put in the field, as Ben got Buddy out. He had everything he needed there.

"I would put him in the corral by my barn but he might not get along with Cloud. He is younger and Cloud is very dominant."

As soon as Mary and Beth were told that Ben and Josh were leaving with Sarah and that she had found something special, they of course had many questions that Sarah was not willing to answer yet. She wanted Ben to be the first to know. The three rode out within a few minutes. Sarah rode quietly, but Josh talked excitedly. Ben smiled at the boy thinking that it didn't matter what the surprise was, because it had already been worth the effort. Josh was enjoying the adventure. Sarah slowed Rusty to a walk and finally stopped in the shade for a rest.

"I think we should rest the horses." They all got a cool drink and when Josh noticed a wild apple tree with some small fruit still on it, they nibbled a few bites here and there where the insects and birds had not spoiled the fruit.

"These are sweet now, but they were very sour when I stopped here hunting." Ben picked a handful of the small apples and gave some to each of the horses.

"Let's get moving," said Ben. "We won't get back before dark if we go much farther. How far is your surprise?" he asked.

"Not much farther. It's just past the next bend where the river flattens out."

"I have only come this way a few times," said Ben. "Once with Slim Parker when he was looking for a piece of land with good soil and a couple times hunting." She directed Rusty to the edge of the water and stopped, looking puzzled.

"I think it was right here, but I can't see it now. The angle of the sun is lower in the sky and the rocks are hidden in the shade. I know it was here," she said as she dismounted and walked into the water, feeling for rocks. She picked up one in each hand and held them up where the sun could hit them. "There," she said, "That's what I brought you to see."

"You brought us all this way to see rocks?" Josh said it with disappointment. Ben took one of the rocks in his hand and held it close enough to study.

"This isn't just a rock, Josh. I think Sarah has found gold!" Josh took the first rock he could reach from the river and studied it.

"I don't see any gold."

"Try again Josh," Sarah encouraged him. He felt around under the water and brought up a handful of smaller stones. Several of them held the sparkling metal.

"It doesn't seem possible that it is that easy!" said Ben. "I don't understand why white men think that the yellow metal is so important, but if you are pleased then I am glad that I found it."

"The question is what we should do about it?" said Ben. "We don't own this land, and none of us qualify to file on it. We already have pieces of land.

"Ben, God showed it to me, and he must want us to have it, just as he did the blue stones for the people. Josh was busy filling his saddle bags with stones from the river. Ben chuckled and decided he would do the same. As he stepped into the water he slid and ended up sitting in the river. Sarah and Josh started to laugh and they all laughed until tears were in their eyes.

"See" she said, "Gold is good. It is already making you laugh." They were still giggling when they mounted and headed for home, eager to show the rest of the family.

"My backside is cold!" said Ben, and they all started to laugh again.

"Ben, that man that you hired, should we tell him about the gold?"

"It isn't a good idea to tell anyone about it," said Ben. "Josh, don't mention the gold to anyone except family, until we figure out a way to own the land on both sides of the river in that area. Even then it will be hard to keep people from taking it," he said. Sarah was quiet. She was thinking that perhaps what she had found for Ben was trouble.

It was dark when they walked their horses across the river near the big oak and stopped at the hut. Mary had taken Nattie and Eli and gone to Jed's house to wait for their return. Ben added a few small pieces of hardwood to the fire in the hut and then they continued on down the path around the lake. As they drew near they could hear laughter. Jed was teasing David about being bucked off of the smallest mustang in the corral.

"She has a bad temper. She tried to bite me, too," said David defensively, as Sarah walked in. Sarah knew the voice, before she saw his face.

"Sharp Knife!" she exclaimed. She ran to him and wrapped her arms around him. "Oh Sharp Knife, I thought you were dead!"

"Sarah! I have been waiting for you. I told your family about our friendship and that I have been looking for you, but Sarah, why did you think I was dead?" Sarah couldn't believe her eyes. She breathed a prayer of thanksgiving to God for answering her prayer and then explained about seeing his shirt, and not recognizing him in the dark.

"I imagined the worst."

"Brave Sparrow, I am so glad that we are together again after such a long time. I have come to find you, to take you back to the people to be my wife. I don't want to be apart anymore. Will you come with me?" Sarah was shaking.

"Sharp Knife, I have missed you," she said. "I have carried you here in my heart, but I am not ready to go with you. I have unfinished business here. These people are my family."

"Sarah we need to talk about many things," he said. "We can start tomorrow. I will come to your house when my work is done for the day." Sharp Knife held her close for just an instant and then walked out and slowly led his horse up the path to the little cabin. He was humming.

Josh was about to burst.

"Can I tell them now Dad?" Ben nodded. "We have gold! There is lots and lots of it, a whole river full of it!" Mary smiled at Ben and wanted to know what the boy was talking about.

"I think Sarah should tell you," said Ben. "She found it." Sarah shook her head and told Ben to go ahead. She was still reeling from finding Sharp Knife.

Ben explained and then he and Josh went out to the horses and brought the samples they had. Mary and Beth each picked up a stone and held it near the lantern to watch it shine.

"It sure looks real!" said Beth. They hadn't grasped yet what a large deposit of gold could mean to them.

Jed went right to the heart of the problem.

"Sarah, did you find the gold on your property?"

"No. It is quite a ways up-river where it bends and then flattens out."

"Sarah how well do you know this Sharp Knife?"

"I have known him all my life. He is a good and honest man, a good hunter and a respected warrior of the people." Ben figured out where Jed was going with his questions.

"Sarah, are you in love with him?" asked Ben.

"I'm not sure. I do love him but I don't know if I'm in love with him. That's the only answer I can give you right now. I'm going to take Rusty and go home now. I am tired and I need to pray and do some thinking." After they helped her carry in the stones from her saddlebags, she said goodnight. The room was quiet.

Jed suggested that Ben walk out to the barn with him. When they were out where they could not be heard, they talked privately about putting the gold samples where they couldn't be found and waiting to see what developed between Sarah and David.

"You know, don't you that if they get married, that could be the answer? David could file on that land," said Jed.

"If he finds out about the gold and Sarah decides not to marry him, he could file anyway and he would own the gold. We need to warn Sarah, and pray about it," said Ben. He was concerned. "This seems like more of a problem than a blessing."

The men worked hard with the mustangs all the next day and it was evening when David finally rode up in front of Sarah's pretty little cabin.

When she answered the door, he handed her a fishing pole he had made and took her hand as they walked to the edge of the river. They sat holding the poles with the lines in the water and talked for hours. They filled in the time they had been apart, telling each other in detail, all that they had done.

"You can't imagine how frustrated I was when Ben told me that his sister had gone off for a few days to rest," he said. "I had all I could do to keep myself from following you," said Sharp Knife.

He told her his name and the story of his parents.

"So you see, Sarah, we aren't that different. Sometimes I can't make my mind up whether I am an Indian or not, but I am sure that I want to be with you." For a moment he was quiet. They could hear the night birds calling to each other and the gentle rattle of the willow leaves mixed with the sounds of the river. He continued,

"I plan to work here with your brother until you know that we were meant to be together."

"This is all so much to think about," said Sarah. "It will take time for me to get used to calling you by a different name." He joked about them not catching any fish, and then he took her hand again and walked with her to the path near her cabin.

"Goodnight Sarah," he said, as he reached for the reins of his horse.

"Goodnight David," she said, with a smile he could hear more than see.

Sarah sat at the table with a cup of chamomile tea, hoping that it would help her relax enough to rest. It was late but she felt that she was at the beginning of an exciting journey.

David rode slowly back to the little lake cabin. He was delighted with the way the evening had gone and he was sure that with time he could convince her to marry him. If he had to, he was willing to stay here with her family. Actually he had decided that he liked Ben and Jed well enough and they all seemed pleasant and treated him with respect.

As the days sped by, David saw more of Sarah. It had become a nightly routine to go for a walk after the evening meal. Finally David became impatient with waiting and once again pressed her to go back with him and be married. She looked at him and was sure that she too wanted to marry, but she didn't want to leave her new life.

"David I can't go back to the village to live. I have just found my brother. How can you even think that I would leave?" she was upset and started to cry.

Once again she found herself with one foot in each of two different worlds and it was tearing her heart apart. David looked at her tears and understood. He asked her if she would consider marrying him if he agreed to stay there with her.

"Sarah, I want to make you happy and if living here will do that, this is where we will live. What do you think? Can we be married and live here?" She couldn't believe that he was willing to leave the people and stay there with her.

"David, are you sure that is what you want to do?"

"Yes Sarah, I am very sure!"

A bright smile spread across her face and his as they entered the hut.

"We have something to tell you," said David. "Sarah and I want to get married. We would like to have your approval. I have a good bride price, and I can work hard and I am a good hunter. I have several horses in the village herd that are mine and I will gladly give them to you, Ben, if you will agree to let me marry your sister." David had said all that in one breath. Ben was laughing and so was Mary.

"Sarah, do you love him?" he asked. "Yes, I really do," she answered.

"Then I must ask this. David, are you a Christian?" He turned to the young man to see a look of puzzlement come over his face. Sarah, too, wanted David to believe in Jesus Christ, and the one true God. She wanted her husband to believe as she did, as her family did. It was the only way that they could truly be happy.

"I can't say that I am a Christian. I know about God and His son. I have listened as Sarah has told the words of the book her father read. She has taught me that the Great Spirit is God. Is that what you mean Ben?"

"No, not exactly, but that is a start. I can't say yes to your marriage just yet, but I won't say no. Continue to stay here with us and as we read the bible and talk, you will learn more about Jesus. Be patient and we will all pray that you receive the gift of faith."

When David left the hut, he wasn't smiling any more. He was deeply trouble.

"Sarah, did he mean that unless I believe as you do, that I can't marry you?"

"Yes David, that's what he meant. It is very important."

David swung up on his horse and rode toward the lake cabin without letting her finish what she was saying. He didn't look back at her.

David felt that Ben was being unreasonable. He was thinking that maybe he was more Winahatah, than he realized.

I want so much for him to understand, she thought. Ben and Mary were thinking the same thing. Ben brought his Bible from the bedroom and sat at the table where the lantern lit the pages as he searched for the scripture that he remembered.

"Do not be yoked together with unbelievers. For what do righteousness and wickedness have in common? Or what fellowship can light have with darkness? What harmony is there between Christ and Belial? Or what does a believer have in common with an unbeliever? What agreement is there between the temple of God and idols? For we are the temple of the living God. As God has said: "I will live with them and walk among them, and I will be their God, and they will be my people." Therefore, "Come out from them and be separate, says the Lord. 2 Co. 6: 14-17 NIV.

"Ben, I am glad that you told him how we feel. You were right."

"Mary, I am so grateful that I found you and the boys. I love you all and I want Sarah to have what we have."

"I know Ben. We must continue to pray for her and David, too, now. All of us need to ask that he be given the gift of faith. "

CHAPTER ELEVEN
AN INSPIRED VISIT

Sarah had gone to bed but had not been able to fall asleep. She had gotten back up and walked along the river in the moonlight until finally she had sat down in the grass and leaned against the trunk of an old tree. The rippling sound of the river was soothing. She allowed her thoughts to drift back to the village and all the people there. Suddenly a deep feeling of concern and self-doubt came over her that she could not dispel.

What if I was wrong to leave? What if the soldiers have attacked the village since I left? What if having the blue stones and developing trade wasn't enough? What if the camp got sick again from their contact with the white men at the trading spot? Would Sweet Grass, our young healer, be able to help them? What if Chief Dark Wolf got sick? Who would lead the people? Suddenly she realized that a tear was slowly making its way down her cheek.

"This is stupid," she said angrily to herself. "Who said I was responsible for the people." Finally she recognized her mood for what it was. She was homesick for the people of the village. She wanted to see Moonflower, Snow Star and she even missed Chief Dark Wolf.

A deep sigh escaped her lips as she walked back to her cabin. If I go back to visit, David, will think I am going back for him and Ben and the others will be upset.

"Father, I know I can trust you to clear my mind while I sleep tonight. Help me to know what I should do."

In the morning her mind was no more settled than it had been. Her feeling of concern for the Indian village continued. I must go back to visit. I need to see that they are doing well and then I can make decisions about my life more comfortably, she thought.

She dressed and then began preparing a bundle of things to take as gifts. In a separate bundle she carefully wrapped the white outfit and placed a large piece of chalk with it just in case she might need it. Strange I feel compelled to take it. It would be big trouble if anyone discovered its origin.

She left all the things on her bed and rode to tell Ben and the others what she had decided to do. Everyone tried to dissuade her. She found David working in the barn. She quickly explained that she was going back to the village for a visit and that she would only be gone a few days. He dropped the bundle of hay from his arms and wrapped them around her.

"I knew that you loved the people," he said. "I knew that you loved me. I will come with you. We can be married there and you can be healer again and it will be like before only better!"

"David, stop! That is not what I said at all! I am going back to visit! I want to be sure everything is alright, that's all. You can come, if Ben can spare you, but you must realize right now that you will only be coming as my friend. Have you forgotten what Ben said, when you asked if you could marry me? That has not changed."

She didn't give him time to reply. She turned around and walked out of the barn, mounted Moon Boy, and rode back to her cabin. She was glad she had been firm with David. Now there would be no misunderstanding. She suddenly felt a weight lifted from her spirit.

"I love You Lord, and anyone that I would marry has to Love You as much as I do. Thank you for helping me to decide. Please watch over my family while I am gone. She had forgotten to eat but now as she tied the water bag to her saddle, she remembered to make one more bundle for food on her trip. She didn't intend to hurry and so she put in more than she thought she would need. She added another large water bag to the packs and a waterproof basket to use for the horses to drink from. She decided to start out on Moon Boy and so she tied her bundles on Pretty Mother.

As she rode across the river and headed out onto the prairie she heard David holler. He rode up beside her, excitedly. His face was red from rushing.

"Ben said I could take the time to come with you, as long as I made sure that nothing happened to you and that I brought you back safely. Sarah, I promise I won't mention marriage again. You will have to ask me," he said with a hardy laugh that he didn't quite feel. Sarah was pleased that he had come and even happier about his promise. They rode side by side enjoying the day and each other. So much had happened in the two years that Sarah had been gone. So many things had changed in the lives of the people.

When they came out of the big rocks and approached the woods they were stopped by a young warrior that did not know Sarah. He remembered Sharp Knife and let them pass after some convincing. Spotted Feather had joined the Blue Stone People when Flying Eagle married Snow Star. He was eager to prove his worth and stood his watch diligently.

"They didn't have a sentry by the trees when I left," she said. I wonder what else has changed."

"The camp has grown," said David. "Many families have joined the village since they became the Blue Stone People. Sometimes, I think that so much change is not a good thing." As they neared the pool where Sarah and David had gotten the first and biggest blue stone, they could see that it looked different.

Men of the village had been working and a ledge had been formed by the men prying stones away, one at a time, as they collected the blue stones that the people needed to continue to prosper at trade. The pretty little pool was a bit larger.

Now, more water ran from the hole where the men worked. It ran down the face of the bluff and into the pool. Sharp Knife looked at Sarah and asked her if she wanted to go swimming.

"No, not just now," she said but she was glad that the pool had brought to his mind the same memory she was enjoying. She smiled at him and allowed her horses to go to the water for a drink.

It was growing dark, as they headed through the trees and down a path that was familiar to both of them. It was well worn now and anyone would be able to follow it without directions.

As they rode out of the trees at the back of the lake, Sarah pulled Pretty Mother to a stop. She could not believe what she was seeing. The village had grown in size. Some tents stood along the path to the lake. Others trailed out toward the cornfield. Next she noticed the small building standing near them beside the lake.

"What is this?" she asked.

"It is a church," said David,

There are two black robes that live in it."

"This is exciting news," said Sarah. "How does Chief Dark Wolf feel about this?"

"I don't think he likes it at all, but he says it is good to know your enemy. They are white men. He lets them talk and he listens."

Sarah and David could hear the voices of the people gathering at the communal fire as they circled the lake. They were excited to see their friends and families.

"Over there is a pen with sheep in it. Singing Wind and I brought them back when we returned from our journey. I want to show them to you in the morning."

Before revealing their presence, Sarah and David stopped their horses in the dark. It was then that they realized that they had actually approached the village without seeing another guard.

"David, I don't hear a flute near the horses. Do you?"

"No. It seems that Spotted Feather is the only one that is on duty. Everyone else is gathering at the communal fire."

Although both young people were eager to enter the village, for some reason, they held back dismounting in the dark and listening to the strange cadence coming from the drums. Things felt unfamiliar. The sound was new and strange.

Suddenly Sarah could feel in her spirit that she had been led back here at just this time for a reason. She asked David to approach quietly and to speak to one of the young warriors to find out what was happening.

When he returned, to her side he found that she had changed into her white clothes made from the sacred robe of Talking Mountain. She had removed the saddle from Moon Boy. His back was covered with a white cloth. Her hair and skin were dusted with chalk and he felt a chill as he approached her.

"You look like you are from the spirit world," he said.

"What is going on in the village?" She asked.

"The people have gathered to accept Singing Wind as their new shaman. He has been studying with Standing Lizard. Before him, they had Red Fox but he was killed last spring in his tent by a big wolf. The people have not had anyone to talk to the spirits for them all summer," said David.

"I see," said Sarah. He could not see the smile that crossed her face as she realized that this was why the Holy Spirit had urged and led her to arrive here now.

This was an opportunity to once again tell the people about the one true God. Then she remembered the little church that was here and she wondered if the people were already learning about God from the black robes.

She and David watched from the darkness as Singing Wind staggered out of his tent. He entered the ring of light from the burning fire and stood before the large number of people gathered there. They could see Chief Dark Wolf and Moonflower sitting together, and slightly back, but beside the Chief on his left sat two priests in black robes.

"It seems strange to me that the priests would be at the fire. This celebration is to accept a new shaman for the people," said David.

"I agree. This whole thing doesn't feel right and David; look at the way Singing Wind is dancing. He seems unsteady as if he has been drugged." Sarah felt concern. "Something is very wrong here," she said.

They continued to watch as the drums beat faster and Singing Wind whirled around faster and faster. When he could turn no more, he tried to stop but the world spun passed him and his feet were out of control. He staggered, tripped and fell, landing with his arm in the fire! Women screamed and men shouted, but none ran to pull him away. They froze in fear. Father Bob was the first to grab him and pull him away from the hungry flames. Father Pete had taken longer to raise his heavy body from the blanket, but with presence of mind he had brought the blanket and smothered the flames attacking the young man's oil coated skin and hair.

Immediately, Sweet grass directed that he be carried to the communal tent.

The celebration was over. Singing Wind would never be their shaman now. People stood back from the fire murmuring.

Chief Dark wolf stood, making an attempt to calm the people.

It was then that Sarah walked Moon Boy into the light of the fire. She and Moon Boy stopped; looking like a spirit from another world had just appeared. All conversation halted. It was silent. The only sound was the crackle of the fire.

"Once again the People of the Blue Stone need to be reminded that they are children of the Great Spirit," she began. The people quickly found their seats, looking on in awe as the beautiful woman in white spoke to them from the back of a pure white horse. Even Chief Dark Wolf sat back down allowing Sarah to calm the people.

"Today God has spoken to you in an undeniable way. He is a jealous God. He wants no other gods to be honored by his children. I am Sarah of the Blue Stone People. Do you remember me? God has provided much for you. The village prospers. Young people come to join the village, bringing new skills and new blood to a once old and tired people. You have not seen war here. You have not been plagued with disease for many years. Since God has blessed you, life here has been good. Your crops have grown. Your children are fat. There has been no season of hunger in the village of our people. Why now do you want to anger God by choosing another shaman to honor other spirits? Did not God send a wolf to kill Red Fox? Did He not already show you that He commands the sky and the earth, the rain and the animals? They all do His bidding. He is their creator. His Son Jesus Christ came to earth as a man, to save us from being thrown into a fire that lasts forever!" Sarah pointed at the fire as she continued.

"Singing Wind felt the bite of flames but he lives and will once more guard the horses and if God wills it; he will play his flute again. The Blue Stone People need no one to honor other spirits. They need to honor God through His Son, Jesus Christ. He will give our Chief wisdom. He will bless our crops and give to us from His bounty. If you believe that God loves you and that His Son Jesus came to earth to save you; to forgive you and give you eternal life with Him in heaven, stand and follow me."

The priests were the first to their feet. They had never seen anything like this woman, but they liked her message. She rode Moon Boy slowly out of the ring of people around the fire and slid off his back.

Sarah raised her hands high into the air walking slowly on the path toward the lake. Moon Boy followed her and the priests followed him. David stepped in line behind them. Chief Dark Wolf and Moonflower stood and after a moment of indecision followed the others. One by one it seemed the entire gathering formed a slow procession.

"We love you Father. Forgive our offenses. We did not trust you. Help us to trust. Teach us about Your Son and bless us. Jesus died for us. We accept Jesus as Your Son, our Savior. He came to save us from the fire, and to lead us to heaven. We know because He is your son, He still lives. He will live forever. We want to live forever with You God. Live with us Father God. Live here in our hearts. Make us strong. Make us one." Sarah's voice was loud and clear as it bounced across the surface of the lake. She stopped before the big carved cross. She shuddered at the bloody depiction of the body of Christ upon it.

Beside the little church, turning to face the people, Moon Boy walked beside the cross and then suddenly lifted his gorgeous head and gave a loud, long whinny. It seemed that all of nature was agreeing with her words. The people felt goose bumps run down their arms! Something strong and meaningful was happening!

"If you want Jesus to come into your life and into your heart with His forgiveness, power, and blessings come and kneel here by the cross." The priests chose to lead by example. They knelt. The entire village surged forward. They gathered around Sarah, kneeling, touching her and touching the cross. Some smiled at her. Some were crying softly.

Tears slid down her cheeks as she realized that she was being allowed to see the harvest from the seeds she had planted during the difficult years that she had lived in the village. She glanced around to see David standing beside her. Slowly he lowered to his knees.

"Now I understand a little. Will you teach me a lot more?" he whispered.

"We both have so much to learn," she answered joyfully.

Father Bob stood and stepped near her.

"You are an angel. You have done in one evening what we have been trying to do for months."

"No. I have just brought them to the cross, now you must teach them all what it means, and baptize them." she said. Father Pete hugged her and began to play his guitar. Soon "The Alleluia, Holy, Holy," rang across the lake, as the people sang the song they had learned from him.

Chief Dark Wolf and Moonflower stepped close and each greeted her with affection. Moonflower was crying with joy that her daughter had returned but also she had a new stirring of joy in her heart that had never been there before. She and so many others could feel that this night was very special. Dancing Willow understood more than most that Sarah was speaking about the same Great Spirit that had touched her heart and responded to her prayer by healing her daughter, Blue Stone, so long ago.

The men of the tribe gathered around David and welcomed him back. Each one was eager to hear about his journey and how he had found Sarah. They assumed that he and Sarah were back to stay. David knew that he would not be staying long.

As people talked and sang, Sarah eased her way back to camp. She told Moonflower that she wanted to quickly change her clothes and then see if she could help Sweet Grass.

"You have come back! Sharp Knife, said he would find you and he did." I am so happy to have you back, Brave Sparrow I guess I should say Sarah. Tell me, did you find what you were looking for?"

"Yes, Mother, I did. I have a large family and even though I was with them, I missed you. So you see; we are here to visit, for a few days. Tell me, are you well? "

*****

Zack's work at the lumber mill had provided the prepared logs for their little cabin and by the time that Jed returned to check on their progress, it was up and the roof was on. Men from the mill had pitched in to help build it before winter. Zack would be working at the mill from now on. He worked hard and was well liked. They could comfortably winter through and add on the bedrooms in the spring.

Rachel had worked hard while he was away to make the tiny cabin feel like home. Margaret greeted him with open arms and he couldn't believe the change in the shy little girl. She ran to the cabin laughing out loud and calling to her mother that they had company. Rachel came out and hugged him, leaving prints of flour on the back of Jed's shirt. She was in the process of mixing bread dough. She apologized and after washing her hands, dusted the back of his shirt with a towel.

Jed could see that this little family had worked very hard every waking moment. A new adobe coated oven stood off to the side of the cabin. A large pile of rocks lay near the cabin door. They had been hauled from the river, to build the fireplace and chimney.

A kettle of stew hung near a small fire in the yard.

"Everything has been done so quickly!" Jed exclaimed. "I can barely believe my eyes. You have accomplished so much, since we left you."

"Oh, Jed, it will take a long while to tell you all that happened since I last saw you. The best part is Margaret! She woke up one morning and just started talking again. I am so happy that I have to watch that I don't start crying when I hear her talking. The men from the mill came down and it only took them a few days to put the cabin together. Zack will be home this evening. He is working every day at the mill. There are still lots of things we need to get before winter."

"The women sent you lots of things. I'll go get them off the packhorse. I'm sure he will be glad to be rid of the weight." Jed carried in several bundles. One included a bit of sugar candy for Margaret. She politely thanked him with a big smile when he handed it to her.

"It is wonderful to hear that child talking," he said.

Once inside the cabin, Jed realized that the cabin was constructed as one room with no partition for sleeping quarters. He noticed the board covers for two caches and took the liberty to lift each one, peering inside. He was pleased to see that the first was full of dried meat. The second one was empty.

"I just finished digging that one yesterday. Zack made the cover for it last night. I knew we would need it when the vegetables are ready next summer, and I thought that if we get more meat we could use it. I might dig another one, if we need it," said Rachel. "I think it is good to have lots of supplies on hand, just in case we hit a bad spell."

"You are right about that. I noticed a pile of logs out there to the side. I think that I could make a couple benches out of them. Do you think Zack would mind?"

"Jed, you know it would be a big help. We have wanted to start making furniture but we just haven't had time." Jed nodded and went outside to the pile of logs. He selected several that were about five feet long. "There is enough wood here for a table too," he said to her, sticking his head in the door. She had placed her dough in two pans that set near an open window on top of a barrel. Jed glanced over at the shade under a maple tree near his horses. Margaret was hand feeding them and jabbering away. The doll Joshua had made for her was leaning against the trunk of the tree, wrapped in a scrap of cloth.

Jed was pegging the second bench together when Zack rode up on socks. With a wide smile, he shook Jed's hand and thanked him for coming to visit.

"Those are really needed," he said, when he noticed the project Jed was working on. "Have you been inside?" asked Zack.

"Yes, I was amazed to see a cabin up. You will be warm and comfortable no matter what the weather is."

"It's not big but I plan to add on next summer and at least we will be cozy in it this winter." "It's a nice cabin, Zack. You have accomplished a lot in a short time," said Jed.

"I want to make some beds to get us up off the ground before winter. Right now it is fine. I met a man at the trading post named Calvin. He said he would help with the fireplace so I said I would help him to gentle a new filly he bought, and you can tell Ben we are doing it his way. I think Calvin said he put your fireplace in, Jed."

"Yes he did Zack, and he did a good job," said Jed. Rachel stepped out and suggested they all sit down near the campfire and rest a bit. Zack said he wanted to wash up first and he headed in the direction of the river with a towel tossed over his shoulder.

Rachel was eager to hear any news from back at the Ranch.

"Jed, tell me what has been happening at your place since we left," said Rachel.

"Well there really isn't much to tell. We are just all working hard as usual and the place is sure growing. We fenced another field for Ben. His property extends past the bluff, so really Sarah's cabin is on the edge of Ben's land. He hasn't started his new house yet, but I think we will soon." Just then Zack came back to the fire and sat down with dripping hair and a happy sigh.

"Jed it is good to see you. I am glad that you have to come to Silverville once in a while, so that we get to visit," said Zack. They ate stew and fresh baked bread and laughed together.

Finally Zack told Jed that he had heard some people talking about Sarah in the trading post and he had set them straight about her and told them how she had helped them and doctored him when he was wounded.

"I told them that I owed Ben, Sarah and all of you our lives," said Zack.

"Ben will be glad to hear that you spoke up," said Jed. "Thank you Zack."

"I couldn't keep still. That's just my way, I guess. You can tell Ben that Rose will be opening that school soon and if he would like to bring Josh in here, he can stay with us to go to school."

"That's a generous offer and I'll tell Ben and Mary when I get back," said Jed.

When morning came, Zack had already left for the mill on Socks.

"I'll stay long enough to make the table to go with the benches. It shouldn't take more than a few hours."

"While you are doing that I want to take Margaret to the woods to gather mushrooms."

She said that she would sand the benches and table and oil them when it was put together and that he needn't bother with that part. She and Margaret entered the trees and disappeared from sight. A few minutes later they hurried into camp with a grin on their faces.

In Rachel's basket, instead of mushrooms was a small raccoon. Margaret danced around her mother excitedly talking and asking to hold it. She gently placed the baby in her daughter's arms warning her to take care not to get bitten. When Jed saw what it was they were giving so much attention, he couldn't help but wonder if Rachel realized how much trouble a full-grown raccoon could be. Margaret asked if Jed would build it a cage before he left. He questioned the wisdom of keeping the curious and mischievous creature in camp.

"Rachel the mother will come looking for that baby. She can do a lot of damage. Maybe you should let that baby go, back in the woods before dark," said Jed.

"She will be lost," whined Margaret. Rachel nodded and pointed to the woods.

"Her mother will call her and find her. We must put her back. Jed is right."

CHAPTER TWELVE
HEADING HOME

As he rode home Jed thought about Sarah and his last trip home in the storm, huddling under the hides to stay out of the rain. He wondered if she really would marry David, and if she did, would he want to build on the land where the gold was. Would she move there? They would have to build a house and probably the smartest thing to do would be to fence right away. That would keep people away from the part of the river where she found the gold. He thought about the gift he had for Sarah in his saddlebag.

It had taken months to get a Bible shipped to the trading post. Now maybe she and David can read it together. Reverend Brown had promised he would come to the "S and J" and stay a few days. Jed had invited him. Melanie had giggled and said Ben wouldn't recognize her, when she came.

She now had two children and had gained about forty pounds. She looked a lot like her mother. Jed had not intended that she come but couldn't figure out a way to politely say so.

It was dark when Jed led the packhorse across the river and continued on to his house. The hut was quiet and only a small fire burned in the fireplace. When he opened the door of his house, it too, was quiet. Where is everyone? He wondered starting to feel alarmed.

As he stepped out on the porch to get his bundles he noticed light streaming from the barn and heard voices. Everyone sounded excited, but he couldn't quite make out what was being said.

"Hello," he yelled, as he entered the corral. The door swung open and Josh stuck his head out.

"Hi Uncle Jed, we are all in here, with the new babies."

"What new babies?" he said as he stepped into the circle of lantern light. There in the first stall was one of the mustang mares that they had caught in the long pen at Sarah's. They had handled her and stroked and brushed her enough that she was no longer afraid of humans, but she had not yet been trained for riding. In the hay beside her were twin foals, so much like the big stallion that they were exact tiny copies.

"These are pretty special babies," he said. "They carry the stallion's mark for sure. It is a good thing she had them here where we can let her use the barn. It is late in the year for a mare to have foals."

"Ben this is really something. At the rate we are adding horses, we will have plenty to sell." Mary and Beth were both sitting in the hay near the new foals. Jed bent down and placed a kiss on the top of Beth's head and it was at that moment that he realized that Sarah and David were not there with the others. Mary pointed to the next stall as she stood up placing her finger against her lips to suggest they quiet down. On a blanket, lay Nattie, Lily and Eli.

"Where are Sarah and David," Jed asked. "They have gone to the Indian village," answered Ben, with a deep frown.

"When did they go? Why did they go? Are they coming back?"

"I'm not sure why, but she said she had to go. She said she would be back." Jed watched Ben's face as he spoke. He could see the pain.

Mary looked at Jed and Ben knowing that Ben had silently communicated to him that he was concerned over whether she would return. She put her arm around Ben and felt the tension in his back muscles.

"It is late," she said. "The foals are fine and so is the mother. I think we should all try to get some rest now. Tomorrow will come soon enough and it will have its own measure of work and problems."

Mary picked up Nathaniel, and Jed and Ben each picked up their sleeping children, carrying them to their beds. Beth yawned and followed Jed and Johnny to the house.

Josh was awake for quite a while after everyone had settled in for the night. He was thinking about Sarah and wondering what it would be like to live with the Indians. He hoped she would come back soon. He knew his dad was worried about her. I like David, he thought. It would be nice if Sarah would marry him. He remembered what Ben had said to David, when he had asked to marry Sarah. Josh wondered what it would be like to go through each day not knowing that Jesus was there to help him, to counsel, to comfort, to protect and to be his loving friend. When Josh thought more about it he decided that it would be very hard to live with a whole village of people that didn't know Jesus.

"Heavenly Father, please bless Aunt Sarah and David while they are gone. Bring them home safely. Help David to believe in Your Son Jesus." and... Josh had drifted off to sleep.

Ben had said his own prayers, including the new foals, but the rest of his prayer was much like that of Josh. His prayer was talking to an old friend as he told Jesus of his concerns about Sarah and David, and about the Ranch. He had been relieved when the men had laid out the new accurate fence lines and he had discovered that he had actually built Sarah's little cabin on the edge of his own land. He thanked God for that again at the same time he was realizing that he would have to build another cabin on her acres in order to fulfill the improvements required to keep the land.

"God, she turns twenty one next fall. We have only a few more months to go before it is legally hers. Give us that time without any more trouble, please Lord." Without knowing it, Ben had whispered his prayer loud enough that Mary heard it.

"Amen" said Mary. "Now Ben, relax and go to sleep," she said snuggling down under the covers, and tucking her head against his shoulder.

The rain hit hard against the roof as Beth stood looking out the window, at the dark night. She couldn't see much but what she did see looked like a wall of water. She was glad that her family was cozy, warm and dry, protected from the pelting rain.

She hoped that Sarah and David were not somewhere on their way, having to endure the cold downpour.

She felt restless and had gotten back up shortly after going to bed. The house was quiet. Everyone else slept. She put the kettle on to heat so she could make a cup of tea. After adding wood to the fire she sat in the rocker near the fireplace sipping her tea and wondering why she was unable to rest. It had been a long and tiring day. A smile curved her lips as she thought about the new foals snuggled against their mother in the barn.

Her expression changed to a deeply furrowed brow as she thought about Sarah leaving to return to the Indian Village. She had to admit that she understood why a young woman would miss the people that had raised her, but felt that as an adult,

Sarah should have weighed that against the fact that they were responsible for removing her from her real parents. I hope she returns soon, Beth thought. Ben is very troubled about her being gone. A big yawn reminded her of the late hour. She quietly set the cup down on the table and tiptoed to their bed.

*****

They had said all their goodbyes and their horses stood ready to leave.

"You are a good mother. I am glad that you and father have Snow Star and Watching Owl to keep you company when I am away. You are in my heart. I will visit again one day."

Sarah did not want anyone to see her tears as she swung up on Moon Boy. Her smile was a bit too bright as the tears threatened to spill onto her cheeks. Quickly she turned him and headed toward the little church and the priests standing outside it. David and Sarah stopped just long enough to shake hands and to ask them when they would begin to teach the people about Jesus. Father Bob replied that they were going right away to ask Chief Dark Wolf if he would talk with them about classes they wanted to hold in the church.

"Good," she said.

"We will pray for you," the priests said at the same time.

"And we will pray for you," said Sarah as she eased Moon Boy and Pretty Mother onto the path that led to the trees at the backside of the lake.

They loosened enough of the turquoise to give as gifts for everyone and to make David a handsome necklace.

"Do you think you can make the time to do the polishing, if I can drill them?" David said with a big smile.

"Yes, they will be nice Christmas gifts."

"The best gift of this trip was what happened when you led the village over to the cross. How will we ever explain all that to Ben and everyone?"

"It was exciting wasn't it? David do you think you can explain it all so they understand that you have also been given the gift of faith?"

He looked puzzled.

"I don't even know how I could begin."

As they moved out of the trees, around the last huge boulder, Thunder and Moon Boy were prancing.

"These two horses are young and full of energy. They are enjoying the cold morning. Let's let them run," said David. Sarah reached over and totally removed her lead from Pretty Mother, knowing that with only the weight of the small packs on her back, she would be able to keep up easily. Sarah felt that Pretty Mother would always stay with her.

"Let's go," laughed Sarah as they raced across the prairie. They allowed the horses to slow naturally after the exhilarating burst of speed. The beautiful horses set a comfortable ground eating pace, once they had burned up some of their excess energy. David had leads on his horses from the herd. They had kept up easily. His horses were strong and handsome.

They crossed the Hickory before noon the next day. "I'm glad to be home," said David, as he entered the water with Thunder.

"So am I," said Sarah with a big smile.

Waiting on the other side of the Hickory was their entire family. David was surprised that he was thinking that this was his family. My family, he thought. It felt good.

Everyone was talking at once.

"We have so much to tell all of you!" said David.

Ben hugged Sarah so tight that she thought he would crack her ribs.

"Sarah, please don't go away ever again. I was so afraid that you would not come back."

"Ben, I promise you, I will always come back." She reached for Nattie and carried him for Mary to the hut. "You are all my family. I love every one of you, and I need to ask Beth to make a big pot of her wonderful chili for our evening meal. It will be a party. You won't believe all that we have to tell you. Let's wait until then to tell all our stories. I know that we all have some work to finish first."

Ben shook David's hand.

"Thanks for keeping your word. I know you wanted to keep her there if you could, but you brought her back to us." David grinned and swung back up on Thunder. He had been leading two mares, one a brown and white paint, the other a brown mare with a beautiful gray colt.

"Is it alright if I put these in the far field?"

"Yes, I just filled the water trough and there is lots of grass. Whose horses are they?"

"Mine right now," said David laughing heartily. "Thunder is tired. I guess I'll put him out there too."

"You can ride back on one of the mares that we have been working on. We did a little work with them this morning and then put them all out there. That is, if you can catch one and stay on," said Ben, with a chuckle.

"That sounded like a challenge to me," said David.

David was glad for the friendly atmosphere at the "S and J".

As he rode down the path to the gate, he started to think ahead to the time when he had a place of his own. He wanted to build a ranch with Sarah. I should have talked further with that man at the land office. He asked me if I was there to sign for a piece of land. Maybe I should talk to Ben and Jed tonight about it if we have time with all the other stuff we have to talk about. It will be fun.

David had put his horses in the field and led them all close to the Palomino that Mary liked. With the other horses near him, she felt assurance that he was a friend. He slid his hand over her back and scratched her ears talking softly. David did it instinctively. He didn't have to learn to be gentle, as Zack had. He continued to hold on to the reins on Thunder, but slipped the soft bridles off and released his other two, and placing the gear in his saddle bag. They were in no hurry to move away from him. They drank from the trough and then started nibbling the green grass nearby. She stomped her front foot nervously and backed up a little, when he approached her with the soft bridle. Ever so slowly he slipped it on, letting her smell his hand and the bridle as he talked to her. Patience brought a small victory as he managed to get it on her and buckled.

"Now, beautiful lady, all golden and white, will you walk up to the barn with me on your back?" He held the reins while he freed Thunder of his tack. "Maybe you would be willing to carry just this saddle for me." He slid it up on her back and watched her ears to see if she was showing fear or displeasure. She stomped again, but didn't try to move away.

"Good girl," he said and scratched her ears and patted her neck. Quickly in one fluid motion he stepped into the stirrup and was seated. He sat still for several minutes, waiting for a reaction. She bent her head down and took a bite of grass and chewed it then took another step and another bite.

"Alright girl let's go over to the gate." His direction was subtle as he nudged her with his knees and pulled softly on the rein in the direction of the gate. She lifted her head and walked in that direction.

When David looked up to see how far the gate was, he saw Ben standing there, ready to open it, with a grin from ear to ear.

"I have to tell you David, that I like the way you handle horses, but that Palomino is tired. I took her out for a long run this morning."

"Are you telling me that you watched me go through all that and it was for nothing?"

"No, it was not for nothing. It showed me that you know the right way to go about making friends with a horse. She will always remember you and trust you. Do you want to pick out one of the others or are you ready for a rough ride?"

"You pick one that is near us and tell me what you have done in the way of training with it, before I get on."

"That bay has been carrying big bundles, but always tries to pull or buck them off. The black over at the fence has thrown Jed off a couple times. He seems to think that is part of the game. He plays rough."

"One thing that Falling Stones and I found that we could do to prevent injuries; was to take them in the lake and work with just the bridle. Falling stones broke his leg and hurt his shoulder, trying to ride a new horse in our herd, over hard ground. After that we started using the side of the lake. We led them into the water and slid on bareback. The water tires them out quicker and seems to settle them. It gives them something to think about besides the human on their back; its softer landing, too."

"Maybe we could check a section of the river and use it the same way. We should make sure there is nothing under the surface to injure horse or rider before we try it though," said Ben.

"Ben swung up on Ginger and patted her neck. She is my sweet girl. I pulled her out of the mud bog when she was a baby."

"She's a nice horse. I think I'll stay here and have a talk with that black. I promise I'll be careful. You don't need to stay or worry. I'm just going to introduce myself. I'll be back and ready for that meal at sundown."

When Ben left, David had hung his heavy saddle on the gate and was standing near the black talking softly to him.

CHAPTER THIRTEEN
THE AMAZING STORY

Sarah felt positively giddy when she entered her little cabin. As she put her things that she had taken with her in their proper places, she recognized how blessed she was to have it all to herself again. Beth had been there earlier, anticipating their return and had left a tray with a loaf of fresh raisin bread and a jar of wild apple jelly, on the counter. She had just made that jelly before I left. I know it will be delicious. She brewed a cup of tea and sat down at her table; enjoying a chance to relax and have the sweet treat. Her mind slid back to their arrival at the camp of the people and all that had occurred. I don't know if I can really explain it tonight, well enough so they can appreciate the significance of it. I think I will go out and put both my horses in the field by the bluff and then I am going to do the unheard of. I am going to take a nap!

As Sarah stepped onto her porch, she could see David working with the all black horse. He was just sliding on and off and scratching his ears and sitting on him, leaning forward and talking to him and scratching him, with no bridle or saddle at all. He was just making contact. He picked a big handful of dry grass from near the fence and rubbed the horses back and sides with it. Sarah could see he was talking.

When David noticed that she was watching, he waved and walked near her and the black horse followed him.

"Looks like you have got a friend," said Sarah.

"Yes, we are working on it. Ben said he has thrown Jed a couple times, so I am going slowly. Today I am trying to convince him that humans can be fun. Ben and I plan to clear a strip of the river of any possible hazards and then we can ride the new ones in the water, the way we used to do, in the lake, at the camp of the people.

"I remember seeing men do that, but I didn't know that you were one of them. I saw Falling Stones do it, after he was well again. It took a long time before he could walk without a limp," said Sarah

"I'm a little excited about tonight. Are You?" David asked.

"Yes, but I think it will be difficult to tell all of it so they understand the power that was present at that cross."

"I'm eager for them to believe that the Holy Spirit is doing a work in the people."

"Sarah, I wasn't going to tell you, but you should know, that not all the people followed you to the cross. There were three men that hung back and stayed near the fire."

"Who were they, David?"

"Flying Eagle was one, Growling Bear and I saw one other but I don't know who that was. I just turned to look at the people all following us and noticed them staying back. I'm sorry Sarah. I know you thought everyone came."

"Thanks for telling me, I will pray for them. It just means that they were not ready yet."

"Sarah, I better give Blackie some more attention." David smiled as he turned back to the big black horse.

Sarah decided that taking a nap was not really what she wanted to do. She turned Moon Boy into the field where David was working, and rode Pretty Mother up to the hut. She wanted to visit with Mary.

When she put her into the corral, Cloud came over immediately and nuzzled Pretty Mother.

"I forgot all about you, Cloud. You are handsome. Ben found a winner when he bought you. It looks like Pretty Mother thinks so, too."

"Mary, are you here?" Sarah called.

"Yes, I am over here. I am trying to dye this material. I wanted brown but it keeps coming out looking green."

"Do you have any nuts in the casings? We can peel them off and toss them in. They give off a strong brown."

"Yes, I thought of that but I couldn't go get them. Eli and Nattie are both sleeping in the hut and the nuts are in the barn."

"Mary, I will only be a minute." Sarah hurried away before Mary could object.

"I think we should be careful how we do this, or we will have brown stains on our hands," said Mary.

The nuts were in a big sack that had held flour from the Trading Post.

"I am going to roll the sack back and forth on the grass," said Mary.

"Well, that didn't work," said Sarah peeking in the sack. "I think you were too gentle." She picked up the sack and slammed it down turning it a bit and doing it again and again. When they looked in the sack, they found that she had succeeded in dislodging most of the husks. "They are dry. I can pick the nuts out and we can pour the husks right in the big kettle."

"Mary, I am so glad to be here with you and Ben and everyone"

"Probably not as glad as we are to have you," She said smiling.

"Sarah, look at this before you go. It is a beautiful dark brown. It will be dark even when it dries."

"Don't forget to rinse in vinegar and salt water. That sets the color, so it won't fade as fast."

"That's a great tip. No one ever told me that. I will remember to do it. I will save this dye. It will be good to use again."

Josh came down from the lookout.

"Hi Aunt Sarah, we are all glad that you are back. I was just up on the bluff, I could see David. He is working with the black horse that hurt Uncle Jed's back. I hope he is careful."

"I didn't know that he was hurt."

"He says it is alright, but I can tell it is hurting because he walks kind of funny. He lit pretty hard. He went right over that horse's head."

In her mind, Sarah was already creating a poultice for Jed's back.

"Josh. Where is Dart Away?"

"He is in a small field upriver from your house. He is with Blaze, and Star. Dad said you would like looking out your kitchen window and seeing them. They sure are pretty."

"Josh I need to go back to my house for a little while, before we have our meal together. If you see your Aunt Beth, tell her I am bringing a pan of cornbread to go with her chili, and I will see you later." David and his saddle were gone from the field when she went back, and so was the black horse. David had put his saddle on him and led him, first to the lake cabin and then the river.

With his clean clothes on the bank, David led the horse into the water and scrubbed himself while deliberately splashing the horse's legs and stomach. He slid on and off several times, but did it in one smooth move.

Once he was dressed in his clean clothes, he decided to go back to the lake Cabin and put on his boots for the first time. David was getting very tired.

"Blackie, do you think you could give me a slow ride to my cabin, so I can get my boots?" He slid up tentatively and coaxed the big horse to turn onto the path around the lake. Blackie was fine walking along and enjoying the running conversation coming from David, until Rascal and Buttercup came out of the bushes barking, and startled both horse and rider. He bolted and David wasn't ready for such a fast ride. He managed to stay on as Blackie dashed down the path past Jed's and finally slowed as he ran past the barn and David was able to turn him back and stop him at the cabin by the lake.

David knew that it was crucial in the horse's training that he completed the experience with a pleasant surprise for the horse. He tied him to the railing and ran into the little kitchen where he knew there was a canister of sugar. He reached in and grabbed a handful, dusting it on the cupboard top and floor as he went.

"Blackie you are marvelous. Here is the only treat I have. Have you ever had some sugar? Here boy take a lick of this stuff." David held his palm against the horse's lips. Blackie bumped the hand and spilled some of it onto the grass, but licked off the rest with joy and nuzzled for more. You are a good boy."

With his new socks and boots on and Trading post pants and shirt, David put Blackie in Jed's corral where there was always plenty of feed and water available.

As he tapped on Jed's door before entering, he heard a whistle behind him and saw Sarah sliding off of Moon Boy. She was carrying several bundles.

"You look very much like a downtown gentlemen," she said teasing. "Have we met?"

"Yes, I think we did, the first night I was here. You came out of the door of the lake cabin and brushed passed me. I was sure puzzled at the time. Let me help you with those bundles."

"David, you look very nice and thank you. You can take this one. It is still quite warm. It is cornbread."

Beth opened the door and welcomed them. Lily plastered a hug on David's leg and Johnny carefully took the cornbread so that David could pick her up.

"Hello, Miss Lily, How are you tonight?"

"You went fast on that big horse!"

"Yes, I did Lily. Did you see that horse running? The dogs barked and scared us."

"Just so you know Beth, I would not intentionally ride near the house so fast. Blackie is just beginning to trust me and the dogs startled us."

"Thank You David, I appreciate your explanation. Please take a seat. Jed is just finishing the milking and Ben and Mary should be here soon.

Once everyone was settled and the youngest ones were fed and happy, Ben began by saying that he had kept one eye on David all afternoon and he had never seen anyone work as well as David had with that black horse.

"I appreciate you saying that Ben. I wasn't intending to ride him, but I spent all afternoon with him and he just felt ready to me and I didn't want to lose the moment. Blackie is a fantastic horse. After that fast run and good response for me, I rewarded him with a handful of sugar. I made a big mess in the cabin. Beth I will need to borrow your broom."

"There is a broom and dust pan in the little storage room."

Jed got up from the table and suggested they move into the living room where he could sit in a chair with a back on it. My back's a little tired. That was a reminder for Sarah to get out the poultice she had brought for him. She heated it by the fire and then applied it to his entire back and wrapped him round and round with soft cloth from the Trading Post to hold it in place.

Beth looked at her husband and apologized for not having done that for him sooner.

"I'm sorry Jed. I just didn't realize that you were hurting. You never let on. You know you don't always have to be the tough guy."

"Say no more, Beth, because I didn't notice it either. Joshua told me, that he noticed that Uncle Jed was walking kind of funny. Where is he? He went out as soon as he finished eating."

"Thanks Sarah. That feels a lot better already. Josh has gone to make sure we have a final all clear before it gets totally dark. Beth you don't need to worry about me. You do so much as it is. I don't expect you to keep track of my little discomforts."

Just then Josh hurried in the front door and plopped on the bear skin beside Ben.

"All Clear," he said. "Did I miss anything? Aunt Sarah, I want to hear what happened at the Indian camp."

"Josh, we were just getting to that. Some of this story is going to sound like we made it up, but I promise you, it is all real. David, you can start."

"Alright, if you want me to, but really, it's your story.

When we arrived at the edge of the woods, and circled the lake, it was already getting quite dark. Sarah noticed right away that a small building of logs stood on a hill near the lake. Two Jesuit priests are there now. They erected a big white cross with the figure of a man on it that looks like he is all beaten up. It's really a gruesome thing. It's supposed to be Jesus. We went passed that but stopped there in the dark. Sarah was sensing that something was wrong. A communal fire was burning and the people were gathered around it. The drums were playing with a strange rhythm. She sent me to ask one of the young hunters what was happening. He told me that they had been without a shaman all summer. Red Fox followed them back from the summer council and although Chief Dark Wolf didn't approve, somehow he convinced the people and became their shaman. He must have been very evil because a big wolf went right into his tent and killed him.

So then Singing Wind a friend of mine, went to study with Standing Lizard, a powerful shaman, and he had come back to the village and they were having a celebration to accept him as their shaman but it went all wrong for him. Sarah, I think you should tell the rest."

"I will try. While David went to ask what was going on, I felt compelled by God's spirit to slip into my white clothes and I took the saddle off of Moon Boy and covered his back with the white cloth that Beth gave me. I dusted my skin and hair with the white chalk, like I did when I went to talk to that migratory band by the river. I could feel that something was going on that was very wrong. White is a sacred color to the people and I felt that it would help me to get them to remember what I had taught them about the Great Spirit.

When David returned and told me what was happening, it assured me that the Holy Spirit had sent me there not to visit, but to help the people. We waited and watched. The Chief had invited the two priests and they were sitting on his left. We thought that it was odd that they were there for such an occasion.

As Singing Wind came out of his tent and into the light of the fire, he was staggering. He was dancing and twirling around, but he was out of control. He fell down and his arm landed in the fire. The people were too frightened to run to his aid, but the two priests acted quickly. The young one pulled him away and the older one smothered the flames on his oil coated skin and hair with his blanket. He was taken by two men to the communal tent so Sweet Grass could care for his burns.

The Chief stood up and tried to calm the people but they were standing and talking and not listening to him.

That's when I felt the urge to walk Moon Boy into the light of the fire. They quickly sat down in their places and stared at me. Then I told them, that God was not happy with the people, that they had not remembered that he had given them the blue stones and the chance to trade for new foods. I told them that He gave them rain so their crops were good. They had been healthy and prospered. I asked them why they were trying to accept a shaman to talk to the spirits of old beliefs when the Great Spirit had sent his only Son to die for them. I told them they must honor His Son

Jesus, and to remember that He lives, and loves the people and that if they want to live in heaven, they must honor Him. I pointed at the cross, showing the people what Jesus did for them and then I started to walk slowly to the cross and said if they believed in Jesus and wanted to honor Him, they should stand and walk with me to the cross. The priests jumped up and followed, then David did, and next Chief Dark Wolf and Moonflower. I thought the whole village followed up the path, around the lake to the cross. They knelt at the cross and opened their hearts to Jesus."

Tears streamed down Sarah's face as she told the last part of her story.

"I had talked about God, the Great Spirit, to the people, at every opportunity but I always thought that God was having me plant seeds of faith that would grow under someone else's teachings. God let me see the harvest, and he gave David the gift of faith. David has a lot to learn, but he has accepted Jesus as his Savior."

Beth and Mary wiped away tears as they listened.

"Sarah, we know that you are special, but we didn't understand until now, what you meant when you said that Sarah had to become Brave Sparrow and then you had to become Sarah of the Blue Stone People. They must think you are a spirit at times."

"No Ben, I never wanted them to think that, but by wearing the sacred white, I was able to reach them on a level that wouldn't have been possible any other way."

It was silent in the room.

Finally Josh whispered.

"It feels like we are in a church. You are right Aunt Sarah. That is an amazing Story. How did you feel when you saw all the Indians following you to the big cross?"

"That is something that I probably will never be able to put into words, but Moon Boy sure did. When we stopped at the cross, he let out the loudest whinny I have ever heard." Everyone in the room laughed at that remark.

"Sarah, that's a marvelous thing that you just related and I have a surprise for you that I think will commemorate it very well," said Jed. He handed her the leather bound bible and said that it was a gift from her whole family. She clutched it to her chest and wrapped her arms around it, holding it tightly. Then she stood up, putting the book on her chair and circled the room giving hugs and thanking each one.

When she finally got to David, it was different. She stopped and took both his hands in hers and looked at him with a funny smile on her face.

"David, I know that having another Bible on the ranch, will make it easier for us to learn about Jesus, but while we are learning, will you marry me? You said that I would need to ask you next time. So I am asking."

David wrapped her in his arms and held her tight.

"Yes, Yes, Yes!" He was laughing and crying and so was she. The next thing they knew they were getting hugs from everyone. Everyone was talking at once.

When things calmed down a bit, Jed said he had a surprise to tell everyone and he hoped that it would be met with at least a little enthusiasm.

"When I ordered the Bible for Sarah, it was months ago, but Reverend Brown was in the Trading Post at the time. He volunteered to give Sarah a few simple lessons on the Bible so she would get more out of using it. I met him on the street as I was leaving the settlement. His wife and children were with him. I invited him to come here when he had time and showed him the Bible. Melanie spoke up and said she would enjoy visiting the place again and I didn't know how to politely say that I just meant him so she will probably be here too with the kids. I'm sorry Ben."

"There is nothing to be sorry about. They can stay in the lake cabin and David can bunk in the hut with us or stay with you and Beth while they are here.

CHAPTER FOURTEEN
YOUR GUESTS HAVE ARRIVED

Now that David and Sarah were back, life at the ranch returned to normal. He sought her out in every spare moment as young couples are apt to do when they are in love. They held hands and walked along the river or read the bible by lantern light at Sarah's little table with the blue and white checkered oil cloth.

Some nights, when David returned to the cabin by the lake, it wasn't to sleep, but to work on a project. He had learned the skill of working with silver when he lived with the Omati.

He was making a wedding band for Sarah, with tiny pieces of turquoise all the way around it. He carried it in his trouser pocket in a small piece of flannel. As he walked the flannel polished the silver. They hadn't decided on a date, but he wanted the ring to be ready.

Sarah had an idea forming in her mind. She wanted Moonflower, Snow Star and Blue Stone to see her wedding. She wasn't sure how she could manage it yet, but she was giving it a lot of thought. Sarah remembered Moonflower's tears as she held Watching Owl. She was a good second mother. She should not have to miss the important things that happen in my life. Maybe I should go get her and bring her to my wedding. Surely my family would not feel threatened by one Indian woman.

It would have to be someplace neutral. Chief Dark Wolf wouldn't like it if I brought the Reverend and my family to the village. I doubt if I could talk them into going anyway. I can't bring them to the ranch. That's out of the question. Where could I have a wedding that everyone could attend?

Mary and Beth were sitting on Beth's porch sipping tea and taking a break while all the little ones napped.

"I wish Sarah was not quite so tall. The dress that the women made for me is probably still at the Trading Post. I think it would fit her waist, if we let it out a little, but we would have to lengthen it a lot," said Beth.

"I have a better idea. I don't think she would like it, when she found out who made that dress. But we could make her one here. I have nearly a whole bolt of white cotton. What do you think?"

"That's a great idea. We can both make lace evenings and if she sees that, she won't know what it is for."

"Do you think we should keep it a secret or let her help? She does beautiful bead work."

"You are right. Let's tell her. When she comes down for dinner we can start planning. It is going to take a long time to make, said Mary.

When Beth and Mary told Sarah that they wanted to help her make her wedding dress, she didn't know what to say. She had already begun to bleach the leather, so she could dye it a very pale yellow.

As they talked, a plan formed in Sarah's mind. She would make a matching shirt and pants in the style of the people for David. The women were talking about a totally white dress, with a train. They were thinking about two different weddings.

Then it dawned on her. She could have two weddings. I want my family here to see a wedding in the style of the people, but I also want the Blue Stone People to see a wedding the way that it is done by Christians, with a minister of the faith. How can I do it?

She pondered it for days, while the preparations for each progressed; she struggled with it in her mind.

Finally one evening as David was leaving, she shared her idea with him.

"You want to do what?"

"I want to get married at the summer council and I want my whole family there and I want to get married twice, once the way of the people and then do it again with Reverend Brown or one of the priests the way that Christians do."

"Sarah, you are suggesting the impossible. You will never get the preacher or your whole family to leave this ranch and go where there are hundreds of Indians! They can't all leave here at once, anyway. Who would take care of the ranch? And did you even think about the fact that they would not be welcomed when they got there. I have never seen white visitors at the summer council. Have you?"

"No. I haven't but there has to be a way to do it, without a problem."

"Sarah, I respect you and love you so much that I would be glad to marry you ten times if that's what it takes to make you happy, but what you are planning is just going to end up disappointing you. Pray about it Honey and I will too."

He left with a frown on his face instead of the usual smile.

*****

Moonflower looked at Dark Wolf asleep on top of his furs. He was restless all night, she thought. I know he is worrying about the summer council because we are the host village this year. He needs to trust his people. Everyone has done what they are expected to do already. We have all the food for the feasts for after each day of games. It is dried and preserved. The women have prepared all the supplies for special sweet treats for after the wedding ceremony for the couples.

The men have made special prizes for the winners of the games. They have added silver and turquoise to the handles of the knives and decorated the bows and they have carved many surprises for the younger contestants. They have not allowed me to see those. I think they want everyone to be surprised. It is fun watching the young ones.

Sweet Grass is working on a big pack of medicines to take. She is hosting a meeting for all the healers. She has planned special food to serve them. She told me she has a list of questions to ask, so they can discuss the best way to treat certain injuries and illnesses. She is trying very hard to do her best to serve the people. I am proud of her.

I don't understand why Dark Wolf feels so troubled.

It is warm in here; she thought perhaps that was making him restless. She tied the flap of the tent open and looked at the early morning sky.

The sun was not yet up and already it was too warm. We need rain, she thought.

"Big Spirit, Jesus, do you see how hot it is? Why don't you make rain?" She strolled slowly to the lake with a cotton dress over her arm and a piece of soft leather to dry on.

*****

Sarah had climbed to the lookout. She was troubled. She wanted to think and pray, undisturbed. With her head lowered and eyes closed, they were nearly to the oak tree crossing before Sarah became aware of the buggy. Scrambling down she met Joshua, starting up.

"Don't go up Joshua, it is all clear. Please go tell Jed that his guests have arrived."

Josh was puzzled but when he saw Ben on the path and told him that Sarah said to tell Jed that his guests had arrived, Ben got a strange look on his face and hurried to the crossing. Ben yelled a greeting and waved and said that he would bring the big raft over. He didn't feel like getting wet so he used a pole and the ropes they had strung across, during the building of Jed's house and had put them back up after the raft incident with Zack and his family. He noted they were holding up well. Ben took the big raft over to ferry the Reverend and his family across.

By the time they reached the bank of the Hickory near the path to the hut, everyone had gathered to greet them except Sarah. She had gone home, to freshen up and change her clothes.

Ben couldn't believe his eyes when he got up close to Melanie. She looked more like her mother, than the girl he remembered. Her baby girl was cute in a fancy dress and patent-leather shoes. Ben wondered where she had been able to buy them. The baby boy in her arms was chubby, and wearing something that looked similar to a man's tailored suit, from back east. It certainly didn't look like it was comfortable.

"Hello, Ben. It is so nice of you to invite us to visit. It has been such a long time since I last saw you. So much has changed," said Reverend Brown.

"Hello everyone, I can't try to remember all of your names, but would one of you be kind enough to bring all of our things from the buggy. I will need them."

"Hello Reverend and Melanie. Thank you for coming, I hope that you and your wife will join us at the house for tea, while the lake cabin is made ready for your use," said Ben. He had resolved himself to the fact that Melanie would always act as if she were a step above everyone else, but he didn't have to encourage it. "I know you are used to a much more refined home, but I hope you will be able to make yourselves comfortable there during your stay. He nodded at Mary, making it clear that he was taking them, not to Jed's but to the hut. She smiled and hurried ahead of them and opened the door to the hut.

It was cheerful, uncluttered and comfortably cool inside. After greeting them, Jed hurried back to bring the horse, buggy and their belongings over without mishap. Joshua helped Jed and asked while they were bracing the raft to ferry the buggy across.

"Uncle Jed, why did Dad act that way? He seemed a little funny to me."

"Josh, I'm not sure you will understand this, but I'll try to explain. Your Uncle Ben nearly married that woman but she chose the Reverend instead. So it is natural that he feels a little strange in her presence."

"I'm glad he didn't. We couldn't have been a family if he had. Uncle Jed, why are they here? Sarah said they are your guests."

"Yes, I did invite the Reverend. I hoped that he would be a blessing to Sarah."

Mary was gracious and served mint tea and apple cakes. She offered the little girl fresh milk, but Melanie wouldn't let her have it.

"I never give her milk that hasn't been skimmed and boiled."

"Do you do the same for your son?"

"No, of course not, he is still nursing." She looked around and said that it felt different inside the hut. "What have you done in here?"

"Let me think a moment," said Mary. "We planked the floors, and plastered the walls. That was a very difficult job, until we decided that the ends of branches that stick out of the plaster were useful and that we liked the way they looked. Ben put the pieces of his mother's broken dishes in the wet mortar between the stones of the fireplace when we made it. I like the bits of color that it adds."

"Yes, with no art, you do what you can."

"We have art, Melanie, beautiful original art."

"Where do you keep it?" Her affectation of a southern drawl was becoming more pronounced as she talked.

Mary was becoming more annoyed by the minute, but was trying hard to hide it.

"Look around you, Melanie, at the wood box, or the back of the rocker you are sitting in. Look at the cross on the wall in the corner or the headboard and footboard of the bed and the chest in there. Look at the beautiful work on the baby cradle under the cross. Our home is filled with art."

"Of course it is, Mary. It just isn't the kind of art that I was talking about."

Sarah saved Mary from exploding by coming in the door at that moment.

"Hello Melanie. We have not met. I am Ben's sister Sarah." She had heard enough of the conversation to know what was going on. She decided that she had nothing to lose and this young woman needed to be taught a lesson. I have been at the cabin and it is clean and has fresh sheets on the bed. I made a pallet on the bedroom floor for your daughter, and a beautiful cradle like Mary's was in the barn ready to be taken to the Trading Post and I had our ranch hand move it to the cabin for you. He has taken all his things out of there until you leave."

"Thank you, that was good of you, Sarah. You did say your name was Sarah didn't you? I'm so glad that you got free from the Indians. You poor dear, I heard all about your plight from Helen at the Trading Post. The Reverend and I have been praying for you."

"That's kind of you. The men have the buggy ready and you can go now and get settled in the cabin. There are a few things there for you to eat, plus some coffee, or you are welcome to come to my cabin at sundown. I have made a deer stew and I did bake bread earlier today. Nice meeting you Melanie."

The men were gathered near the buggy talking and laughed out loud just as Melanie stepped out of the hut. They woke the baby and he began to howl in red faced distress.

"Oh dear, now he will scream all the way there until I can feed him." She looked as if she was ready to shed a tear of frustration. Melanie had some issues of her own that she was not dealing with and finding out that Ben and Mary were happy and doing very well, had not helped her lack of self-confidence.

As soon as they entered the cabin she, shoved the screaming baby into her husband's arms and said she needed the lady's room. After looking around, she realized that she would have to take a trip out and around the back of the cabin. She was not happy.

He placed the baby on the bed and began to remove the many stiff layers of clothing she had placed on him. He changed his son's diaper and had put a soft flannel sleeping gown on him. By the time she returned, the baby was playing with his toes and happily drinking water from his bottle.

"Relax Melanie, he was hot and thirsty. He doesn't need to eat again. You nursed him just before we got here. Remember?"

"She looked around as if she was lost. "What am I supposed to do here? This isn't a place for a lady. It is filthy. This is where their ranch hand stays. We are lucky they didn't ask us to stay in the barn."

"Melanie, stop it! You don't have to act like you are royalty all the time. This is a nice cabin, clean and well stocked. Willie likes it, don't you son?"

"Don't call him that! His name is William."

"Melanie, I love you very much. I need you to know that, because I also need you to know, that I can't take much more of your uppity attitude! You were born on a dirt farm. You are not a lady; you are a farmer's daughter. When I met you, you were smart, beautiful, funny, and cheerful all the time. Now, you are not any of those things. What has changed you into this disapproving, unsatisfied woman?"

"I don't know. I just feel ugly and stupid and I feel like whatever I do or don't do, it isn't going to make any difference. I'm turning into my mother! I hate myself and everything in my life. I hate the wind and the mud and the people in town. They are ignorant and can't talk about anything except each other. Some of them have never read a book in their entire life. Help me James, I am drowning." She started to cry and he let her.

The baby had fallen asleep on the bed. He lifted him down onto the soft pallet on the floor where he couldn't roll off and get hurt.

"Melanie, you are tired from our trip. I want you to rest. I will come get you when it is time to eat. I was told the meal is at sundown. Until then rest and think about what we have both said here today. I came to help Sarah, but maybe God put us here to help us."

He suddenly realized that his little daughter had been toddling and crawling around in the cabin unattended. He picked her up and gave her a drink of water from a cup. She gulped it down and patted his face, saying "dada, dada."

"Yes little one my sweet flower, we are going to see if you have any toes in these shiny shoes." He pulled off her shoes and stockings and tickled her feet. He loved to hear her laugh. There hasn't been enough of that, he thought.

Next he pulled her fancy dress over her head and dug around in the satchel of her clothes until he found a bright blue play dress made of soft cotton. He put it on her and a fresh diaper and said they were going visiting. Melanie didn't answer.

He walked slowly up the path around the lake, watching the excitement on his daughter's face. He took her near the corral so she could see the horses. Jed saw him coming.

"I was hoping that you would come over before evening. Sarah said we will all be eating at her cabin tonight. That will be fun. Come in, Lily will love playing with your little girl." Lily squealed with delight when the baby girl was placed gently on the bear skin rug, beside her.

"She is pretty. What is her name?" asked Lily.

"Her name is Violet. I call her my little flower, but I guess you are both little flowers," he said with a tired smile.

"Welcome Reverend Brown," said Beth. "It is nice to see you again. Are you and Violet hungry? I have just made a pan of pudding. I could feed her some and for you I have something a little hardier. How would you like a piece of wild cherry pie and a cup of coffee?"

"That sounds wonderful for both of us. Violet is a good little girl. She seldom whines, but I am sure she must be hungry."

The pie and coffee appeared in front of him before he got settled on the bench at the table. Beth put a bowl of sugar and a small pitcher of milk beside him with a fork and spoon.

She put two small bowls of pudding on the table and scooped up Violet, telling Lily to come have a treat at the table. Beth enjoyed feeding the baby girl.

"She opens her mouth like a little baby bird, laughed Beth. Is Melanie coming over soon?

"No, I don't think so. Willie is napping and I told her to rest, too."

"Reverend Brown, we really appreciate you making the effort that it took to come all the way out here," said Jed.

"Jed, can we just relax and be friends? My name is James, and my friends call me Jim. I want you to know that I have been looking forward to coming here for a long time. I thought that Bible would never get here. I wanted an excuse to come."

"Jim, you don't need an excuse to come. All our friends are always welcome."

"I thank you for that, and just between us, I know that Melanie is a trial. She and I are working on that. I love her very much, but I know she can be very annoying when she puts on that fancy front. I think that she feels that she doesn't measure up and so she hides behind that "southern lady" shield. It's exhausting. I am so sorry. I came to help you folks and I sit here telling you my problems."

"Ben taught us, that's what friends and family are for, to help each other."

"Jim, maybe we can all help with your problem, while you are here. There is no place as genuine, as a campfire on a ranch," said Beth.

They spent the rest of the afternoon, talking about Sarah and David's relationship and the amazing story they shared when they returned from the Indian village. Just as Jim was thinking that he should go see if he could help Melanie get ready for supper at Sarah's; Joshua and Ben rode up to the big fire pit in Jed's yard. Joshua had spotted the big deer from the lookout on the bluff and Ben had allowed Josh to hunt it. He had gone with him, but Josh had shot and cleaned it.

Little Mouse, Josh's horse, pulled the travois like she had done it many times. Josh proudly brought wood and placed it in the fire pit, while Ben untied the deer and slid it onto the grass.

"Josh, after you wash off the travois; please bring the drying racks from the barn and then put Little Mouse in the corral. She did a good job, and so did you, son."

Jed and Jim came out to see what they were doing. Beth stuck her head out long enough to tell them that they should bring the drying racks from the barn and someone should tell all the other ladies to come to prepare the meat for drying. She put an emphasis on the word all and smiled at Jim.

"Does she mean Melanie, too?" asked Jim with a chuckle. "I am going to enjoy watching this."

"Yes Jim, but she should put on something made of cotton, so that it will wash easy. If she didn't bring anything like that, maybe we can find something she can wear. Tell her when we are blessed with fresh meat, it has to be taken care of right away or it will spoil."

"I am going to tell her right away."

"Wait a minute Jim, I think Beth has something she wore just before Lily was born that should work for her."

Beth dashed in and came out with a dark green cotton dress that spread out as it went down. Jim carried Violet back to the lake cabin, whistling all the way. They stopped at the corral to pet his carriage horse and he noticed the good supply of fresh water and abundance of hay available. I like it here, he thought. These are good people.

After the first shock of being asked to wear a maternity dress, it sunk in that she was being expected to help slice up a deer and prepare it for drying.

"Mel, no one here dresses up. Beth has on a brown cotton dress and no shoes. Mary will be here soon to help and so will Sarah. It should go fast with so many working.

"I really wish you wouldn't call me Mel. That isn't my name."

"Yes, it is from now on, and when you hear it, it will remind you that we don't put on prideful airs." He put Violet on the bed and changed her diaper and then sat beside her and pulled off his boots and socks. "I haven't gone barefoot since I was a boy," he said grinning.

"I think you have gone out of your mind! Where is your dignity? You are a man of God!"

"It's over there on the floor, by my boots," he said laughing. "Did you feed Willie?"

"Yes," she said, "Are you going to try to keep both of these babies out of harm's way, while I cut up raw, bloody meat?"

"I am sure I will have help from our friends. We will be fine. Come on girl. Be a good sport. Pull your fancy shoes off and don't hang back."

Jim found that going barefoot wasn't easy in the rough grass and stones of the path. He was happy to sit down on the grass when he got to the fire. He had a baby on each arm and they both were fascinated by the fire and the lake. Willie had not learned to crawl yet, but Violet had already taken her first unsteady steps and could move on all fours very quickly. Beth solved his dilemma by slipping a harness on Violet and fastening it to the apple tree. She put a blanket under her and provided a few toys she had not seen. She offered her a cup of milk which she drained and then took the butter cookie she was offered and bit it with the few front teeth that she had.

"I saw that," said Melanie. "Are you trying to make my child as fat as I am?"

No one answered. They weren't sure if she was kidding or angry. The woman that arrived earlier would have been angry.

"It's alright. I'm joking. I think I need to learn to laugh at myself and my own flaws."

Her admission was like a breath of fresh air. They had all been nervous about how they would deal with her all evening, and now her apology, made it really feel like a gathering of friends.

"I have put on this queen's tent, as requested. I understand that our young hunter has shot a deer and I am to help preserve the meat. Well, let's do it." She leaned over to Mary and gently took the sharp knife from her hand. In one quick stroke of the knife she had separated a large chunk of leg meat from the bone. She sliced through it so quickly that before anyone else settled down to the job at hand, she was working on another big chunk.

"I was raised on a farm folks, don't look so surprised," she said laughing. Jim's laugh was the loudest.

Sarah came slowly down the trail from her house with the hot meal in a bed of hay in the wagon. She had stopped at Mary's and picked up a few more bowls and plates, forks and spoons. Beth had plenty of cups to add to the ones Sarah had brought. With the stew near the fire and the big coffee pot there too, it began to feel like a picnic. Jed thought about the night that everyone in the settlement had come and they had all gathered at a big fire by the lake after all the work of building the house and planting the garden was completed. With the deer meat drying on the racks, the area was cleaned and the hide rolled up until morning when it would be worked and turned into soft leather.

Old Stump, Rascal, Sunshine and Buttercup were a short distance away, each enjoying the meat covered leg bone they had been given.

David had been working in the barn and finally decided he would approach the group. He was not sure of his social graces. Things were done differently in the camp of the people. He extended his hand to the visitors, first to Jim, introducing himself as David Sharpe.

Melanie was trying, but was not completely able to guard her tongue.

"I know about you. You escaped the Indians, too, didn't you?"

"Yes, I did. You must have been talking to the woman at the Trading Post," said David smiling. He sat down on the blanket next to Sarah and she handed him a bowl of stew and pushed a cracker into his mouth, before he could make any further reply.

"What? I didn't say anything," he said defensively.

Melanie had carefully fed little bites of the vegetables and meat from the stew to Violet. She dunked a piece of bread in the broth and let her suck on it. The baby girl grabbed her mother's hand and held it with both of hers.

"She likes your cooking Sarah," said Mary, trying her best to be nice. Her nerves were still on edge from the abrasive way she had been treated by Melanie earlier.

"Mel. Do you want anything else; more stew, or are you ready for a taste of that wonderful wild cherry pie, with your coffee? I had a piece this afternoon and it was exceptional."

"Beth, it looks delicious, but I think that unless I want to always have to wear tents, I better start training my appetite as well as my attitude."

"Honey, don't be hard on yourself, but if you are sure, I'll eat your piece for you," said Jim. Everyone laughed at his joke and Beth gave him an extra-large piece, and then turned to Melanie and handed her a clean plate and fork with a small slice.

"Mel, never refuse the pleasures of life, just a rein on the quantity and you will be a twig, before you know it. You are a beautiful woman." Beth didn't know the significance of the nickname Mel.

CHAPTER FIFTEEN
GENUINE BLESSINGS

Jim spent the next day mostly with Sarah and her new Bible. In the afternoon David joined them and it was after dark when they finally tapped on Beth's door, to accept her offer of chili and cake with nuts and sugar glaze. This combination had become one of the favorites at the ranch.

"Beth, the day has slipped away. We are sorry to be so late. Is that offer for chili still open?"

"Yes, it is. Mel just left. Jed is helping her get the babies back to the cabin and into bed. He will be back soon. Jim, did you make good progress with Sarah and David?"

"I'm not sure which of us learned the most. Sarah is a very spiritual girl, strong in the faith. David is definitely a believer, but he has some strong feelings about things that are not biblical. We were working on that some today. I asked Sarah if there were any believers here that had not been baptized. She said she didn't think anyone was. She couldn't remember ever being baptized."

Jed stepped in the back door.

"Hi, Jim, I am pleased to report that your little ones are tucked into bed and sound asleep. Mel said that if I saw you to tell you that she was making coffee for you and would be up for a while and not to hurry."

"Jed, I am sad that it is necessary for us to leave tomorrow, so we can be back at the church in Silverville, for service on Sunday morning, but I was thinking that we could make time for a baptism service here, first thing in the morning. We have the river, or the lake, and if any of you are so inclined, I would be proud to get wet with you." He laughed out loud and seemed so much happier than he had been when he arrived.

"Jim, I will pass the word, for sun-up at the lake by the fishing platform. Does that sound like a plan?"

"It does Jed. Thank you."

"Beth, I'll be right back." She could see him smiling in the light from the front window as he walked to the corral.

In the morning, when Reverend Brown stopped his buggy on the path by the lake, he was excited to see the entire family of the "S and J" there waiting for them. Mel stepped down holding Willie in her arms. Jim had Violet on his lap. Their babies were wearing only a diaper and Mel had put the green maternity dress, back on.

"Good morning, everyone, and a very good morning to Our Father God, for I know that he is pleased that you are all here. I hope that it is to participate and not to watch. I am happy to tell you all that I have the honor of baptizing my own wife this morning, and it was her idea that we also baptize our babies and claim them as members of God's family." Everyone cheered and applauded. Jim stepped into the water and walked out until it was up to his waist. He reached for his baby son and held him while Mel removed his dry diaper. "Dry diapers are hard to come by," he said laughing. Then his face became serious.

"William, my son, I baptize you, In The Name of the Father and of the Son and of the Holy Ghost. You come from the darkness to the path of light that leads to our Father. Amen. As he said it, he scooped water with his hand and poured it over William's hair and tummy and dunked his legs in the cool lake water. William let out a loud howl, starting to cry. Mary took him, wrapping him in a warm blanket and immediately secured the dry diaper back on him, and dressed him in a comfortable gown. Violet was next, and then Melanie. Each person at the ranch was baptized in the lake and the last one was David.

"That lake will never seem the same to any of you. When you walk this path, you will remember how God's grace used the water of this lake to wash your sins away and to write your names in The Lamb's Book of Life."

They talked and applauded as Jim and Melanie turned their little buggy around and went back to the cabin to put on their dry traveling clothes.

When Sarah received the message from Jed, about the baptism in the morning, she knew that everyone would be hungry after the ceremony. She had bread dough rising and decided to turn it into cinnamon rolls. They were wrapped on her table waiting. Sweetened tea for the youngsters was keeping warm and a big pot of coffee for those who wanted it, was hot and ready.

As soon as they had all enjoyed the breakfast rolls, Jed, Ben, and Josh, helped to ferry the buggy across the Hickory and their new friends left waving and smiling. Mel held up the green dress as they drove away. She had asked Beth if she could keep it as a reminder of their stay and all the blessings she had received while she wore it.

She had stepped into the water of the lake, with it on, but it would always mean much more than that. It would hang in her closet to affirm the promise she had made to Jim, that she would always be Mel.

*****

Mary had finally decided that Adam could climb to the lookout once in a while, with permission; and he could take a turn to make sure they had an all clear. He was proud of his new position as back up sentry, and listened intently as Josh explained where and how he was to check the entire field of vision.

Johnny too, had grown into new duties. He was official egg gatherer and chicken caretaker. He was responsible for feeding and watering both his mother's chickens and his Aunt Mary's. It didn't take him long to ask why they kept chickens in two places. Mary laughed and told him that maybe by having two pens, they could confuse a fox and he would forget first one pen and then the other as he ran back and forth trying to choose.

"That's a story, isn't it Aunt Mary?"

"Yes Johnny, it is. All the chickens were your mom's, but she was good enough to share with us so we could have eggs at our house, too. We like having eggs for breakfast, and eggs so we can make pancakes and birthday cakes, don't we?"

"I guess so, but I get tired when I have to work. I like playing with Sunshine and Buttercup better."

"Everyone gets tired when they have to work, Johnny. I get tired when I have to cook, and wash dishes and sweep the floor and pull weeds from the garden and... hmm. I guess he didn't want to hear anymore." Mary laughed when she realized that Johnny had left the hut, slipping out quietly.

*****

Sarah still didn't understand why Helen had said the hurtful things she had, but Reverend Brown had convinced her that it was necessary to forgive her. He pointed out that David had not reacted badly, when he heard that she had been talking about him. He had decided that Helen lived in a small environment and didn't know what she was talking about and that it really didn't matter.

"Sarah, would you consider getting married in the church in Silverville?"

"Perhaps," was her answer, she and David had a lot to discuss.

*****

Ben had ordered two wagons of lumber for his new house, and six windows, two large ones for the front, a smaller one for over the kitchen sink, and three medium ones for the three bedrooms, he had planned. Their house would be comfortable for his big family

It was hot and dry, a perfect day for building, when the wagons from Tom's lumber mill rolled up to the crossing. The two wagons with lumber were followed by another wagon carrying the windows, nails and all the other supplies Ben had ordered including a hand pump and pipe to bring water inside from the well.

Adam was alone tending the lookout when the caravan of wagons and riders appeared. This was his first time to spot anything on the prairie other than animals. He was excited and thrilled that he was the one to bring the news that he could see something coming.

"Daddy Ben, Daddy Ben, Uncle Jed," he yelled as he ran to Jed's corral where the men were working with the horses. "There is some big stuff coming up the trail. I saw them and I saw lots of men on horses, too."

"That's great Adam! You are a very good sentry," said Ben, as he hurried to climb up and see what it was and how far away they were. Jed stood at the bottom waiting for verification. They had been eager for the building supplies to arrive so they could get started. It was going to take a while to build a house that large and they wanted it closed in and roofed before winter.

"It's Tom and his crew. I'm so glad to see them. Josh, tell your mom, Beth and Sarah. They will need to do some serious cooking, for these men. I don't see a chuck wagon. I didn't expect there would be one."

Josh quickly put a bridle on Little Mouse and headed out to spread the news.

Mary was smiling broadly, holding Eli's hand and feeling mixed emotions. Ben was determined to build her a big, beautiful house, with lots of room for their growing family. She knew they needed the additional room, but in her heart, she would not like moving out of the hut. Ben and the hut, had offered her security, warmth and love when she had needed it most. She could feel a warm embrace, each time she entered.

"Here comes the first load, Mary!" Ben was like a little boy, laughing and so excited that he couldn't stand still. It took most of the day to get the wagon loads ferried across and the empty wagons across and reloaded so the supplies could be drawn to the building sight that Ben and Mary had chosen. It was a year later than Ben had planned. He thought he could do it before Nattie was born, but it hadn't been possible. Now, it was really happening!

Tom and his crew were focused and efficient. They had unloaded the supplies before dark. They had not stopped for food, until the last board was stacked and the empty wagons taken back across the Hickory. From there, they walked eagerly to the big fire and wonderful smell of the ready and hardy meal in front of Jed's house. Some of the men commented about the fun they had building Jed's house as they washed their hands and faces in the lake and prepared to enjoy the well-earned meal.

The first rumble was so slight that Beth didn't feel it, in the house. The water of the lake danced a little. It looked like a gentle rain was touching its surface. Some of the less observant men that stood talking hadn't noticed it at all.

Next they all felt a slight sway of the ground and the lake water splashed. The horses in the corral quickly ran into the barn, but another rumble and vibration sent them all running back out. Some of the men hurried to Jed's corral trying to calm the horses, fearing that some might get injured. The big work horses that had pulled the wagons were tied to trees along the river, where they could reach both grass and water. They stood still and seemed unaffected. Beth held Lily in her arms as she came out of the house fearing to start down the steps in case they would start moving. Mary had Nattie in her arms and Eli and Adam both ran to Ben for protection. Josh stood near the men wide eyed, showing the fright that everyone felt. Sarah sat down on the grass, still holding the large basket of bread she had sliced and just brought out of Beth's kitchen. With presence of mind, one of the men took a large knife and retrieved a roast from the flames, where it had fallen.

"It's crispy on the outside but fine inside," he said. He pulled the other two big roasts a safe distance from the fire just in case they would experience another tremor. A few minutes passed quietly, and everyone began to relax. David rode up on Blackie just as Ben started to say grace. They listened as Ben said a prayer of thanksgiving for the food and for the wonderful provision of supplies for his new home and then lastly he said, "Thank you Lord that the movement has stopped and we and the "S and J" are all fine. David, I know you went to check the hut, the stock and Sarah's place. Is everything fine?"

"Yes, a few things fell on the floor, at Sarah's. I picked them up. I checked all the stock."

They filled their plates with the wonderful food and some of the men did not hesitate to go back to the big kettles for a second helping.

"I hope all of you have left room for a piece of pie, or cake. We have both," said Mary.

"Ben, we talked about it before we got here and we will stay a couple days and help you get the frame work up and the roof beams in place. That should get you started enough that you and Jed, David and Josh here can get it closed in before winter. I feel bad that I didn't bring it sooner like you wanted, but the truth of it is, we had a small fire at the mill and that held things up a bit. No one was hurt and the mill is back up and running now. We lost one of our best saws though. It got hot and sparked the fire."

"Tom, you aren't obligated to do that, but I would be a fool to refuse the help. Thank you. I have to admit that I was feeling a bit concerned about us being able to put it up and get it roofed and all. I am sorry to hear about the mill fire. That's the first that I heard about it."

"Well, it was scary for a while, all that sawdust just fed the flames, and we decided the best thing was to wet everything around that building and let her go. Like I said, nobody got hurt and that's the important thing. We have a lot of family men working at the mill and I sure didn't want to lose anyone."

"You are a good man Tom. I appreciate you doing this for us. You are probably a bit behind with your orders because of the fire. Last thing you need is to be gone with your crew for extra days."

"I feel it is the right thing to do and we intend to do it. So say no more about it. Besides you have women on this ranch that really know how to feed a man. Why would any of us want to leave?"

The men laughed and agreed and before long they had all gone down under the big trees by the river and had bedded down for the night.

Later, when Ben and Mary closely inspected the hut they found a few small cracks in the plaster on the walls. A basket had fallen, spilling the last of the nuts, and some dirt had sifted down on the floor of the bedroom.

"This is a wonderful, strong home, Ben. You built it and it will still be here for your grandchildren to enjoy."

Josh came in and said he had gone up on the bluff and poked around making sure there were no boulders loose enough to fall and that it was really too dark to do a good job of it, but he planned to check again first thing in the morning.

"Dad, did anybody check the chickens and the horses tonight?"

"Yes, Josh, all the animals are bedded down and happy. You need to get some rest. Tomorrow we have a house to build." Josh liked the sound of that. He liked being included in the work of the men. He had felt proud when Tom had mentioned him as he was talking about them getting the house closed in before winter. He could hear his father's prayer for safety for everyone as they worked tomorrow and another thank you for the buildings not being damaged and no animal or person being harmed during the earthquake.

Ben snuggled close to Mary and told her that he knew how hard it was to do all that extra cooking and to still have to take care of Nattie and Eli.

"Soon Honey, Soon. It will all be easier for you."

"Adam, are you awake?"

"Yes Daddy," he answered with a giggle.

"You have an especially hard day tomorrow. You will be our sentry at the lookout all day. I need you to be extra careful up there. Even a small loose pebble could cause your foot to slip and you could take a terrible fall. We need you to be very watchful. We will all be busy. You have to be our eyes."

Adam didn't answer. He had fallen asleep. Josh tiptoed closer before he spoke.

"He is asleep Dad. I hope he doesn't doze off, up on the bluff."

"Did he have to say that," said Mary? "Now I'll be worrying about that."

"Adam is older than Josh was, when he started going to the lookout. He will be fine. Get some rest.

The women had made a plan and divided the work. Meals were planned for the next few days. Breakfast was slices of leftover roast deer meat, with fried potatoes and scrambled eggs, with fresh bread, butter and jam. Two big pitchers of fresh cold milk stood on the end of one of the tables. Fresh hot coffee was ready. Beth's table, Mary's, and Sarah's were placed on the lawn with their benches and blankets were still on the grass if some of the men preferred.

"This looks like you are ready for a party, said one of the men to Beth. We all appreciate the hard work you ladies are putting into the meals for us. Just so you know, Tom says for us to fill up good, this morning because we won't be stopping until near sundown. We won't be back for lunch." He filled his plate generously, and then poured several cups of coffee for others before sitting down at one of the tables.

"Dear Lord, we thank you for all this good food," said Tom, as he set his filled plate down. "You ladies sure make a man feel like he can eat all he wants. You have cooked a bounteous meal. We all thank you." He stuffed his food in as if he was starving and urged his men to do the same.

"This day isn't getting any younger he said as he gulped the last of his coffee and was already walking to the work site before some of them got their plates fixed.

Lily and Eli were in the house on the bear rug playing with the blocks. Nattie had been fed and was back asleep in Lily's bed. So far, the women were managing to keep things under control. Sarah had come with the three wheeled wagon the night before and in it along with the food she had managed to put her big kettle that she used for dye making and making batches of soap. Last night she had set it near the fire and nearly filled it with water from the lake. They washed the dishes in it and rinsed them in another big kettle. They turned the dishes upside down on the oil cloth table tops to dry. Very quickly, they were done with the cleanup and they were able to sit down and have their own breakfast.

Lily and Eli were fed some of the leftover potatoes and eggs, and then Beth decided they needed a break and put them back in the house with a butter cookie. A pan and spoon for Eli to bang on, was keeping him busy. Lily, though not much more than a baby, cuddled a rag doll that Beth had made for her.

"Are you sure there is nothing they can get into?" Mary was nervous about Eli's inquisitive nature. "He is apt to get into anything."

"We will be able to hear, if he quits banging. I can see them through the window. Relax Mary. He is having a good time."

"It is good that Tom told the men that they couldn't come back until sundown. That will give us time to make a good meal for them. We have lots of vegetables in the garden. We even have some in the baskets from last year. Let's make a big stew with potatoes and dried deer meat and a lot of everything. Anything we can fit in that biggest kettle," suggested Sarah.

"That's a good idea, but I want to take some sandwiches down at lunchtime with a pot of coffee, said Mary. We have plenty of bread and lots of the roast left."

"Do you think that Tom will mind if we stop work to give the men a sandwich and coffee?"

"No, he will be hungry by then too. He isn't a small man. He will be glad to have a snack.

Sarah turned the water out of the big kettle and cleaned it thoroughly.

"If you don't mind, I would like to make the stew. You both have babies to keep track of and I know that you will want a peek at the progress they are making on your house, Mary. Maybe you could go down and take the lunch in the little wagon and we will stay here and watch the little ones."

"Thank you Sarah. You are thoughtful. I have to tell the truth. If we were not doing so much work, I would be down there most of the time. It was a lot of fun to see Beth and Jed's house take shape. Sarah, I do have a lot of dried vegetables left in the hut, and our garden is ready to start harvesting for this year. I need to go check on Adam and when I come back, I'll bring them. Will you watch Eli for just a few minutes? Nattie should sleep another half hour at least. Oh, no, I don't hear Eli banging the pan!"

Beth and Mary both jumped up and dashed up the steps, with Sarah right behind them. They stopped in the living room and stood there stunned. In the middle of the kitchen, stood Eli, covered in black ashes from hair to toes and not seeming to mind it one bit.

"Thank God I let the inside fire go out last night. I knew we would be doing our cooking outside and it's so hot that we didn't need it. I think we need to take him to the lake," said Beth. Mary started to laugh, and so did Sarah and Beth. They laughed all the way to the edge of the lake.

"I have some mild soap. I'll go get it, and something to dry him off." The fact that this could have been a terrible accident was beginning to sink in, as Mary stripped her son's clothes off and dropped them into the edge of the lake.

"I told you he would find something to get into. I never imagined it would be the ashes of the fireplace!" Beth, I'll help you clean the mess in there after I get him cleaned up."

"That Eli, he got all dur dee. I telled him no, but he got dur dee," said Lily, sounding quite indignant that Eli hadn't minded her. Beth scooped her up, grateful that Lily had not decided that the ashes looked like fun. She could have.

"Lily you were such a good girl." Beth carried her out and put her favorite blanket by the little apple tree. She slipped the harness on her in spite of Lily's objections and tethered her there. She handed her the rag doll and a piece of fruit leather. "That is a surprise for being a very good girl." She hoped that would remove some of the sting that the little girl felt from be fastened. Lily was pouting.

Beth wasn't taking any chances around the lake or the campfire.

Mary lathered Eli from top to bottom and he whined the whole time. Once she had him dry and dressed she scrubbed his clothes and put them on the line to dry. Nattie was awake and complaining. Mary was looking a little frazzled.

"Mary, I'm going down and check on Adam and I'll bring back the dried vegetables for the stew. Do you want me to bring a big pan of potatoes from my storeroom? I will never be able to use them all before the fall?"

"That would be a big help, if you don't mind. Also bring my peeling knife, and a big basket with all the rest of my wild apples. They are getting wrinkled. We can turn those into applesauce. It will make an easy desert."

Beth came out the door as Sarah was getting up on the wagon to leave.

"Mary, I changed Nattie, he is on the bear skin, chewing on a block. You should take a break and hold him in the rocker and nurse him. I have Eli and he is not getting out of my sight. I cleaned the kitchen floor and everything is back in order. Relax," said Beth.

Mary appreciated the chance to sit and hold her baby son, more than the other women could have ever realized. She was trembling inside and close to tears. I am a terrible mother. He could have been badly burned or killed, she thought. Thank you Jesus that Beth had let that fire go out.

Beth sat on a blanket playing with Lily and Eli. Johnny came over and sat down on the grass looking downcast.

"What is the matter with you? You look like you just lost your favorite toy."

"Mom, Dad said that I have to stay here with you, that it is too dangerous at the new house. I want to help make the new house, too. Josh is there!"

"Dad is right. I think you will have more fun here with Eli, Lily and Me."

"They are babies!"

"Well, I know some babies in the barn that you love spending time with and that mare is so happy when you talk to her and brush her. Everyone is too busy. She hasn't had any love today. Did you know that Joshua tamed Little Mouse with no help until the very last few lessons? He started just as you are with that mare and her twins, by being a good friend and talking and brushing and making sure they have everything they need. You can go in there if you want to. Remember to stay to the side or front of the mother. No horse likes people to stand behind them."

"Thank you Mom," I know to be careful. She hasn't had all her lessons yet."

"Johnny, even the horses that we ride every day will kick you, if you walk up behind them. Take this water bag, and half of one of the sandwiches, that Aunt Sarah is making and you may have your lunch with the twins. Come check with me before you go anywhere else. If I need you, I want to know where to find you."

"Sure Mom." Johnny took a half-sandwich and the water bag and ran in the direction of Jed's barn. He stopped on the path when he saw a big frog jump into the water. It quickly swam away. "I will catch you some day, and you will be my pet. I saw you sitting under the fishing platform on the other side. Maybe I will ask Mom if I can go fishing later." He disappeared into the barn and Beth breathed a sigh of relief, knowing that he would stay in there as long as she let him. He lost all track of time when he was with the foals and their mother.

CHAPTER SIXTEEN
A SERIOUS INTERRUPTION

Mary came out of Beth's house smiling with Nattie in her arms.

"Let's all go down and see how they are doing. We can use the wagon and pile all the sandwiches, cups and coffee pot in there with us. Sarah they look good. Thanks for doing that while I was in with Nattie. That rocker is so comfortable that I could have gone to sleep. Beth thanks for watching Eli. Would you put him here in the corner of the hay where I can make sure he stays put?" Beth laughed at that remark.

"I guess it will be quite a while before he gets a chance to get into any more trouble. We are all keeping an eye on him. We are tucked in here safe and comfortable, Sarah. I wrapped a blanket around the coffee pot and it is being stabilized by my feet. Just go slow." Sarah drove the three wheeled wagon carefully over the well-worn path. Beth felt a pang of sadness as they rolled up river, passing the lake and garden and the hut came into view. She had warm feelings about the hut and had enjoyed being there with Ben and Jed. That was a long time ago. I hope they maintain it. I would not like to see it ignored.

Ben saw them coming and greeted them with a big grin while plucking Eli from the corner of the wagon.

"Oh, you brought food! Hey guys, they brought sandwiches and coffee. Break time!"

"We didn't think the men should work all day without some lunch. I hope Tom doesn't mind," said Mary. Ben helped her down and the men gathered around Beth and Lily as she handed out sandwiches and cups of coffee.

"Uncle Ben is making a new, big house," said Lily

"How can you tell that it will be a big house, Lily?"

"I see the stuff over there. See?"

Eli squirmed to get down, and Ben let him. He ran to the outline of the house and stepped inside, jumping up and down.

"Daddy, is this my new house?"

"Yes, Eli. Here is where you will sleep. We will put your bed here, and you will be able to look out the window at the horses, and Natty's bed will be here. Out the window you will have a swing, on that big tree over there and a tree house in the top." Eli's eyes grew larger with excitement as Ben explained to his son, the plans that he had.

Mary leaned her head on his shoulder and said that it all sounded wonderful.

"Dad I hope you don't mind but I wanted to see up close what the men have done, and I am a little hungry."

"Adam, what kind of a father says his son cannot eat? I am glad that you came down for a little while; there are lots of sandwiches here, and a water bag on the back of the wagon. Get a sandwich and come over here and I will show you where your bed will be." Ben had rested his arm around the lad's shoulders as he directed him to the far end of the house. "This will be a room for you and Josh. There will be a window in that wall and you will look out at the field where the yearlings and untrained horses are kept. You will be able to see Aunt Sarah's house from here."

"Dad this house looks really big! It will be fun to live here, but it will be farther from Uncle Jed's. I almost forgot to tell you that I saw a big deer on the edge of the trees. He was there earlier, but when all the banging started he hurried down river. I think it scared him."

"If you see him again, let me know right away and we will hunt him. It will give us fresh meat for the men."

"Dad, where is Johnny? Everyone else is here."

"I don't know son, ask Aunt Beth."

"Adam, I heard you asking about Johnny. He is having his lunch with the foals in the barn. Did you see anything else interesting while you were up there?"

"No, but I saw some horses; they went up river. There was only about ten. It is sad. It was the same stallion that Dad and Uncle Jed caught in the long pen."

"Adam, that is not sad. He is free and happy and he has already gathered a small herd. He will find more with time. It is wonderful that we can count on you to be at the lookout. I feel safe knowing that even though we are pounding and have a bigger fire, we are safer, because you will warn us, if Indians are on the prairie. Thank you. Do you need anything before you go back to work?"

"No Aunt Beth, I am fine.

"If you wait just a minute you can hitch a ride with us. We are leaving now."

Sarah helped the women and children to get safely in and settled. The coffee pot and cups were gathered and they were all on their way.

When they got back, Lily and Eli were given their lunch and tucked in for a nap. Nattie slept on the Bear skin and the preparation of the stew was finished. Mary made the applesauce while the place was quiet.

When Beth peeked into the barn to check on Johnny, he was lying on top of the mare, talking in her ear and gently brushing her neck.

"I'll never let them sell you to a soldier. You are my horse. I will take care of you. You are a sweet girl and a good mama too. I like your babies. They are so cute, but I like you even better. You are my best friend. I think I will name you. You are Sandy. Do you like that name? I like Sandy because that is the color you are and your babies are that color too and so, you are Sandy. I love you, Sandy." He wrapped his arms around her neck and just stayed there. She didn't seem to mind at all. Beth was concerned but didn't want to startle them, so she quietly backed up.

When Beth was back near the gate of the corral, she softly called his name.

"Johnny, I need you. "Where are you?"

He came quickly out of the barn.

*****

Tom and his crew left earlier than planned. Mathew Morgan arrived with bad news.

"Come back as soon as you can. Many of the people in town are sick and the children are very ill, with fevers. It seems worse for them."

Sarah questioned him to gain knowledge as to the kind of sickness. He said he didn't know, but he knew they had very high fevers and had trouble swallowing.

"Sarah, you can't be thinking of going to the settlement to nurse them. You will catch whatever it is and be sick. Besides, they don't know you. You aren't a doctor. They will not let you in their homes. Sarah, no, I don't want you to go." Ben was distraught.

Within an hour, Sarah had pulled Moon Boy and Pretty Mother from the fields where they had been grazing peacefully. She had collected bundles of all the plants that she had and placed the large pack on Pretty Mother. She took several kinds of teas and honey to make infusions. She instructed Jed to get her a big pile of willow bark and to bring her many of the plants that fight infection.

She knew that it would be necessary to gain their trust, before they would let her help them. Tom questioned Matt further, wanting to know if Gentle Fawn, his wife, was ill, or their children. He said he wasn't sure, he hadn't heard that they were but that when he left, he had seen Sam putting a closed sign in the window of the Trading Post.

"Ben, we have had many people from the settlement here. Any of those men could have been carrying the sickness. I need you to make a tea and crush at least two of the plants in it that fight infection. Make it sweet so that you can get the children to drink it, too. Make sure you put some in a bottle for Nattie, just add more water. Add some mint, sugar or honey. Have everyone drink at least two cups and you must, too. Drink lots of fresh water and have Mary make a big pan of soup with lots of broth, eat light and rest. No one should work tomorrow. You and David can care for the animals, and that is all. Read the Bible Ben and pray. Pray that I can help them. I am going back with Mathew. Do you mind if he takes Sundown? His horse needs rest."

"We will do what you say, but what about you? You should drink some too?"

"I will be fine. I will be making lots of medicine when I get there. Tell Beth to wash all the clothes that anyone wore while the men were here with strong soap and to give a bath to the children right away and put them in clean clothes. Everyone must take a bath and change clothes. It is good that the men were not in the houses." Ben had seen Sarah take charge once before when Zack was injured. He knew that it was useless to argue with her. This must be part of the healer training she got from the Indians, he thought.

David came forward and said that he was going with her. He had been in the communal tent many times when she had made infusions and various medicines. He insisted that he could help. He was going.

"David, you might get the sickness. I want you to stay here."

"I am going."

Josh had put Mathew Morgan's saddle on Sundown and one of Ben's on Moon Boy so that Sarah would have the use of the bigger saddlebags.

"Thanks Josh, I appreciate that."

Mary hurried out of the hut with two big bundles.

"You need to take these and water bags for yourselves. You don't want to eat or drink in the settlement. There is plenty of food in there for you to share for a few days. Make yourselves a little camp. Don't stay with anybody even if they seem well. I hope it won't take any longer than that. David, you take good care of her and make sure she doesn't go non-stop. That's what she did when Zack was so sick."

"Don't you worry, I already thought of that. I have my little tent and these. He slipped the blue stone necklace over Sarah's head. He was wearing his. It won't hurt for the people in Silverville to know that we still hold a bond with the Blue Stone People."

"God will go with you. We will pray unceasingly for you until you return, said Ben.

Sarah swung up on Moon Boy and led Pretty Mother across the river. It was obvious that she was not going to linger for long goodbyes. David took the lead for Pretty Mother and fastened it to her saddle. David rode Thunder, on her right. Mathew Morgan rode Sundown on her left and the three allowed the horses to stretch into a distance eating smooth gate. They stopped on Mary's land and David added water to the water hole. The fence was standing firm and strong. The slight tremors they had felt had not disturbed it. The cattle looked fine.

Sarah sat with her back against a tree with her eyes closed. The men thought that she was resting, but really she was remembering Singing Lark's instructions. She didn't want to miss a thing that might make a difference in the healing of this sickness. These were her people. The life she had lived had made her different. They didn't know her.

"God help me to help them, just as you did in the camp of the people." She prayed silently.

When she opened her eyes, David reached for her hand and helped her up. He handed her the water bag and then a piece of dried meat. She took a quick drink but refused the meat.

"Do you think the horses are rested enough? I would like to arrive before dark."

Mathew looked at David and said that it was a good thing that all the horses were young and strong.

"Has anyone from the ranch ever ridden into town in one day?"

"Yes, it's a hard trip for the poor beasts, but with the bridge, it can be done." David didn't like pushing Thunder at the pace Sarah set. Sundown's father had given him the advantage of strength beyond the norm.

When they tied their horses near the Silver River, it was in the same spot that Jed had tied Ginger, years earlier when he and Ben had been there with Beth for the first time. Matt had directed them to the spot and helped them set up the little tent before walking across the open area in front of the Trading Post and hesitantly opening the door to his blacksmith shop. He led Sundown into a shelter he had built for his own horses and gave him food and fresh water. His home stood only a few yards behind it. He prayed that God had spared his family from the illness before he entered. Lizzy met him with a smile and a hug.

"The girls and I are fine. How are you?"

"I'm not sick, but very tired. I need to sleep. Sarah is going to make medicine to fight the infection and I want us to learn how to make it."

"Who is Sarah?"

"She is Ben Slater's sister. She came back with me to help. She knows a lot about medicines and healing."

"Is she an Indian shaman?" Helen said some things about her when I was in the Trading Post.

"Don't believe anything that woman says. Sarah is here to help. She came even though she knows that people have been talking about her. One thing she said was that anyone who has been near a sick person should take a bath and scrub their clothes. Lizzy, you and the girls haven't been near anyone sick have you?"

"No. I kept them home and we made soup and baked cookies today. I am teaching them to embroider and they worked on that this afternoon. Are you hungry?

"I'm starving."

Wash your hands and I will fix you a bowl. She poured some coffee for him and put out a plate of sugar cookies.

He saw the large fire burning in the pit near the street and realized that it was Sarah and David, making the medicine.

It was then that Mathew realized that they had not caught up with Tom and his men. It is a good thing that their wagons were empty, he thought. Mathew loved horses and as far as he was concerned, misusing one was a terrible crime.

At least the teams didn't have to pull a load, he thought. Matt walked out his door and across the street where David and Sarah were working.

"I am going to rub down your horses. I already did Sundown," he said. "I hope Tom and the men had sense enough to give theirs a little break. I know they were concerned about their families. Do you want me to walk down the street and ask at each house to see how many are sick and tell them all about the bath and scrubbing their clothes and to eat soup and to come in the morning and get the medicine when it is done?"

"Thanks Matt," said Sarah, "First I think we need to get Sam and Helen to open up so we can get what we need. I need canning bottles to put the medicine in."

"I can get them to open up or I will break the door down!" said David.

"Calm down David, that shouldn't be necessary," said Matt. "They know me. We just need him to hand out the supplies. We won't go in."

"Tell him I need honey and Sassafras roots, lots of both if he has any."

"How much do you need?"

"Tell him I will need enough supplies and bottles to take one to every house."

David and Matt pounded on the front door of the Trading Post but no one came. Matt went around the back and pounded on the back door. Sarah could hear the noise out front in the street. Finally she could hear voices.

Through the window, she saw Sam carry a lantern into the store and set it on the counter. He placed two boxes of bottles on the floor by the front door, next she saw him fill his arms with metal cans and smaller boxes. Lastly he put a canvas bag on top of the pile. The front door opened just long enough for him to shove the pile out on the porch and it slammed shut. She heard him set the latch and watched him take the lantern back through the curtain that separated the store from his living area.

David and Matt carried the supplies and set them down beside Sarah.

"Are they ill? Is his family sick?" Sarah was worried.

"No, they aren't sick, just scared. They aren't going to open up until everyone in the area is well again. I tried to tell them about the bath and washing their clothes but Helen said she would bathe when she wanted and no one was going to tell her how to care for her family." She had said more than that, but he was not going to relate it to Sarah.

"Well at least your persistence got us what we need for now. Matt do you have another big kettle or tub?"

"I'll go ask Liz. Sarah, is there anything else you might need?"

"This should do for now."

Matt returned with the tub, carrying it carefully by its two ring handles. Inside was a large pot, filled with fresh coffee, and a stack of cups. Beside them was a plate of fresh sugar cookies.

He set it down gently and said that Liz sends her love and she and the girls are praying for you and the town."

"She is thoughtful. Thank her for us when you go back."

Efficiently, Sarah added some honey and the sassafras root to the many herbal medicines she already had brewing.

"I am so glad that Lizzy had two big laundry tubs. David carefully helped her to pull the strong infusion away from the fire. We can let it cool and strain it while the next one is cooking.

"With so many people in the settlement and out in the lumber camp, you will need to make a lot," said Matt.

"If I make it strong, the families can add water and we will only need to start with one quart bottle at each house."

"David I am going to need more of the infection fighting plants.

As soon as it turns light enough I will search the area for them. You and Matt should rest now and I will stay here and keep the fire going."

Matt headed home without a comment and quickly returned with several blankets and an old hide.

"This should make a cozy bedroll for you near the fire, Sarah. I noticed that you didn't bring one." He put them down on the grass and spread them out. "I'll be back in the morning to help visit the houses and deliver the medicine. Most of the people have met me at least once or twice and they are more apt to talk to me." He knew that Helen had spread her stories at the store and that people were not likely to trust Sarah, especially if they knew who she was.

David, spread his bedroll beside Sarah's and said he would take the first shift.

"When the infusion matches the other one, I'll pull it away. We can bottle all of it in the morning." With a little coaxing, she sat down and had a cup of coffee and a cookie and then she surprised David by dipping one of the clean cups into the first infusion and poured it into his cup. She did the same for her own. After her first sip, she poured a bucket of water into the brew.

"That is really strong and bitter," said David.

"I brought sugar. I better add some now while it is still hot." She poured a generous amount into the brown-black liquid and stirred until the grains of sugar were completely dissolved. Showing self-discipline, she added a bit of sugar to her cup and a bit more coffee and drank it down without stopping. David managed to drink his, but shuddered and gagged.

"That is awful stuff," he said. "I sure hope it works."

In the morning, at first light, Sarah nudged David and asked if he would watch the fire while she searched for plants along the river.

He rubbed his eyes and sat up. She had placed a cup of coffee in his hand.

"I hope this cup doesn't taste like the last thing that was in it," he joked.

"No, I washed it out. It is just coffee." She walked away towards the horses, where he could see her talking to them and giving Thunder and her horses a chance to graze on a new spot as she tied them a little farther up the Silver. She made sure that they could still reach the river for a drink. She continued on until she found the plants she was looking for, but when she saw the purple flowers on some plants, she pinched a leaf and waited to see if her fingers became numb. They did. She returned to the fireside, with a double bundle. "These do not grow near the ranch. I can make syrup to coat their sore throats. It will make it easier to drink the medicine."

She is amazing, thought David. He watched as she produced a package of wild cherries from one of her bundles and crushed them into a soup kettle, that she had taken from Gentle Fawn's porch. She poured in sugar and crushed two of the plants into the pan and covered them with water.

"When that boils, it will be ready. We will strain it into one bottle. They just need a spoonful to coat their throat so that they can swallow the medicine. It will numb their tongue, too. Maybe they won't mind the taste as much."

Matt crossed the street bringing two plates of eggs and fresh baked biscuits slathered with butter and jam.

"Oh, that sure looks good," said David. "Thank you Matt."

"Thank you Heavenly Father. Please make our work here successful and help us as we work to heal the people that are sick. Please strengthen them and give them your blessings," prayed Sarah. Amen they all said.

Quickly, both plates of food were enjoyed and washed down with another cup of the bitter medicine.

Sarah insisted that Matt drink a cup.

"Now I think we are as ready as we will be." She had strained the syrup into one jar and screwed on the lid. The first batch of medicine was strained and already in jars with lids. David had noticed that as soon as she woke him.

"I think we need to get this to each house as soon as we can," she said. Just carry as many as you can without dropping any. I want to start down at the end of this street."

"The settlement is so quiet that it is eerie," said Matt. "Usually I see people at sunrise and hear doors banging and kids out playing."

A family had started a cabin in the trees just passed Rose's house. There was a tent and a cooking fire going and a woman was lying on a blanket near it. A tall gray haired man came out of the trees leading a horse. He had downed a tree and cleaned it and several others earlier in the week, now he was attempting to drag them up where he could use them for his cabin. It was easy to see that both the homesteaders were sick.

"Good morning neighbor," said Matt with a smile. "I'm Mathew Morgan. My blacksmith shop is down on the other side of the street, across from the Trading Post. "We haven't met yet. I'd shake your hand but as you can see my arms are full of bottles."

"Whatever you are selling, we don't want any!" His voice was gravelly and tight.

"We are not selling anything," said Sarah. It is easy to see that you and your wife are ill. Many of the people in this settlement are sick. We have made medicine. It may help. Is your throat sore?"

He nodded.

"Our girl is real bad. She's in the tent."

Sarah set the bottles she was carrying in the grass and looked around for basic utensils.

“I need a pan, and some water and a spoon,” she said to the man. He pointed to a large kettle by the fire and a big cooking spoon, before he collapsed. Matt did his best to soften his fall, but couldn’t catch him because of the bottles he held.

“I will be right back,” said matt. He ran all the way back to the spot where Sarah had prepared the medicine. He picked up a satchel and emptied its contents on to a blanket. He did the same with a second one. Then he covered what he had dumped out with the old hide. He returned with the empty satchels and proceeded to carefully slide the bottles in one at a time.

Sarah was in the tent with the girl. She backed out holding the bottle of syrup and a teaspoon. She filled the spoon and lifted the woman’s head enough to put the syrup in her mouth. She did the same for the man. He had revived when David had placed a wet cloth on his forehead.

“My girl,” he said. “Help my girl. My mouth feels funny inside. I can’t feel my tongue.”

“That’s good. It should make it easier to swallow some of this medicine.” She poured a half of a cup and filled it the rest of the way with water. “Drink all of this.” She held his hand with the cup up to his mouth until he had finished it. She did the same with the woman. “They need to drink water. They have high fevers. David, force him to drink water.” She sat the woman up and placed her arm behind her. “You must drink water.” Sarah was insistent. “How long has it been since you have eaten?” Neither of them answered. They were asleep.

Sarah turned to Matt and thanked him for the satchels. "I was in such a hurry. I wasn't thinking clearly. The little girl is dead." The mother is really bad. I can't do anything more for them until we get the medicine to all the houses. Let's go."

"I'll go get a shovel and bury the girl in the trees," said Matt.

"No, Matt. There may be more. We need to hurry." Rose didn't answer her door, but it wasn't locked. Matt turned the knob and called out to her. She answered from her bed.

"Don't come in. I'm sick. You will catch it."

Sarah, knelt beside her and repeated the simple routine, first syrup, then medicine and followed it by water. They placed the medicine and a pitcher of water next to her bed. Sarah noted that Rose was not as ill as the first family had been. Rose was able to explain that she had tried to help them until she became sick, too. Sarah warned her that the medicine would be bitter, and that she should mix it with water.

"We will be back," she said. "She needs soup. They will all need soup." They are too weak to cook."

CHAPTER SEVENTEEN
STRENGTH TO CARRY ON

Sarah was most affected when she found that all of Reverend Brown's family was gravely ill. Melanie had tried to help others until she was no longer able. Violet lay in her crib and William was in his. They found Melanie on the floor in her kitchen. She had been trying to make soup but had collapsed. The fire was out and the vegetables from her garden lay on the counter.

David carried her in and placed her on the bed beside Jim. Sarah started with Violet and stripped her to her bare skin.

"She will die if I don't get her fever down! Matt, strip William and then take their blankets out and soak them in the river." Violet tried to cry, but only a little squeak came out. "She is so little, Please God show me what to do for her and how much medicine I can give her." Sarah dipped her finger in the syrup jar and let Violet suck on it. She did it again, and then gave William a tiny bit on a teaspoon. She had to search to find a baby bottle. Finally she saw two in a pan of water. They had been used and Melanie had been preparing to clean them. Sarah took both bottles to the river and washed them over and over.

"How much should I use Lord? I don't know how much medicine I can give them." Sarah's hands were shaking as she poured an ounce of the bitter infusion into the bottle. She filled it to the top with warm water and shook it. When Matt came running in with the dripping blankets, Sarah immediately wrapped violet in one and placed the bottle in her hands. "She is big enough but I think she is too weak to feed herself."

Sarah sat beside her on the floor holding the bottle until Matt had wrapped William.

"David, please hold this for her." She fixed the second bottle the same way and handed it to Matt to feed to the baby boy. Tears were in Sarah's eyes as she struggled to spoon the syrup in Jim and Melanie. She couldn't wake them up. Finally she did the only thing she knew to do. She dumped water on them.

"You have to wake up! She shouted. She shook Jim and blotted his face with a cloth forcing the spoon in his mouth. He choked and coughed and opened his eyes. She did the same to Melanie. Finally she was able to prop them up and get them to drink some of the medicine. They were burning up and went back to sleep before they had taken enough of the infusion to do any good. She snatched the blanket from the bottom of their bed and ran to the river with it. She raced back with it dripping all the way. Spreading it over them, Sarah continued to pray and shake them until they had finished a cup of medicine each and had taken a cup of water. Sarah returned to see the men cradling the little ones with tears in their eyes, too. They all loved this little family.

"We need to move on. Put a diaper on them and put them in their beds with no other clothes and no blankets."

The next house was a young couple that had been working hard in the woods, cutting logs for a barn. They had not visited anyone in the settlement for several days. Matt explained about the sickness and gave the instructions on what to do. He stayed back from them and left the bottle of medicine on the grass.

"Stay away from everyone. So far, you are the only ones we have found that are not already sick. Dump a bucket of water on the medicine bottle and let it dry there in the sun before you touch it. Just keep doing what you have been. You can't help. You will just get sick, too. We will do what we can. Follow the instructions carefully. It tastes terrible, but drink it anyway," he added.

"Tell me about the babies, are they alright?" The young woman asked.

"No, answered Matt. They are all very ill."

They spotted smoke curling up in the trees down river on the Hickory.

"Let's go back and start another batch of medicine and a tub of soup. We can use our horses to go to the lumber camp and the houses near the mill." Sarah was also thinking of all the men stationed in the fort. God how can I help so many?

"There are several houses beyond the fort. We need to check them too, said David and what about the fort?"

When Sarah asked Matt if he could write, he laughed.

"Sure I can."

"Do you have paper and a pencil?"

"Yes I am sure that Liz has some."

"Good. Please get it."

"Sarah, what are you planning on doing?" asked David.

"I am going to have Matt write down the instructions and give them to the man in charge along with a lot of the medicine. It is very quiet in the fort and no one is on guard at the gate. There are too many men for us to try to take care of all of them."

Sarah was worried. She was running out of supplies. She took inventory and found that she had just enough of everything for two more tubs full. "I will make one and give the ingredients for the second batch to the cook, if he is well enough, he will be able to make it, if not someone else will have to do it.

When Matt returned, with his paper and pencil, she made the batch of medicine while he wrote down the directions. She measured each ingredient and had him mark them, and wrap them as they went along.

"Now we need you to get Sam to part with some more of his bottles."

He hurried around to the back of the house and tapped politely. Sam came slowly, and Matt knew instantly that he was ill. Sarah knew it too, when she saw him shuffle into the store and unlock the front door. Matt slipped in the back and checked the family as they had the others. He stuck his head out long enough to indicate to Sarah that she was needed. Sarah was in the middle of making another batch of the syrup. She pulled it aside and took in a bottle of medicine and the nearly empty bottle of syrup. She could see Abe and Henry in their beds. Helen was asleep and Sam walked shakily back and lay beside her.

"How long have you been sick?"

"Since this morning, but she got sick during the night and the boys were a little sick when we put them to bed last night."

Flashes of painful memories kept interrupting Sarah's thoughts as she tried to work and do what needed to be done, as she had at other houses. She knew this woman would be repulsed by her very touch.

"Matt, will you help the adults? I am going to see what the children need." They were fevered and Henry wouldn't open his eyes when she talked to him. She returned to their beds armed with a pan of water and two cloths. She wiped their faces and arms and legs and finally Abe started to make a whimper.

"Thank you Jesus," she said out loud. With a half of a teaspoon of syrup in each child, she handed the jar to Matt. She had to work hard to get the children to take the medicine, but finally they had done all they could for now.

Outside, David was making the biggest batch of soup possible. He had scrubbed one of the tubs and was cutting into small pieces, all the food that Mary had sent in the two big bundles.

When Matt came out he saw what David was doing and said that he was going to raid some gardens. David had brought out two more cases of bottles, and had them ready for the next batch of medicine.

When the syrup was done, Sarah poured half of it in the bottle they had been using and bottled the rest for the fort. Matt had the recipe for it, too. She carefully wrapped the plants that were the main ingredient. Don't touch them; Matt or your fingers will get numb.

Take all these ingredients to the fort and find someone capable of making the medicine and following the instructions. David and I are going up the Silver to check on the families along there. After that, the three of us will head for the lumber camp."

Sarah was glad she had a saddle to use. She put it on Pretty Mother and filled her saddle bags with the things she would need. David slid bottles of the medicine in his saddlebags.

Matt had ridden to the gate of the fort with his horse burdened with bundles. He pounded on the gate until his hand was sore. I have a really bad feeling about this, he thought. He rode back to the Trading Post and borrowed an axe. He went to the side wall and hacked a hole big enough to push his bundles in and crawl in after them. Many men lay in the dust, where they had collapsed. Matt went to the mess hall and found four men, ill but ambulatory. He gave them the bundles and written instructions, and told them to make the medicine before they were too sick to do it.

When he looked up toward the commander's office he saw a soldier stagger out, carrying a full bottle of whisky in his left hand. In his arms he had another, and in his right hand he had one that was nearly empty.

"Soldier, are you in charge?"

"No, but I'm the one with the whiskey," he slurred.

"Where is your commander?"

"He is sick in his bed. Everybody is sick, but me."

Matt walked to the man and led him into the mess hall by pulling on his shirt sleeve. There he took away the whiskey and poured him a cup of coffee, black and strong.

"You have to get sober. You are in charge here! Do you see these men? They are sick and they are trying to make medicine to save the lives of the men in this fort. Can you read?"

"Yes, I can read. Give me back my whiskey."

"You can have it back when the medicine is made and the men have all been taken care of."

"I don't need to make medicine. I'm not sick."

"Drink that coffee!" Matt ordered.

Matt spotted a bottle of mustard on a shelf. He dipped out a spoonful and forced it down the man's throat. It acted as an ipecac and the man emptied his stomach right there on the spot.

"Drink that coffee or I'll purge you again," said Matt.

Outside, Matt lifted the bar on the gate and swung it open. He started a fire in an existing pit in the middle of the parade ground. He needed help. He couldn't do all that was needed here. He had to get help. With two big tubs half full of water he started dumping the ingredients half in one and half in the other. Without realizing it he had also dumped in the plants for the syrup. He dumped in sugar and honey and suddenly he recognized the error.

The four men that had been standing in the mess hall earlier were now sitting on benches laying their heads on the tables.

I need someone that knows what they are doing. I wish I had another woman like Sarah. That's when it hit him. They had not gone to Tom and Gentle Fawn's home yet. It was on the main street right next to the Trading Post and across from his Blacksmith shop. What if they are all sick? He thought. We even used a pan off her porch but none of us knocked on that door to see if they were alright!

Matt was frightened for the people of the settlement and the men of the fort. He worried about his own family. He had slept in his shop to avoid taking the sickness into his house.

Guilt for overlooking her house, worry and a need for help drove him to knock on her door.

"Gentle Fawn, how are you, Tom, and the twins?"

"We are well. Tom is not here. He stopped when he arrived, but then he went to the lumber camp. I haven't seen him since. I heard that some people are sick. I saw someone cooking medicine near the street last night."

"I forgot to stop here to ask about your family. I guess it's because it is so close to the shops and not near the other houses.

"Gentle Fawn there is one young couple in the woods, building their cabin, beyond the Reverend's house. They are well. Do you think you could trust them to watch the twins? Gentle Fawn, I need your help. The soldiers are very ill. I found one soldier that was well and he was drunk. Please Gentle Fawn will you come?"

"I don't know those people. I don't want Anne and Stormy to get the sickness and how can I know that they are good people?"

"I know, these people are not your people, but they are Tom's. Please Gentle Fawn. I can't do it all alone."

"If they will come here to watch the children, then I will help you. I don't want to take them out where the sickness will find them," said Gentle Fawn. He could tell that she was more concerned about her children's care than for herself being exposed to sick soldiers.

"Thank you, Gentle Fawn, I will go get them. Gather anything together that you think will be helpful."

"Please God, Please God, Please God, he prayed to the rhythm of his horse's hoof beats as he hurried back to the camp of the young couple. They were not there! He called out, but got no answer until he turned his horse to leave and saw the woman through the window of Reverend Brown's house. She had Violet in her arms, feeding her a bottle with what looked like a mild blend of the medicine.

"Oh, thank you Jesus. Thank you God," he said as he ran up the steps.

After an explanation that took longer than he wanted, he talked her into coming to take care of Gentle Fawn's children. The woman stopped at the river and scrubbed her arms, hands, face, and even her hair. She splashed water on the front of her dress over and over. Gentle Fawn watched from her window and thanked the woman for the effort and discomfort. She gave her a dry dress to slip on, and hung the woman's wet one, on her line. She quickly gave Norah a few instructions and showed her where things were that she might need and told her that she had stew on the stove and when she got hungry she should eat and feed the children. "I will take good care of them. Please don't worry. I love children."

Matt had not asked where her husband was and now that he and Gentle Fawn were on their way to the fort, it was too late to ask. They rode in the open gate and went to work immediately. Like Sarah, Gentle Fawn was a take charge type person.

"You there, get these men out of the sun. Put them over there against the wall."

She had given the order to the man whose stomach Matt had emptied. He was carrying a coffee cup and Matt checked to make sure that it was coffee inside it. Together they carried them and made a row of sleeping soldiers on the grass in the shade from the high fence.

"They look dead," he said. "How do you know they are not dead?"

"Because you idiot, they are breathing. God help us save these men," Matt prayed out loud. "Go put wood on that fire and stir that medicine."

"Who said you were in charge?"

"I did," said Matt.

Gentle Fawn had looked in all the buildings and had counted forty sick men. She had found two that were dead.

"Major Bennet and his wife are both very ill. I didn't see any children."

"Thank you Gentle Fawn, that is helpful to know."

"Mathew, there are buckets and spoons and things in the kitchen that we can use to take the medicine to the men, but I tasted the medicine. It is bitter, and it made my mouth feel strange. What is in it?" asked Gentle Fawn."

"I made a mistake. Sarah gave me directions but I forgot and put the two medicines together. The syrup numbs and it was supposed to be made separately and given to them first, but I put the plants in with the rest."

"It is a good thing. They will not taste the bitterness as much and it will help their throats, too," said Gentle Fawn. There is a room off the kitchen with supplies, I will see if they have sugar that we can add."

"Soldier, I am sorry that I was so hard on you. What is your name?" asked Matt.

"Just John, is good enough." He was surly and had a bad headache.

"Thank you John, for helping us. Let's go in and get a container to hold some of this medicine and as soon as we add something more to sweeten it a bit, I think we should start getting some of it into them. We will need to follow it with a cup of water. Can you bring that big bucket full of water?"

Gentle Fawn hurried out with an empty bucket and a pan full of sugar. She dumped half of the sugar in each of the tubs and handed a big spoon to the soldier.

"Gentle Fawn, this is John. John this is Gentle Fawn. She has volunteered to come here to help us save your comrades."

She looked at him with sympathy.

"This has been a terrible experience for you. How did you stay well when everyone else was getting sick?"

"I don't know. Just dumb luck I guess."

"God has blessed you, be glad," she said smiling at him.

"How can you smile when people are dying here?" he snapped at her.

"We will do what we can. God will do the rest. Some will die. Some will live. We can work, we are well, and we should be glad of that."

It took a long time, before they had gone through the routine of medicine and water with everyone. They placed a cup by each soldier and used it just for him. John and Matt took over and that freed Gentle Fawn to explore the kitchen and she soon had a pair of huge pots bubbling on the stove with a nutritious concoction in each.

Matt buried the two soldiers inside the wall of the fort and printed their last name on boards and shoved them into the soft dirt piled over each grave. Their tags were put on the desk in the office.

They made another round through the buildings forcing the men to drink the medicine and water. On the third round, they brought warm soup. The meat and vegetables had been crushed into a pulp that they could swallow.

When Gentle Fawn suggested strongly that John and Matt should drink some of the medicine, they resisted until she told them, that unless they did, they could not have the special meal she had waiting for them.

The four sick men that had been in the mess hall had been moved to their cots and she had the dining hall scrubbed. Gentle Fawn brought out glasses of cold milk and then three steaks nearly as big as the plate they were on.

"I don't think the commander will mind. He has a field with many cows in it near the back wall of this fort." I have one more thing. She came back with an apple pie and pot of coffee.

"Woman, you are amazing. I was starving. I can't remember when I ate last, thank you," said the soldier.

"Thank You Gentle Fawn. Tom will be proud of the job you are doing here," said Matt.

"I think tomorrow will be much like today. After that we should see some of them getting a little strength back," said Gentle Fawn. She didn't acknowledge the compliment.

CHAPTER EIGHTEEN
CAN WE DO IT?

"Sarah, I think we should rest before we go to the lumber camp." David wasn't thinking of himself. He was concerned that Sarah might get ill if she didn't eat or rest."

"I can't David. I have to take them medicine and check with the people in the settlement that we have visited to see if they have taken any more of the medicine, and bury that poor little girl and maybe Violet and William."

She was exhausted and had invested her heart in each person that she helped. She feared that her medicine wasn't enough, and worried that they weren't doing enough. Her tears slid silently down her face as they rode back down the trail beside the Silver.

David understood her distress. They continued on, returning for more bottles of medicine. They found another family camping near the fort. They were also ill. A man, his wife and two big boys were in their bedrolls. The oldest boy was able to explain that they had been in the settlement two days earlier and had bought supplies and their father had not felt well then.

"He ate stew last night but said his throat was awful sore," related the boy. He listened and Sarah felt confident that if she could get the first dose in them, that he would be able to follow her directions and help his family.

"It was good to see Rachel and Margaret well and the new folks next to them were well. Rachel said that Zack had been home just for a few minutes last night to check on them and that they only had one sick family at the mill. Melanie's parents were sick, but not so bad that they couldn't help themselves. They will take the medicine and drink lots of water. Minnie had food prepared that they can eat."

They saw the gate to the fort standing open before they could see inside. They rode in slowly, first seeing the tubs of medicine, pulled away from the dying fire. Sarah gasped when she noticed the soldiers lying in the grass by the fence. At first she thought they were all dead. A solitary cup placed beside each soldier testified that they had been given medicine.

She and David heard voices and hesitantly stepped down from their horses.

"Hello, Matt is that you?"

"Yes, David and Sarah, come on in. This is John and Gentle Fawn. They have been helping."

"Hello, Thank you," said Sarah.

As David shook John's hand, Gentle Fawn jumped up and hurried to the kitchen. She could tell with a glance that these two people had been doing the same thing they had.

"Please sit, I am making food for you," she yelled from the kitchen.

Before long Sarah and David were thanking God for two beautiful steaks and fresh apple pie.

"We needed that," said David. "You are kind to leave your family and come here to help."

"Those that are well should care for the sick. That's how it is. We have forty sick soldiers here, but I know we can do it. We will get them well, with God's help."

Sarah and David felt encouraged as they changed to fresh horses and then quickly checked the families they had visited earlier, on their way to the lumber camp. The last family on the main road was the one where the little girl had died in the tent.

A young man sat beside their small fire stirring a pot of soup. The mother of the little girl still lay on her bed. Although her eyes were filled with tears, she seemed a little stronger. She was sobbing inaudibly.

David and Sarah recognized him from the other side of the settlement. He extended his hand and said he was just a neighbor trying to help a little.

"My wife, Norah, is watching a woman's twins, while she is at the fort, nursing the soldiers."

"Yes, thank you for helping. We met her a little while ago. We stopped to check on the family. She said her name is Norah."

"Yes, we are new here. I'm Nicholas Russell."

"The gentleman that was here earlier, where is he?"

"I don't know. He walked into the woods while I was burying his daughter. He is very sick. I tried to stop him."

"Which way did he go? Asked David as he slid down off his horse and headed into the woods on foot. The young man pointed.

"I understand their grief. Norah and I lost our little boy to measles a year ago."

"I am so sorry. Please tell David that I have gone to the Reverend's house to check on them, and I will be back as soon as I can."

"You don't need to go there just now. I gave them all some medicine and I took soup over for the adults and gave the babies each some milk and changed their diapers. The little ones are much better than they were when I first saw them. Their folks are still pretty sick, but it looks like they are all going to make it. I'll go there on my way home and I think I should put some light clothes on the babies for tonight. I covered the Reverend and his wife with a light sheet."

"Nicholas, you are an angel. I needed to know that. I was so worried. Tell David, that I have gone on to the lumber camp."

"Wait," he said. "What is your name?"

"I am Sarah, of the Blue Stone People. I am Ben Slater's sister."

"I've heard of you."

"I'm sure you have," she said sadly, as she rode away.

*****

Sarah could hear the sounds of men at work as she neared the lumber camp. That is a good sound, she thought. It means they are well. She stopped on the edge of camp as she heard someone yell "Timber" and then heard the sound of a tall tree crashing to the ground. She looked around for someone she could approach, to ask if anyone there was ill. Cookie saw her and walked over to ask what she wanted.

"I need to know if anyone in this camp is ill. I have medicine."

"Yes, good thing you come. Follow me please. You fix leg? He has much pain. No doctor here. You doctor?"

Sarah was not prepared to help a man with a broken leg. It was badly swollen and should have been set hours earlier.

"When did this happen?" she asked.

"Before lunch, right when I ring bell, a tree kicked him when it go down."

"Cookie, I will need cold wet leather to wrap it and strong tea made with willow bark. Do you know how to make it?"

"We can do it," he said, as he hurried away. He lifted the canvas, covering the side of his chuck wagon. Inside he had many cooking and healing herbs all hanging in dried bunches. Sarah searched through with her eyes but didn't see the ones she needed to put the injured man asleep.

"What do you have for pain?"

"We have whiskey!" he said with a smile.

"Good, get it please and make him drink a lot of it. I am going to search the edge of the river for what I need. I will be back as soon as I can."

Sarah found willow trees. They were the easy part, but to find the plants that fight infection she had to go a long ways.

Finally when she returned, Cookie was doing what he could to ease the man's pain. He had given him nearly half a bottle of whiskey and the man continued to moan.

"He needs more, and I need to make an infusion of medicine. I need a pan."

Sarah suddenly realized that if she poured a bottle of the medicine she had with her, and added lots of the willow bark, she would have what she needed.

Just as she knelt beside the injured man, David and Matt arrived with a slowly drawn wagon. In it, covered with boards held down with heavy rocks, was one tub full of soup and another of medicine.

The relief to have them back working with her was apparent on her face.

"Thank you Jesus," she said, as she hugged them both at once. How is it that you are able to come? Are the soldiers better?" she asked Matt.

"No not yet, but Gentle Fawn made another tub of medicine with her own ingredients and one of soup and said we should bring them here and you don't say no to Gentle Fawn. She is a lot like you, Sarah. She has a man named John at the fort helping her and she was worried about the lumber camp and her husband, Tom.

"John is a good help, now that he is sober, I have his liquor in my saddlebags. I think he took it from the commander's office, but anyway, I didn't want to leave it where he could find it. Gentle Fawn has enough to deal with, without having to deal with her only help getting drunk."

"I am so glad that you were able to help the men at the fort, but now we have another challenge. This man broke his leg hours ago, and it is swollen. I won't be able to set it for him until some of the swelling goes down. I wish I had ice."

"I go get ice from cold shed. How much you need?"

"Cookie, Thank you, I didn't realize that you had it here. Please can you fill that small pan with pieces?"

"I'll help him said Matt."

"Wait, Matt, did you say you have whiskey in your saddlebag?"

"I need to give some more to this man, but Cookie had only a half of a bottle."

"That's a far better use for it, than the soldier had," he said laughing. He got it and handed it to David to open. It was a full bottle.

Matt hurried in the direction that Cookie had gone.

"I don't think the sickness has reached here. When I asked the cook, if anyone was ill here, he immediately told me about this man. I haven't been to the saw mill yet."

"I think I better ride over there and see. If I don't come back soon, you will know that they are sick."

"Alright David, I am so glad you came." She hugged him tightly and didn't want to let go, but she did. "I hope you are back soon."

"Me too," he said.

After David left, she gave the man a cup of the infusion. The liquor was starting to take effect. She gave him another cup, this one filled with whiskey and he drank it down.

"I needed that," he slurred, "that other stuff was awful!"

With his leg propped up high and wrapped in ice, the pain subsided.

"It's not so bad," he slurred. "I am tough. I can take it." She smiled at him and was about to pour him another cup of whiskey when his chin dropped onto his chest. He had passed out.

"He sleeps long time now," said Cookie. "That's good, no feel pain. I go cook now. You tell, if you want help."

Matt asked if David had gone to the mill, and she replied with a nod. She was praying and searching the man's leg muscles, attempting to see how bad it was.

"When the swelling goes down a little more, I think we can set it. I will need you and David or Cookie to help me. I will need four smooth boards and some pieces of leather, also some cloth to wrap it and make it stable." She was thinking out loud, and Cookie was listening. He scurried away and quickly returned with everything she had mentioned.

"Thank you," she said. "Can you help me for a few minutes?"

"We can do it," he said. It was his favorite saying. "I pull food away from fire. I come right back."

"He is a nice little man," she whispered to Matt.

"Have you ever been around a man from China before?" asked Matt.

"No." She couldn't say more. Cookie was back and enjoying the feeling that he was helping to fix a broken leg.

She explained the procedure thoroughly and showed the men where to place their hands. They pulled, and she pressed, and prayed. She feared that the bone was so shattered that their help would be minimal, but finally she felt a thump, and a big smile broke across her face.

"Hold steady, hold it steady," she said as she packed it with the willow bark and medicine poultice and wrapped it tight with the ice cold leather. She returned the ice pack, and then more leather.

"We will leave it up and wrapped like that until the swelling goes down some more and then we will put the boards on. Thank you both. I couldn't have done it without you."

"You do good work. Now please help sick people in tent by trees over there."

"Cookie, you should have told me about them right away."

"Woman got sick and then two men. I put them in tent in trees. I give whiskey and soup. That why whiskey most gone."

"Oh Cookie," Sarah exclaimed as she ran to the tent he had indicated. Matt followed, bringing a quart jar of the medicine and three cups and a jug of water.

"Matt, the only one alive is the man on the right. Please lift him out into the fresh air."

Sarah walked back to the cooking fire, where Cookie was working. He looked sad, but determined to do his job as camp cook.

"Cookie, it's a bad sickness. That is why I came. Many people in the settlement are very ill. When did these people get sick?"

"Four days ago. Just sleep and very hot, not want soup, not want whiskey, not want water. I make take, but they not get better."

"You did all you could. You were near them, are you feeling well."

"I not get sick." He turned away from her. He didn't want her to see the look of complete failure he was feeling.

"Cookie, you did a very brave thing, taking care of them. You were right to put them separate from the rest of the camp. It stopped the sickness from spreading and I couldn't have helped your friend with the broken leg without you. This camp is very lucky that they have you to take care of them."

"Did people in tent die?"

One is alive and Matt is caring for him. Your coffee smells wonderful, could I have a cup?" She sat on a log near him and he gladly poured her a cup. Then without asking, he made her a sandwich of fresh baked bread and meat.

"You eat and rest," he said.

David returned from the saw mill then, but only to switch from the horse to the seat of the wagon.

"They need this bad, several families are down with it, and Tom is trying to stay on his feet, but I can tell he won't be much longer. Several of the men that were at the ranch are getting sick, or already are."

A stone of fear settled in Sarah's heart as he drove slowly away with the wagon containing the tubs of medicine and soup. God please protect our families. Protect Ben, Mary and their boys. Protect Jed, Beth, Johnny and Lily. You are the great physician. Lord, your grace protects Matt and his family too. Norah and Nicholas have been working near the sickness, and Gentle Fawn and John, and my David and I. Please keep us well so we can serve as your hands.

"You cry? Why you cry?" asked Cookie.

"God bless you, Cookie. I hope that you stay well. I am going to the mill. Please tell Matt to stay here. Help him to put the boards on that leg, before the man wakes up. When he does, he can only have medicine from the smaller pan and soup, no more whiskey."

She followed David, to the mill and found it was just as he had said. They worked as an efficient team and got medicine and water in everyone that was ill, while the soup heated.

Once the wives, that were well, saw what to do, they were glad to help. They went with Sarah and administered the next round of medicine. Sarah explained about scrubbing the clothes and washing themselves and the sick ones with soap and water. She told them about using wet blankets to bring down fevers, if it came to that.

"The two tubs belong to the fort. When they are empty and things return to normal, you will need to see that they are returned. I am sorry but we must leave now. Others need our help. Ask God to help you. He is the Great Healer. We will pray for all of you."

David drove the wagon back to the lumber camp and picked up Matt. He was very glad to see them.

"We did what you said, but he is complaining something awful," said Matt.

Sarah adjusted the wrappings on the leg and gave him another cup of the strong willow bark infusion. They left Cookie looking a little overwhelmed when he heard he had to make sure everyone in camp took a bath with soap and water and put on clean clothes, and that included him. He was glad to have the medicine for the man with the illness and she felt confident that he would do his very best to see that both men got well. Matt had marked the graves of the woman and man that he had buried. They were husband and wife, they had no children.

On their way back through the settlement, they checked every family and were joyous to find the sick ones were getting better. Gentle fawn was back at her house making a huge kettle of stew to share with anyone that needed it. Sarah told her that Tom was ill, but that he was recuperating, and being cared for by some of the wives of his crew members.

"He is a strong man. He will be well soon." She said. "Norah was a blessing to me. She baked cookies with Anne and Stormy ate many. She took good care of the twins. She washed all the clothes she could find. She is a very nice woman. I will be her friend always."

"How is it that you are here? Are the soldiers well enough to care for each other now?"

"No, but a small, very late, wagon train came down the trail, along the Silver and it had an escort of soldiers; they are there, in the fort now and John is considered a hero. I told them that they should keep the people of the wagon train out of the settlement or fort, until the sickness is gone. They agreed. The new people are camped along the trail near the Silver until it is safe for them to come."

"Gentle Fawn, I am Sarah, of the Blue Stone People. It is good to know you. Thank you for your help at the fort. I have been told that we are a lot alike."

"I have heard about Ben Slater's sister. I knew that I would like you, as soon as Helen started to talk. With my house next to the Trading Post, I hear much, but say little. The baskets that you sold in the store were very beautiful. I cannot do work that is so lovely. Perhaps one day we will have time, and you can teach me how. I was at your brother's place once, when the people of the settlement built Jed's house. Ben is a nice man. I met him when they first came with Beth. I will not keep you. I know you are eager to move on. Sam and Helen and the children are doing alright. You don't need to stop there, if you want to hurry. Just leave a bottle of the medicine you made and I'll see that they get it, so they can continue taking it."

Sarah gave her a quick hug and handed her a bottle of medicine from her saddlebag.

"I will come visit you," she said, "I hope you will be my friend also, she added with a big smile, as she turned her horse toward the Reverend's house.

David had just been there and said it was wonderful, to see what a good job Nicholas had done there.

"The whole family is getting better. Melanie was sitting in a chair with Violet on her lap, feeding her a bottle of milk. Jim was sitting up in bed, reading the

Bible and Willie was on the floor playing. Norah and Nicholas were certainly good neighbors."

"Yes, they are good people."

"Matt, you should take a bath in the river and then go home. Thank Liz for all the things she loaned us and the food she made for us and the batches of soup that she made and delivered. I hope to get to know her when things are better. I will pray that you and your family stay well. Take a cup of that medicine tonight and have them take some too. It will help you all to stay well. Thanks for all your help. God bless you."

She took her saddle off Pretty mother and put it on Moon Boy, fastening her satchels and empty bundles on Pretty Mother. David rode into the fort and returned their horse. Thunder was rested now and they had cared well for him. John greeted him with a hand shake and big smile.

"They are getting better, David. I don't think we will lose any more," he said proudly. Thank you to all of you for coming and bringing the medicine."

David waved as he rode out of the open gate. He heard John shout.

"Someone close that gate and fix the hole in the fence, too!

CHAPTER NINETEEN
GOING HOME

"David, we need to scrub in the river and our clothes, too, before we pass near the people of the wagon train."

"Sarah, I have an idea that will protect them and spare us the trouble of wearing wet clothes on our way. I understand that we need to check the Brigg's place and Rachel and Margaret and the new folks along the Silver, but we can do it by riding the back line of their properties. None of them are fenced. That way we won't go near the wagon train at all."

"That's a good idea. I didn't think of that. Let's do it."

They cut across the grass and around bushes and trees and found that the first two families were getting better. Next they rode through the woods and saw Minnie out hanging a wash.

"Hello, you are looking well. How is Calvin?"

"He is up and getting around. He is not totally well, but a whole lot better than he was."

"That's what we wanted to hear, Ma'am. We are just going along and checking on everyone. We will be heading back to the ranch as soon as we know that everyone is doing better."

"You two youngsters have been a real blessing to all of us. I just want you to know how much you both mean to folks around here. Thank you for everything you did. I heard about that young couple that helped care for Melanie and Jim and my grandbabies. We can sure be glad for new people moving here, that are like that. There's a wagon train up river just waiting for folks to be well so they can pull on through. They are late in the season as it is. They certainly didn't need sickness to stop them. You can be sure we will all do what we can for those folks when the time comes."

"Thank you, Ma'am, we will be praying for everyone in the settlement, at Tom's lumber mill, and at Fort Connor. You take care now and don't do more than necessary for a few more days."

"We will be praying for you youngsters, too," she said waving.

"Let's turn around and use the bridge. It will be a lot faster," suggested Sarah.

"I was just going to say that."

Matt saw them ride by and waved with a big smile. They knew that if he was in his shop and smiling, that things at his house must still be alright.

"I don't know how we could have done it without that man," said David.

"Yes, God sent the help we needed. He always does."

Sarah was thinking of the man at the lumber camp. He wore a braid down his back, like the people, but he looked so different. His eyes slanted up. He looked like he was smiling even when he wasn't. He will have a difficult time with that man with the broken leg. I left all the directions I could and he knows where the trees are so he can get all the bark he needs to make more willow bark tea. I know he can do it.

I am so glad that I met Gentle Fawn. She was so nice and worked so hard. Almost all of the people in the settlement were really nice. Norah and Nicholas were a wonderful help. We might have lost Violet and William if they hadn't helped them.

"Sarah, Sarah, slow down. Why are you pushing the horses so hard? I am sure the people at the ranch are fine. Tom's crew didn't get sick until they were back and near other sick people. No one was sick at the ranch."

"I am sorry David. I didn't realize that I was."

"Let's stop near the base of the falls and jump in for a swim. The sun is high. It will dry our clothes and we can rest the horses there."

"I can't relax until I know that everything is alright at the ranch, David, but you are right. We need to stop and scrub ourselves and our clothes and the horses can graze and rest."

Thunder came over as soon as David stretched out on the grass to dry off. He nudged at David's head.

"Hey what are you doing? I know you haven't had any attention for a few days. Sorry Thunder, but I don't have any sweets."

"David, I think I do. Gentle Fawn wrapped up some of the sugar cookies that Norah made and she handed them to me as I was leaving. They are in my saddlebag. We can give them all a treat."

"She handed the package to David, holding on to one big cookie. She broke it in half and gave each of her horses a treat and some scratches. You were both so good. I hope you know how much I love you," she said. She watched as Thunder got his treat and the attention he was craving.

As David settled back on the grass munching a cookie and holding the package, she suddenly felt playful and flopped down beside him.

"I hope you know that I love you, too, but I am not going to let you eat all of those cookies." She grabbed the package and bit both that were remaining.

She ran along the bank laughing, holding a cookie in each hand.

"No you don't, you can't get away with that," he said laughing and catching up quickly. He grasped both her wrists and took a bite from each cookie.

"Now miss cookie grabber, what do you think of that?"

"I think you are, are, are, the most fantastic man in the whole wide world and she wrapped her arms around his neck and kissed him. She stopped her kiss, because she started to giggle.

His arms were around her and he was puzzled why she was giggling until he heard a loud snort near his ear. Thunder had walked over and gently finished both cookies.

"Hey you greedy boy, that was our entire lunch," said David.

"Well, I think we have to move on anyway or it will be late when we get home," said Sarah. "My clothes are getting dry."

They rode side by side, with Pretty Mother trotting along behind on a long lead. David had put it on her. He worried about having an encounter with the stallion.

When Mary's cattle came into view, they saw Joshua there on Little Mouse. He had filled the watering hole and was repairing a wobbly post.

"Joshua, we are so happy to see you. Is everyone at the ranch feeling well?"

"Sure Aunt Sarah, we are all fine, just really busy. Dad and Uncle Jed have been working on our new house every day from sunup until sundown and the rest of us are trying to keep all the other work done." He slid up on Little Mouse and leaned forward scratching her ears without even thinking about it.

As they started out toward home, a frown crossed his face as he thought about the reason the men had left so quickly.

"Are the families that were sick, getting better?"

"Yes they are," answered David. "Your Aunt Sarah was able to make the medicine they needed. She saved their lives Josh."

Sarah rode along not saying anything. David could tell that she was thinking about something from back at the settlement.

"David, the family with the little girl in the tent, did you find the man that walked into the woods?"

"No, Sarah, I didn't."

Joshua seemed to instinctively know not to ask questions about it. They rode along quietly.

Adam spotted them from the top of the bluff and everybody gathered at the crossing. The hugs given that day meant so much more than they ever had before.

As usual Beth and Mary had lots of food prepared for their meal and the talk was mostly about the new house.

The little ones grew quiet and Eli and Nattie cuddled together on the bear rug, with Sunshine and Buttercup. Beth had kissed Johnny goodnight and Lily was tucked in bed.

"Ben would you mind reading a few verses of scripture before we all leave? Please read Psalm 103 the first five verses. My reading still needs improving. I love to hear you read. Your voice sounds like Father's. Psalm 103: 1-5 NIV. "Praise the Lord, my soul; all my inmost being, praise his holy name. Praise the Lord, my soul, and forget not all his benefits-who forgives all your sins and heals all your diseases, who redeems your life from the pit and crowns you with love and compassion, who satisfies your desires with good things so that your youth is renewed like the eagle's."

"God was working with us in the settlement. He keeps all His promises. He forgives and I must do the same," said Sarah. "He heals all diseases and renews our strength."

Ben read and then they prayed together, thanking God for his healing power and protection for Sarah and David and all the people that had nursed the sick. He thanked God for bringing them back safely.

It was well after dark, when Sarah opened the gate to let Moon Boy in the field near her house. Pretty Mother was back in with Cloud and the other white mares. Everything seemed back to normal. The full moon shone on her cabin door as she went to open it. She read the words Ben had carved in it. "Home Sweet Home." For the first time their meaning was completely absorbed into her mind and soul. It is a sweet home. When I am at the "S and J" I feel wrapped in love.

She slid out of her clothes and into her nightgown without lighting a lantern. Her curtains were open wide and she could see Dart Away in his special field. When the weather was cold or damp, Jed made sure that he was in the barn, but on warm nights, he left the door open at the back of the barn and Dart Away sometimes preferred to stay out in the field. He was treated with tender loving care. They knew how precious he was.

As gratitude for the security and love that filled her heart, she whispered, "Thank you Lord that I have Ben and this family and thank you that we still have Dart away."

She fell asleep praying for the healing of all the people that had been touched by the illness in the settlement.

Sarah woke to the sound of pounding. Ben and Jed were putting the first roof boards on the new house. David was on a ladder, handing up another board that Josh had brought from the stack. She stepped around the back of her house where she had a better view of their work and was amazed at the large skeleton of a house that had appeared while she and David had been gone.

I better go see Mary and find out what I can do to help her today. She had pulled on her leather clothing, and took a fast walk down the path to the hut. Mary was not there. Adam was up on the bluff at the lookout and yelled good morning.

"Mom is in the garden. If you want to help, you better take some baskets with you. She said yesterday that she was going to pick everything that was ready and slice it for drying." He was talking as he climbed down. "You can tell Mom and Aunt Beth that we have an all clear and that I am starting to clean the stalls in Dad's barn now."

"Thank you Adam, I will pass on the good report." Sarah watched Adam as he stepped through the corral gate and latched it. He went to each horse in the corral and gave them scratches. She couldn't hear his words but she could tell that he was talking to them as he went. She noticed how tall he was getting. The hut was dark except for the light that filtered through the trees and into the bedroom windows.

The fireplace had not been used since the weather had turned hot. She knew where the empty baskets were kept and took four. That is probably all I can carry, if they are filled. Rascal and Stump walked on the path behind her. When she greeted Mary and entered the gate, the two dogs continued on and settled under the trees in Beth's side yard.

"Hello Mary, Adam said to tell you that we have an all clear and that he is cleaning the stalls in Ben's barn."

"He has been volunteering to do many chores since Ben and Jed have been putting all their time into getting the house closed in before winter."

"It was just an outline on the ground when we left. The men didn't get much done before they had to leave."

"Well, all the boys are growing and before long this ranch will have a crew that is as tall and strong as Tom's," said Mary proudly.

They worked together picking the ripe tomatoes and filling their baskets.

"Sarah, I was thinking this morning, when I was alone, before you came out, that I owe my life to you. Can you even imagine what my life would have been like, if you hadn't helped me escape?"

"Yes, I know what it would have been. You would have been a slave wife for Growling Bear, if he had gotten what he intended. Chief Dark Wolf has never allowed that in the camp of the people. Only promised women that want to marry are wives in the camp of the Blue Stone People. I am so glad that you are here for me to talk to and for Ben to love. You have made him happy. I can see it in his face. You are a good wife and mother."

"Thank you Sarah that was a lovely thing to say."

"I hope Beth has her eyes on Eli. He will try anything if you aren't looking right at him."

Sarah smiled remembering his ash caper.

"I think I have all that I can carry. Where do you want to wash and slice these?"

"I have a set of lines in our barn, but Adam is working in there. Let's walk over and see if we can do it in Jed's. That way I can check on Eli and Nattie, too."

"Beth was amazed at the full baskets.

"It will take the rest of the day to slice and string all those. I will send Johnny back with a couple pans for washing them and I will put the knives inside one of them. I am sure he is sitting on top of Sandy. He never gives that horse a minute of peace. Just tell him to come, when you see him."

"Beth was right. She knows her son," said Mary. Let's leave him be. I don't like the idea of a youngster carrying knives even if they are in a pan and I want to check on my boys." Mary was glad to set her baskets on the ground near the barn. Her arms ached from the weight.

"Hello Johnny," said Sarah softly. She didn't want to startle the boy or the horse. "How are you today?"

"I am good but sort of sad. Dad says that Sandy and the twins are going out in the field tomorrow. I won't be able to see her as much. She is my favorite horse in the whole world."

"Why is she your favorite, Johnny?"

"Lots of reasons, but the best is that she likes me and listens when I tell her things. She is so beautiful and I can sit on her and she doesn't try to dump me off. Dad says she is wild, but not to me. I think she will let me sit on her even in the field if I can get on her. She is quite tall. Here I just climb on the side of the stall, but out there, I can't do that. That's why I am sad. She is my only friend."

"Thank you Johnny for telling me. I will think about it and Pray. You should pray about it, too. God always answers prayers."

"I know, but Mom says He doesn't always answer the way we want."

"That's true. Here comes Aunt Mary. She has two big pans. I need to help her fill them with water so we can wash the tomatoes."

"Aunt Sarah, I think I will go in and help Mom. She says it is a big help when I play with Eli." He went to the house but his body English betrayed his mood.

"What's the matter with Johnny?"

"He is sad because Jed is putting Sandy out with the other mares and foals."

"What is sad about that?"

"He is worried that in the field, she will no longer be his friend."

"I'll bet that he is wrong. Slim told me that once you win a horse's trust, it lasts a lifetime. Beth told me that once Sandy is totally tamed, Jed is going to give her to Johnny. He knows that it is rare that a boy would pick a grown horse over a pair of foals."

It was quiet in the barn for a while and then Mary asked Sarah if she had decided where she would have her wedding.

"I haven't had much time to think about it. I haven't even decided when," she laughed. "I started my dress and his outfit too, but there hasn't been time to work on them. I have been wishing one thing. I would like to have a Christian wedding, but I would like us to wear the wedding clothes of the people. If it were possible, I would have two weddings. I would like to have the people that raised me, to be there, and also Blue Stone. She was my first and best friend.

Mary, don't look so shocked. I would never bring people from the Indian camp to the "S and J" and I am sure you have no desire to ever see Growling Bear again."

"You are right about me not ever wanting to lay eyes on that man again, but it is a fun idea to have two weddings. You could have an Indian ceremony here for us, and a Christian one for them there. You said that the Jesuits have built a little church. Maybe you could have them perform the wedding."

"Well, Mary, you have given me food for thought."

"I was thinking as we were riding up the Silver River, checking on the families, that I was seeing a few trees down and it got me wondering if the people had any damage or injuries during the ground tremors. I hope not. I can't help but worry a little about them. I took care of them all and trained Sweet Grass before I left. I guess it is her job to worry about them now."

"How close were you to their camp?"

"Not close at all. Can you remember the night ride in the woods and then the long trip back with Ben and the soldiers?" They are east and north of here, by at least a two day ride."

"Do you think it was worse in that direction?"

"I have no way of knowing, but the more I think about it the more I feel concern. Our wonderful lookout hasn't spotted the people going to the summer council yet. He should soon." Mary could see that Sarah was worried and probably wouldn't feel better about it until she saw the Indians going to their summer meeting.

"We have talked our way through slicing all those tomatoes! It is always fun to see them hanging high and dripping. I wish we could figure out a way to catch all that juice. It would make a good base for soup."

"We could can the rest of the tomatoes in the garden, but the store is out of bottles. David and I used every single one the Trading Post had before we were done distributing medicine. Maybe that's an idea for next year. That sickness cost them a bit of money. I hope people clean and return his bottles."

"I hope they don't. It serves them right the way that woman talked to you."

"I am trying to forgive her. I know I should, but it is difficult. She had gossiped about me to most of the settlement. Whenever I said who I was, they had heard about me from Helen."

"Land a Goshen! That's such a terrible thing. That had to make it even harder for you," said Mary sympathetically.

"It was hard on everyone, but it's done now and so are we! I'll wash the pans and knives and return them to Beth and let's go quietly just in case she has the babies asleep," said Sarah. She had guessed correctly.

The children had eaten their lunch and were down for naps. Johnny had forgotten to do his chores and was not proud of his basket of eggs when he came in with them.

"Mom, I think I didn't feed them yesterday either. There are too many eggs for just one day. I am going right now and do your chickens Aunt Mary. I am sorry. I forgot. I think the chickens are mad at me. They are really hungry. Mom I'll clean out the pen as soon as I come back. I feel bad. I didn't do my job," he said hurrying down the path.

"I gave the chickens feed yesterday and enough water to do them, but I didn't tell him. I want him to be more responsible." Beth was grinning. That horse, Sandy, is all he can think about."

"I fed mine mid-day too," said Mary. "Aren't we a pair?"

"I made you both a sandwich to go with some tea, I have mint brewing. Is that alright?"

"That will be good. I am hungry now that you mention it. They laughed and took the tray out on the porch.

"Josh was here about an hour ago and took back lunch for all of them at the new house. He said that they have the boards on one side of the roof on the main part now. Mary, you must be very proud of that boy. He is growing up so fast," said Beth.

"Yes, you know I am. Did Adam come down for lunch?"

"No, Mary, I haven't seen him. Maybe he had lunch with the men at the new house."

Just then, David rode up fast.

"Jed and Ben said for you to go in and take cover. Adam spotted two riders and Ben went to the lookout to see if he recognized them. They weren't coming from the settlement. They were two Indians heading across the prairie at an angle and heading up river. He said to just go inside and be quiet until you get an all clear."

"Thank you David," said Mary as she and Beth scurried inside. Sarah stood on the path beside David.

"David, this has me puzzled and a little worried, too. This is the time when all the people should be traveling to the summer council."

"Yes, I think they were sending messengers in the direction of the council. Do you think they are sick too? Maybe they can't go this year."

"David, I am concerned, but I don't think it is sickness. Do you remember when you remarked about the trees uprooted when we were checking the farthest places along the Silver? I am wondering if the tremors we felt at the ranch got stronger in the northeast. If they did, that could have caused damages or injuries. Maybe that's why we have not seen the people on their way to the summer meeting."

"Sarah, it could be either one. They see white people at the trading spot and they could get the sickness there."

"David, I am worried."

Sarah, there is nothing we can do for them. Pray and God will send them help if they need it."

"Yes, but what if we are the help he is sending and we don't go?"

"I don't know Sarah, but for now you should go in the house with the other women."

He turned his horse around and rode back to the hut. Sarah could see him heading toward the path to the lookout. I'll bet all the men are up there. Sometimes they are like little children. I'm sure that the riders are out of sight by now.

She went in and picked Nattie up and cuddled him.

"You are such a sweet big baby boy. One day I would like to have a son like you. You have a fat tummy and a cute smile and chubby toes," she played with him until Lily became jealous and wanted attention, too.

Sarah scooped her up and sat her on her knee with her right arm around her.

"Lily, you have a pretty bow in your hair today. Do you know what color it is?"

"My bow is blue."

"Yes it is and it matches your eyes and your dress."

Eli chugged over and patted Sarah's knee.

"Mary, would you take Nattie. I think Eli would like a little fun." As soon as Sarah had Eli balanced on her left knee she started to bounce them up and down.

"Wee! Ride the horses, faster, faster," she said as the children giggled and held on to her. When she stopped, they both said "more, Aunt Sarah, more".

"Alright, are you ready? Here we go!" They all laughed with the children as she bounced her knees again.

"Wee, go horses, Go, faster, and faster."

When her legs could take no more she put them down and said that the horses were tired now, but they will be back to play next time. The children were satisfied and their mothers had been temporarily distracted.

"Beth, and Mary, I am sure that something is wrong at the Indian camp. I can feel it inside my heart. It could be the sickness or perhaps the tremors we felt were worse where they are, but I feel that I should go. I will be leaving in the morning. I hope that David will go with me, but if I must, I will go alone."

She walked out the door and up the path swiftly. When she found Ben, and Jed, Josh, Adam and David in a huddle at the base of the bluff, she stopped long enough to tell them that she would be leaving and why. David announced that he felt concern, too and would be going with her.

"Ben knew there was no point in trying to dissuade them. He had tried before. Actually he was starting to understand her a little, partly because as they had worked on the new house, David had related the many different situations they had found in the settlement and how Sarah had known what to do at each.

"She gives orders like a Chief," he said with a proud smile. Jed soon found himself on the receiving end of that ability when she stopped again at their gathering. She had pulled an all brown mare out of the field and had fastened a saddle on her. Jed I need you to take a satchel and fill it with clean healing plants. Pull as many as you can without depleting the patch. I have none left in my cabin so if you would; please hang a few to dry in there. I am going to go while it is still light and gather more of the plants that I want to take with me."

"Sarah, the horse you are using is a good one, but she is not completely trustworthy yet. Be careful getting off and on and tie her when you stop to gather."

Beth and Mary both packed food for their trip and filled extra water bags. Beth had slipped in a large jar of salve, made with clover, bear grease and a bit of the healing plant mixed in. David thanked them gratefully. They had so much to take with them that a pack horse was needed.

There were no white clothes or chalk in Sarah's bundles and she wore the comfortable clothes she had made while acting as healer for the people. David had on his cowboy hat, he had gotten used to it and liked that it shaded his eyes but the rest of his clothes looked like any man in the Indian camp.

CHAPTER TWENTY
AT THE CAMP OF THE PEOPLE

When they arrived, Sarah's worst fears were confirmed. The orderly camp was not recognizable. The communal tent was down. Many family tents lay on the ground. The lake was brown and churned as the new springs stirred the mud from the bottom constantly. The only thing that was the same was the small church. The cross was gone, only the pile of stones marked where it had stood.

They stopped but the priests were not there. She noticed that the cross lay on the floor of the church and had been cleaned. She knew it would have been muddy. Everything she saw was wet and covered with mud.

"David, what has happened here?"

"Look over there, I see Chief Dark Wolf. We should talk to him first."

"Where, is he?"

"Over there, with the men. They are trying to decide what they can do for the big tent so they can raise it again."

"It looks like everything has been violently pushed back, away from the lake."

"Chief Dark Wolf, Greetings," said David.

"Hello, Father," said Sarah.

He stood looking at them as if he didn't comprehend that they were there. The shock of what had happened to him, his family and the people, was written on his face and frozen in his eyes.

He turned as if he was about to walk away.

"Father, what has happened here?" He stopped and finally acknowledged them, by answering.

"Your God has taken his anger out on the people once again! He shook the ground and tipped the lake into the tents of all of us. Some are injured. More are hiding in the woods. They fear that He may do it again, and your mother and Sweet Grass are badly injured. They were under the heavy wet leather of the big tent. We had to cut the seams to pull them out."

"Where are they?"

He walked away then without saying anything more and slumped down on the small knoll that still remained a place of consolation and meditation for him.

They inquired of the men and found out that Falling Stones and Running Deer had ridden to the summer council, hoping to bring back a healer and to tell them what had happened.

"They left here two days ago, I think," said one of the men.

"Can you tell me how Moonflower and Sweet Grass were injured?"

"They were in here," said Night Hawk. "I am sorry Sarah. One of the big poles fell on them. We are trying to get the ropes back in place so we can pull it away with the big horses. We have got to fix the base and repair the leather seams before we can stand it up again."

"Thank you Night Hawk. Can you tell me where they are?"

"We took them over there. The priests have been doing their best to care for them.

Why is no one cooking? Where are the women?"

"They ran into the trees and are frightened. The ground has growled and moved twice now. They fear that the ground will shake again. Or the lake water rise and dump on their tents again. Two are there in that tent. One is sick and the other is Big Flower. She just sits and won't talk. Her son, Cub, is with Growling Bear, over there.

The priests have been making food and delivering it. They stood on the hill there in front of the church when it started. I saw what happened. The whole hill lifted up, church and all and that's when the lake looked like it tipped and it dumped water over the whole camp. Fish were in my tent! I was lucky. I was able to put my tent back up quickly. None of the poles were broken. I pulled the wet furs out of it so they can dry. They should be worked, but there is no one to do it. I don't know where my wife, Spotted Fawn is."

"Night Hawk, you have all been through a terrible ordeal. I think what we all need is a big fire. If the women see it, perhaps they will come back. Will you help me?"

"Yes, but we will have to go far to get dry wood."

"We will do what we must, to get things back livable."

David helped and soon they had a modest sized fire blazing.

"Night Hawk, has anyone gone to round up the horse herd?"

"No they scattered and they are not back. Gray Cloud has been helping to get some of the tents back up."

"Ask him to come here please." A few minutes later Gray Cloud came, looking glad to see them.

"Hello Gray Cloud. How are you?"

"I am alright. But so much is wrong that I don't know how we will get it all back the way it was."

"You can't. It will be new and different. It will be better," she said, "You will see."

"Do you have your flute?"

"Yes, I keep it here." He pulled it from a leather case that hung on his chest.

"Good, please go to the usual place that you sit, and play as if the herd was there. I think some of the horses will return when they hear the familiar sound. I noticed Coyote sitting on the rock of the herd watcher. Does he have a flute?"

"No I haven't sensed that he wanted one. I will talk to Singing Wind and perhaps he will make him one."

"That is good, Gray Cloud, but for now, let him ride among the rocks and the far woods and to the north, to see if he can find any horses and bring them back. The poor things are frightened. Play Gray Cloud. It will give comfort to all who hear it." He smiled as he walked toward Coyote.

Sarah ducked into the Chief's tent that Night Hawk had indicated. It was larger than most family tents but crowded. The priests had provided dry furs for them to lie on and she could see a kettle of stew near the door, with bowls and spoons that someone had collected.

"Mother and Sweet Grass, hello, how are you doing?"

"Sarah! Oh Sarah, I am so happy that you have come," said Moonflower, with tears in her eyes. "It is good that you have come. We have never needed you in the camp, more than we do now."

"Night Hawk told me that you were both injured when the poles of the big tent tipped over. Where are you hurt?"

"Your mother has been teaching me to sew. We were sitting together when the ground began to shake again and harder this time! The pole came down and hit my arm and shoulder. Your mother has a bad leg. The pole was on her leg for a long time until the men cut open the seams on the tent. Then they helped me out and were able to lift the pole up. They were holding it on a big rock but the rock tipped and the pole rolled off the rock and hurt her ankle and foot."

"I heard that the priests have been helping. Did they make willow bark tea? What have they done for your injuries?"

"The older one made us willow bark tea and he put some grease on my arm and the scrapes on her leg, but that's all. He brought that stew a little while ago."

"Sweet Grass, are your legs hurt?"

"No, I told you, it is this arm and shoulder."

"Sarah was frowning.

"Step out here where there is room for me to check your injuries."

Sweet Grass did as she was told, but preferred to stay inside. She felt safer being cared for. Outside the tent something more might be required of her and she sensed it.

Sarah examined the shoulder and arm and decided that it was comforting that Sweet Grass really needed.

"I think that the Great Spirit loves you very much. That heavy pole could have hit your head and killed you. Instead all you have is a bruise and scrape marks. Here, is a piece of cloth, it is dirty, but it will make a good sling. You will only need to use it for a day or two. Take this fur in your good hand and sit on one of the logs near the fire." Sarah stuck her head back in long enough to tell Moonflower that she was taking the stew near the fire and that she would be right back.

With Sweet Grass out of the tent, Sarah was able to check her mother's more serious injuries.

"The priest did a good job of wrapping your leg. The bone is broken, but it feels like it is back in place. Your ankle and foot are badly bruised and scraped, too, from the weight of the pole and rough bark, when they rolled it off of you. Can you move your ankle?"

"Yes, but it hurts a lot when I do. He packed it with willow bark."

"I will make a poultice. I brought many of my medicinal herbs with me. As soon as I get it made, I will put it on for you but in the meantime I will have a couple men help you out of here so you can sit by the fire, too."

David and Night Hawk carefully took her to sit near Sweet Grass. Someone had found a willow back rest and they put her where she could use it and be comfortable. Sarah returned to the fire with several pans, pots and cooking spoons. She found a brightly colored blanket that had once been beautiful, now in the mud being trod on. She pulled it up and tossed it over a thorn bush to dry.

"The sun and breeze is drying the camp. We need the women back to work the hides and furs or they will be ruined. David, see if you can find a drum and someone to play it. Also get someone to start bringing wood for the fire."

Sarah tied Moon Boy, Thunder and Pretty Mother near the center of camp where they could easily be seen. She knew that everyone would recognize her white horses. She started the plants simmering in a big pan, near the fire and then when she spotted the priests, she hailed them and asked them to bring their guitar and tambourine.

"We need the sound of a celebration. Please do your best to get something going that will bring the women back. They sang and played and once Moonflower got relief from the poultice she clapped and sang as loud as she could.

Sarah carried several big kettles to the edge of the lake and carefully found a place where she could fill them with the brown water and placed them within easy reach of the fire. Next she wandered the camp collecting drying racks until she had so many in a row that it was reaching all the way around the fire.

Morning Dove came back and sat down next to Moonflower. They began to talk.

"I am sorry Moonflower, I felt like a coward, hiding, but I couldn't make myself walk back across the open grass where the tents and everything lay in the mud. I knew you were in the tent and needed help. I should have come to you. Please forgive me."

"Morning Dove, there is nothing to forgive. You could not have helped me. It took many men. Thank you for coming back now, and soon things will be back to normal. You will see.

Next Dancing Willow and Blue Stone came out of the trees. She held Happy Song in her arms. Sarah hugged her and asked them please to sing as loud as they could. Snow Star came with Watching Owl. She was wrapped in the white rabbit fur blanket that Sarah had made so many years earlier. Somehow, Snow Star had kept it clean and dry. Dancing Willow and Blue Stone clapped and sang. People were talking, laughing, and singing.

Slowly Big Flower walked across the camp and took Cub from Growling Bear.

"We are going to be all right," He boomed. "We are going to be all right!" Big Flower laid her head against his chest and finally she was able to release the tears and fear, knotted up inside her. She sobbed and held tight to him. Chief Dark Wolf walked back from his little hill and sat down on a log near Moonflower. Other families were slowly reunited after days of panic and separation.

Sarah stood up in front of the group gathered at the fire and simply said that her heart was rejoicing.

"You look puzzled. I am joyous, because the Great Spirit has protected the Blue Stone People. You have all sat at communal fires where your shaman has danced and chanted for the many spirits that he knew. You now know that the Great Spirit is the strongest, the fiercest, the mightiest, the most loving and caring of all. This terrifying event could have killed many. Not one person was killed. We have two women with healing injuries." More people slowly joined the group, coming out of the trees from every direction.

"I have gathered some drying racks but I am sure that we can find or make many more. All the meat and dried foods in the caches must be brought out, rinsed in clean water and dried or it will rot. No one will have food to eat. The furs need to be greased and worked or they will be hard. The water in the lake is good and fresh. Dip in a pan and wait a little while. The brown that we see is sand being stirred from the bottom of the lake. I filled these pans just a few minutes ago. All we need to do is pour it into a different container. It is clean and clear. The sand is on the bottom of the pan.

We can rinse the meat and hang it on the racks and it will be good. Let's all get busy before the meat spoils."

Many families strained to remove the wet fallen tents and wet furs and hides so they could open their caches. Some brought pans and kettles filled with lake water. The activity and voices brought still more people from the trees and surrounding area.

Chief Dark Wolf stood and wrapped his arms around Sarah.

"You have done what I couldn't. They will recover now. Look, I can see people at every tent. Soon things will be livable here again. Thank you, Sarah. Can you stay a few days? I need to talk to you about something important."

"I need to tell you and Mother something. It is a good thing." She motioned for David to join her. She took his hand and looked at him with a big smile. "David and I are going to be married. It will be here, in the little church and Mother you will be able to see my wedding. We will have a celebration feast and the people will be happy again."

Moonflower hugged her and then she reached for David and pulled him down where she could hug him, too. Snow Star was so happy at the news that she was bouncing.

"The camp is a muddy mess. How can we prepare a wedding and a feast?" she asked.

"Well I think we will all have to work hard to clean things up," said Chief Dark Wolf laughing out loud.

When the priests heard what she had said, they were concerned.

"She is not a Catholic. We don't know if she is even baptized," said the older priest as he headed back to the church.

"We must pray about this and get the cross put back up right away. It can't lie in the middle of the floor any longer."

The people worked hard the next few days to restore their camp. They were excited to hear that there was to be a wedding. Blue Stone worked harder than most. She had managed to keep her wedding dress and Running Deer's wedding shirt, clean and dry.

Their tent's location on the far back side of the lake, and the fact that she had wrapped them in old hides greased on the outside, just in case it rained when they moved back from the Omati all had been fortunate circumstances. She had hung the bundle with them in, high in the tent out of the way. All that aided in preserving them from being ruined. Sarah and Blue Stone spent many hours adding leather to the bottom of Blue Stone's dress so that it would be long enough for Sarah.

"It is a darker yellow than his shirt, but it looks like it is a red top and yellow skirt," said Dancing Willow when she saw what they had done.

"We have done wonders considering that most of the dyed leather in camp is stained with mud. Try it on, with the head piece, Sarah," said Blue Stone. "You look beautiful. This is so wonderful. I never dreamed that my special friend would wear the dress that I made and wore," said Blue Stone. She looked like she was about to cry.

"Don't you dare cry? This is a very happy time," said Sarah. "Now I need to do something about footwear and I need to ask Mother a question. I will be back later," she said as she slipped the dress and head piece off and carefully placed them in Blue Stone's arms.

"I can't believe it. Our Brave Sparrow is getting married," said Dancing Willow. She placed the dress safely inside her tent and hung it high with the shirt. Running Deer had made cross braces in their tents and the clothes would stay on them out of harm's way.

"Mother, how are you feeling today?"

"I think my ankle is much better, and I can't tell about the leg. It aches, but I am satisfied that it is healing. Sweet Grass is much better. She has taken the sling off her arm and I saw her scrapping a hide over in the shade earlier."

"That is good news. Mother do you know where the gray wolf fur is, that hung in the communal tent?"

"I think that the furs and all the meat have been removed. You should ask Sweet Grass. She has had women working, but I can't say who has done which ones or where they have taken them. The men made a lot of new racks for us and the meat was salvaged. That is the meat from the big tent over there. Sweet Grass found bags of wet salt and used it to rub every piece. She has been working very hard."

"Thank you, Mother." She spotted Sweet Grass helping to clean out a tent on the far side of the camp. "I think that tent belongs to her brother and his wife. All the other tents are up and opened to dry out. Theirs is the last one."

"Sweet Grass, How are you?"

"I am well. My shoulder aches a bit but mostly I am fine."

"That is good news. I have a question for you. Do you know where the big wolf fur is that hung in the big tent, the fur from the wolf that killed Red Fox?"

"Sarah, I don't know. The men brought armloads of heavy wet hides and furs to us over near the church.

Many of us were working them. The ground there was never covered with lake water so it was a dry place to lay them all out. The priests said they didn't mind. Did you notice that they put the cross back up?"

"Yes, I noticed. Should I go over there and look? Are they all still there?"

"I don't know. I think so."

Sarah checked every hide, but the big gray wolf fur was not among them. She asked the priests.

"Hello Sarah. Tomorrow is your big day. David was here earlier. We have talked a lot with him. He is a nice young man," said Father Peter.

Sarah laughed at that remark.

"Of course I agree with you. I have a question. Did either of you see a big gray wolf fur here, when the women were salvaging the furs and hides. Many remain, but the one from the wolf that killed Red Fox is not here."

"Yes, Sarah, it is here. One of the women took special care to scrape and oil it until the leather was soft again. Come in the church and see. I hung it on the back wall for all to see each time they come. I didn't damage it. I sewed loops on the back so it can be easily taken down and put back up. I have been brushing it. I must also confess that I rubbed a little yellow ochre on its sides, so it would look the same as it did. I hope that is alright."

"That is perfect. At the end of our wedding promises, I want to wrap it around our shoulders as we leave the cross. Is that going to be a problem?"

"No not at all. Are you sure Sarah that you don't want a Catholic Mass and a longer service?"

"I'm sure, Father Bob, I just want to do what we discussed."

The camp was clean, and all the tents stood farther back from the lake, but in their proper positions according to status. Many had raised the ground in their place, to help keep rain and mud out. The flaps still stood open to allow moisture to leave. The grass in the linings was pulled out to allow air to circulate. The main area around the communal fire was dry now and the meat had been placed on huge woven mats waiting for the last bit of dampness to leave the inside of the caches.

*****

Everyone had made an extra effort to dress in their very best clothes. Much of their clothing had been ruined or badly damaged, but each had located, polished and now donned their heavy stone necklaces.

No song to the sun god would echo over the lake this morning or any other morning from now on. The old woman was the last of her belief in the camp and she had given up the ritual.

Moonflower giggled nervously as Chief Dark Wolf and Flying Eagle carried her to a place of honor on the grass where she would be able to see the entire ceremony. Flying Eagle, Sleeping Bear and Snapping Turtle had left before Sarah and David arrived and they had promised Chief Dark Wolf that they would not return until they had enough fresh meat to feed all the people.

They had returned after being gone four days, just before dark with two deer. It was perfect timing for the wedding feast. Snow Star and Blue Stone had proudly prepared them both for the large fire that burned in the center of camp. Small fires burned in front of many tents, as good scents filled the air. Although much of the food they had prepared to take to the summer meeting was ruined, the women had managed to salvage some of the dried foods they had gathered and now they were doing their best to make a worthy wedding feast for a very special couple.

The lake had continued to fill until it was necessary to make a new path to walk around it. It now was stable and the edges were starting to clear. They hoped that in time all of it would be clear enough to drink without waiting for sand to settle.

Sarah was not displaying her usual, in charge, behavior on this special morning. She had been so busy during her time in camp, that she had not had time to acknowledge the serious step that she was about to make. It wasn't that she was questioning her decision. She wasn't sure why she was so nervous. She could feel herself tremble as she slipped the beautifully beaded wedding dress, over her head. Moonflower's tent was the second largest, and the only one large enough for Sarah, Blue Stone and Snow Star to all stand up in, at the same time. The big community tent had not yet been repaired and Chief Dark Wolf was determined to wait until the ground was totally dry before standing the big poles up again.

The messengers had returned from the summer council but after delivering their report, were unable to convince any of the healers there, to come back to the camp of the Blue Stone People with them. It was just as well, now. Sweet Grass was nearly healed and Moonflower's injuries had been dealt with and she too, would be well by the end of summer.

Dancing Willow was pleased that her husband and son were both back in time to attend the wedding. Running Deer was proud that David would be wearing his wedding shirt.

Sarah's hair had been washed and braided in many small braids. Now that it was dry, the braids were carefully removed, leaving a full head of wavy blond hair to compliment it, the head dress was placed on carefully and fastened.

"You are almost ready. I want you to wear this. I will get it back from you when you change out of the dress."

Blue Stone slipped the single Blue Stone, on a cord of yellow yarn and blond hair over her head very gently. She kissed Sarah on her cheek.

"There, my sister, you are ready and you look very beautiful."

Snow Star wrapped the white rabbit fur blanket around Sarah's shoulders.

"Wear this, just until you stand beside David. It is so special to me. This will add another memory that I can tell Watching Owl's wife someday."

"Thank you Snow Star. I am blessed to have two sisters. I love both of you. This day is so special for many reasons. If I am correct, it is August 29, and it is my birthday, too. I am twenty one today."

The priests were thrilled to be officiating at their first Christian wedding. They had drawn lines with powdered chalk stone, on the grass, and had asked the people to seat themselves on either side. This left a six foot wide isle for the couple to walk on.

Everyone was there, seated and excited. What a difference Sarah has made in the people in less than a week, thought Chief Dark Wolf as he sat down beside Moonflower.

Both Gray Cloud and Running Deer had practiced with Father Peter, and now with the guitar and a soft drum beat, the music most loved by the people began.

David whispered into the tent.

"Sarah, are you ready?"

"Yes, David, I am ready," she said as she stepped out to see a very handsome man, wearing a yellow leather shirt and dark brown leather trousers. His hair was shorter than the men in camp, but he had let it grow since his one haircut. It was freshly oiled and braided with beads that matched the ones on the shirt he had borrowed. "You look very handsome," she said as she slipped the white fur around her shoulders and took his hand.

"There are no words to say how lovely you look. Sarah, how is it that someone so special would choose to marry someone like me?"

"Silly, I love you. Let's do this," she said with a big smile.

The beautiful music, played softly and sung softly, greeted the amazing couple with praise to God. They walked slowly, beside the lake, across the grass between the people and stood, in front of the cross, where Sarah had led the people to the Lord. Father Bob started the ceremony with a prayer of blessing, first for the couple and then for all the people gathered there. The promises were said first by David and then by Sarah, each made a special effort to say them loud enough to be heard by everyone. Finally the ring that David had made with love was placed on her finger. David kissed her and held her a bit longer than Father Bob would have suggested, but the people loved it. The flutes, guitar and drum changed from the soft sound to one of joy and celebration as Sarah slipped off the white rabbit fur blanket and both of them were covered in the huge gray wolf fur.

"Sarah, come under my protection," said David loudly. The people applauded and laughed as he kissed her again.

They led the people to the feast and Sarah took one final circle of the fire in front of all the people, greeting each as she passed by, wearing the beautiful dress, before she slipped into Moonflower's tent and changed into the clothes she had worn when she arrived. Blue Stone stepped in and received the dress on her arms and then Sarah returned her single blue stone, necklace. Sarah kissed her friend on the forehead before she stepped out to find David outside, holding the yellow beaded shirt. He handed it carefully to Blue Stone, thanking her again for allowing him to wear it.

"This Blue Stone binds us together. You will always be my sister and friend, she said as she hugged Blue Stone. We will leave early in the morning. I may not see you both then, but perhaps next time I do I will see you wearing this, too." Sarah slipped a large gold nugget into Blue Stone's hand and then she turned to Snow Star to reveal a second gold nugget equally large and beautiful. "This one is for you, Snow Star. The craftsmen of the Blue Stone People will be able to make something beautiful to hold them," she said as she stepped out of the tent with a big smile.

"David, the people are nearly back to normal, and you my sweet, funny, and wonderful man will always be my only love. We are forever together, but tonight you should enjoy the fun of the celebration and your friends, because we must leave at first light tomorrow to go home and plan another wedding."

"That's the Sarah that I know and love, practical and matter of fact. Sarah there is no one here that I want to be with, more than you."

They walked, hand in hand, until it sunk in what she had said about another wedding.

"Sarah, are you serious?"

"Come on, let's go to the feast,' she laughed.

In her pocket Sarah had one last gift. She had a third nugget, just a bit larger than the other two. She hugged Moonflower and placed it in her palm.

"Thank you mother, for all that you did for me and all that you taught me. Thank you for loving me."

When it came time for the little ones to go to bed, Sarah stood for just a moment to speak.

"We want to thank all of you for the love that you have shown us tonight and through the years as we were growing up with you in this camp. If you desire to give us a wedding gift, which some of you have indicated, I would ask this? Instead of gifts to us, give your hearts to Jesus. Love Him and Thank Him that you all are alive and the camp of the people is back in order. Thank Him and Praise Him each and every day. Be glad that you are safe and together, and you are **The Blue Stone People.**

AN INVITATION

If you do not know Jesus, as your savior but you would like Him to be, please pray the following prayer. Invite Him into your heart. Commit your "New Life" to Him. He will be your constant companion, counselor, comforter, and protector, The Holy Bible tells us that He will never leave you or forsake you.

"Dear Jesus, please forgive my sins. Give me grace and strength Lord, so that I will not commit them again. Come into my heart so that I can start a "New Life" with you as my companion. I want to live according to your will and commandments. Bless me Lord and lead me in a life that is pleasing to you. In Jesus' Holy name I pray. Amen"

If you prayed that prayer, you are saved. You are born again. Your soul is whiter than the snow on the highest mountains. The angels in heaven are rejoicing as they write your name in The Lamb's Book of Life.

Get a Holy Bible and begin to read it. Find a good Bible believing church and start attending, so that you can learn more about Your Heavenly Father. What a wonderful God we have!

If you wish, you can sign your Bible and date it as an outward sign that you are saved. Tell someone. Rejoice!

I will pray for you. God bless you. Louise Bouck.

ABOUT THE AUTHOR

Louise Bouck is a follower of Jesus Christ. She and her husband, Dale Bouck, live in Arizona. Together they have raised six children.

Until an early retirement from her fulltime job in 2000, not much time was available to allocate to writing or art. With many interests, Louise enjoys painting on location. The lush greenery of Michigan, her home state and the abundant flowers in her grandmother's greenhouses and flower shop all encouraged her eye to appreciate the colors and beauty of nature.

Later after moving to Arizona, the rugged landscape of the mountains and desert stole her heart and took her artistic soul in a new direction.

Paintings in many media cover the walls of her studio as she has deliberately turned her creative side more to the discipline of writing.

Hesitantly she withdrew from the art gallery where her work was sold and left the position of resident artist at the local Historical Society Museum. Louise has written a series of Christian; Bible based stories that she is now starting to release for the first time as she works on still another story and another painting.

BOOK TITLES IN THE NEW LIFE SERIES

More than Survival
Life's Many Journeys
The Land's Heritage
The Story of Sarah
Together
The Blue Stone People
Teewahpanee the Boy, Two Feathers the Man
The People of the Lion
The Lion's Den
Just the Beginning

www.ingramcontent.com/pod-product-compliance
Lightning Source LLC
Chambersburg PA
CBHW050714180626
46814CB00002B/430

9781943984046